Finding Liberty

Blaine Staat

DEC 2007

Linear Wave Publishing
Liberty, KY

For reprint permissions, questions, or feedback on this book or articles containted therein, please direct inquires to info@linearwavepublishing.com.

Linear Wave Publishing
P.O. Box 177
Liberty, KY 42539
www.linearwavepublishing.com

Library of Congress Control Number: 2007905477
ISBN: 978-0-9767196-0-1

Cover Photograph by John Dickinson. Used with permission.
www.motionworks.com.au

Printed in the United States of America

To-day we would pass through the scenes of our youth like travellers. We are burnt up by hard facts; like tradesmen we understand distinctions, and like butchers, necessities. We are no longer untroubled – we are indifferent. We might exist there; but should we really live there?

We are forlorn like children, and experienced like old men, we are crude and sorrowful and superficial – I believe we are lost.

- Erich Maria Remarque
All Quiet on the Western Front

to Catherine

for staying with me during the whole trip and
never letting go of my hand

Contents

Forward

Several years ago I was asked to introduce a day-long training session for a large group of people at my company. This was known as a "kick-off", and for 10 minutes I went through my corporate spiel, always upbeat and clever, letting everyone know how great the day was going to be and how lucky they were to be there. I was quite proud of myself. I thought I had done very well.

My boss, however, thought I was terrible, and he was mad because I had taken a valuable opportunity and squandered it. It was boring. It was garbage. It was schlock. "You have to tell them a story," he said. "Where we've been, what we've done to get where we are, and where we're all trying to go. *Tell them a story!*"

So that's what I do now. I tell stories.

The 32 stories that make up *Finding Liberty* were written over a period of 2 years and appear (more or less) as they were originally published in *Making It Home* magazine over the same span of time. All of them are different, and yet at the same time, all somehow seem to be integral pieces of a larger whole.

I make no claim to actually knowing what I'm talking about. Truly, I am no expert. These stories are simply the thoughts and perspectives that I gathered once I stopped listening to the noise of the world and, instead, shook the rust off of my mind and started thinking about things for myself. If these stories have any value to you, it would be my wish not that you would agree with them, but that they might prompt you to take a step back, open your own mind, and think for yourself. I can safely promise that if you do, you will be amazed.

Before you continue, I should let you know that my grammar is not always perfect. I sometimes confuse subjective and objective prepositions. I've been known to dangle a participle or two. I have a tendency to interrupt myself a lot. And I often start sentences with conjunctions. Some of these things I do by conscious choice, some by accident, but that's simply the way I tell stories. I have to trust that those things won't be so blatant or offensive that they get in the way of the stories themselves. Hopefully, I haven't left out something *really* important (like an entire word), but if I have, please accept my sincere apologies upfront.

1

Looking for Mayberry and Finding Liberty

It started with question: *Why do I not feel as happy as I used to feel?*

It was a valid question, but it was puzzling at the same time, because it didn't seem like I should have been asking it in the first place. After all, everything seemed like it was supposed to be as it should. I was married to a wonderful woman. I had beautiful children. I lived in a very nice, distinctive house in a neighborhood that was envied. It didn't seem like there was a problem with that at all. And my career had blossomed pretty well since leaving the Navy a decade before; between 2 companies I had received 17 promotions, pay raises, or combinations of the two. I wasn't fearful of losing my job, was well liked, and I was at a point in my life where money was not an issue anymore. I could pretty much buy anything I wanted or needed.

Nonetheless, I *was* asking it, and I was frustrated because the answer wasn't immediately obvious to me. I just couldn't figure it out. For all intents & purposes, I *should* have been happy. I had the wife, the kids, the career, the money, the house, the cars, the pets, the clothes, the toys . . . you name it, I either *had* everything – or had *access* to everything – that I had been working for my whole life. And yet, I was *less* happy than I was back when I started, when my wife Catherine and I had to sit home on Saturday nights playing Scrabble because we didn't have money to do anything else. Something wasn't right here.

One of my first reactions to the problem was to increase the inventory of what I already had: More shoes, more watches, more tools, more toys. So I gradually added all manner of stuff to my household. Then I added all manner of stuff to store my stuff in. Then I added all manner of stuff to clean the stuff that I had my stuff stored in. But even though these things did provide a temporary relief with their "newness", they were ultimately nothing more than distractions whose initial excitement rapidly faded.

So that wasn't it.

Okay, maybe it wasn't what I had, but the *quality* of what I had. Maybe what I needed was a *better* car, *better* clothes, *better* furniture, and a more expensive beer to wash it all down with. Again, while these things would occupy my mind and my time for awhile, they ultimately only distracted me from addressing the underlying problem. (I have to tell you that in hindsight I feel very fortunate that I had stopped in my efforts of trying to "improve" the things I had before I got around to trying to "improve" my wife!).

It didn't matter what I did, the result was always the same; a temporary fix, then a letdown. It was almost like getting drunk; You feel good for awhile and all of your problems seem to melt away, but eventually you sober up and suddenly realize that you're right back where you started, except that another day has slipped through your fingers. All that I had for my efforts was a ton of junk that I neither wanted nor needed and the memory of the effort and money that it had taken to accumulate it. And every year I could feel the emptiness inside of me growing a little more.

I knew I had a choice to make. I could either continue tipping up that bottle of distraction – it comes in so many flavors: purchases, travel, clubs, work, etc. – and let the years slip by even as the underlying disease continued to eat at my soul, or I could sober up, figure out what was really wrong, and try to do something about it.

I try to live my life by pushing on doors to see which ones open for me and which ones don't. Doors that are open I walk through; doors which are firmly shut I leave alone. I also feel that some of these doors are always in flux; opening or shutting depending on the season of our lives. Some things that may have been out of the question to me years ago might now be an option, and vise versa.

Before I could figure out how to fix my problem, I first had to find out what the problem was, so I finally stopped distracting myself and instead started looking around and paying attention to what I saw, what doors were slamming shut in my face, and what doors were opening to provide a possible alternate path.

As is often the case with people, we sometimes see only what we want to see (I'm certainly no exception), and because I was firmly looking for things that I wanted, or *thought* I wanted, I was blissfully overlooking all of the things that were available to me. In other words, I wasn't seeing the doors that were open, or if I did see them, I wasn't paying attention to them because I simply didn't care.

Much easier for me to see are the doors that are shut or in the process of shutting. I notice these more because they are usually harbingers of news that I don't want to hear, telling me that I can't have something I want. I find that when I see these, I often figuratively close my eyes, put my hands over my ears, and loudly recite "*La, la, la, la, la, la!*" until the coast is clear. But by taking the time to see the doors that are closing, and to *accept* them, it's much easier to see the ones that are opening.

What I saw - once I took the time to look - was that there were clear signs that I should change the current path of my life. I saw doors shutting on me all over the place, things I didn't like, things that all agreed with each other that time for a change had come.

I was tired of my job and the time, stress, and sacrifice that it demanded. I was tired of the traffic, tired of ironing my clothes every night (or paying for dry cleaning), tired of getting to work earlier & earlier and getting home later & later. I was tired of meetings, and email, and logins & passwords, and PowerPoint presentations, and airports, and cell phones, and Blackberries, and expense reports, and off-sites, and performance reviews. I was tired of hurricanes, road construction, petty bickering, entitlement, and uppity homeowners associations. I'd had enough of aloof neighbors who didn't speak to you, who "outsourced" their children's friends to other neighborhoods, and whose primary concern was with keeping up with the Jones'. I was shocked at my property tax increases, choking on debt, and fearful that my homeowners coverage could be cancelled at any time (that last one was kind of a special "Florida only" hurricane bonus).

All of these things, and many more, were weighing on me, and all of them seemed to me to be doors that were already firmly shut or in the process of shutting. And all of them were telling me the same thing: *you are on the wrong road!*

There's a stereotype about men regarding the fact that they don't like to stop and ask for directions. As with most stereotypes, there's a lot of truth to that, and a lot of reasons why. Men don't like to be wrong. We see asking for assistance as a sign of weakness. And we don't like walking away from something that we've already invested our time into. I had been on this particular road for *12 years*, making a name for myself, building my career, providing more and better things for my family. You might imagine my dismay when I considered all of the effort, the stress, the sweat, and the work that I had gone though to get this far, only to realize that the whole time I'd been heading in the *wrong direction?*

The society & culture that we live in is constantly telling us how we should live our lives and what we should value, and I had been feeding from that trough since I was a child. No surprise then, that I would feel disillusioned with what I'd accomplished in my life and what I'd become when I realized that it wasn't at all like I was told it would be. Admitting to ourselves that we've made a mistake, even when we *know* we have, can be very tough. For me, it took a couple of years to fully accept it.

But during this time, as I was coming to grips with accepting what I didn't want out of life, I also had time to ask myself what I *did* want. And the answer was surprisingly simple: I didn't want *more*, I wanted *less*. Less stress, less stuff, less debt, less traffic, less time away from my family. Fewer bills to pay, fewer things to fix, fewer numbers to remember, fewer channels to watch. I wanted to get away from the gadgets and gizmos and contracts and all of the other things that were dominating my time, ruling my life, and bleeding me dry.

In short, I wanted a simpler life. One were I could still be a "productive member of society", but on *my* terms. I wanted to spend time with my family and enjoy it, without the baggage of fatigue or stress or worry. I wanted time to think, people to laugh with, and dirt roads that led to serene fishing holes. As silly as I may sound, what I wanted was Mayberry.

So during this transition of thinking and accepting, Catherine and I began getting ready for a change. We didn't know exactly what would happen or when, but we knew *something* was going to happen. Over the course of a couple years, we quietly began clearing all of the unneeded stuff we had accumulated out of our home. We worked on paying down our credit cards, and paying off our cars. We started looking at our home as a potential buyer would, and I methodically began painting, patching, and repairing. And all the while, we kept constantly looking at what possibilities were out there, where we might live, and what we might do.

One bright Monday morning, it all finally came to a head. I told my boss that I didn't feel like continuing, and we worked out a transition plan that would phase me out of the company in another month and a half. I went home early that Monday and told Catherine what I had done (I hadn't planned to resign when I went in that morning): the die was now cast; we had no choice now but to do *something*. After listening to me tell my story, she smiled and said, "*Look what I found this morning.*"

What she had found was a beautiful house over 100 years old that had been completely renovated and was priced – for those of us used to the Orlando housing market – for a song. We could buy it outright with what we would make from the sale of our current home and still have plenty left over to smooth our transition. Catherine had been so excited that she had already called the owner and talked with him about it, even before she knew I had quit my job. The house was located in a tiny little town called Liberty, KY.

You may think it foolish or silly, but both Catherine and I took this to be a sign from God. You can call it fate, or destiny, or whatever you choose. I don't really know much about all of that. What I do know is that I had just permanently closed a major door in my life, and *immediately* another door had opened.

We made plans to drive up and take a look; at the house, at the town – at Kentucky for that matter – with the mindset that this was going to be our new home unless something drastic told us otherwise. Quite to the contrary, everything we saw, heard, or ran into reinforced in our minds that this was to be our new home. I even loved the name: Liberty.

So two months later, there we were, and since that time I've been happier than I've ever been in my life. There wasn't even a "breaking in" period; we felt at home our first night here. I won't bore you with all of the details of why I like it here, but consider the fact that when I get in my car to go somewhere, I actually go somewhere. Granted, dodging the 3 stoplights in town sometimes creates a challenge, but usually not. Usually, I just walk anyway. Oh, and from what I'm told, they don't have too many hurricanes here either.

I love my home, I love my town, and I love the people. I feel *complete* here, and I think that God has led me to this specific little town for a reason, although I haven't the faintest clue as to what that might be. I'll find out soon enough, I guess.

I live in Liberty, KY. Like thousands of other little towns across America, Liberty doesn't have a lot going for it by today's standards. There are no bowling alleys, movie theaters, shopping malls, or country clubs. You won't find a Starbucks, a sports bar, a nightclub, or an upscale restaurant. You can't even buy a cold beer or a shot of whiskey.

In fact, there isn't very much in Liberty at all, except exactly what I was looking for.

Peace.

2

Lewis & Clark Abbreviated

"Daddy, can we go camping in the backyard sometime?" my 8 year old son asks.

"Sure," I reply, safe in knowing that a camping trip is well off into the future. It's January – we're still living in Florida at the time and I'm still running a daily sprint in the corporation rat race – and though the landscape is not exactly covered with a blanket of snow, it's still cold enough to keep two novices (this one without even a sleeping bag) indoors and waiting for warmer weather. "But we'll have to wait a few months," I finish.

A happy & excited boy bounces off like Tigger, already imagining the adventure.

"Daddy, is it warm enough to go camping now?" He's back, and he hasn't forgotten the promise. The seasons have changed - perhaps faster than I would have liked - and it is now April. This time, I lift my head to make a serious looking inspection of the outside world through the living room window. Cold weather is no longer an issue.

"I don't know, David," I say with due gravity. "Looks pretty cloudy out there. I think it's supposed to rain tonight."

"Okay, Daddy. But we'll go soon, won't we?"

"Absolutely. Very soon."

A happy & excited boy again bounces off like Tigger. For a moment, though, it seems to me that his bounce is maybe not quite as high as it once was. Must be my imagination, I think to myself.

My son is blessed with an uncanny memory and dogged persistence. His father has been given the gift of procrastination and the ability to prioritize those things that are important only to himself. And so as the weeks go by, the litany of excuses continues:

"Can we do it tonight, Daddy? Can we?"

"Maybe next week, David."

"Daddy's not feeling too well today, buddy."

"It's Wednesday, David. Daddy has to work tomorrow."

"Daddy has to get ready for a big meeting on Monday."

. . . and so on, and so on, and so on.

With each request, my little Tigger approaches me with boundless optimism and excitement, and with each rebuff, no matter how gentle, I can't help but accept the fact that his bounce is a little less than it was before.

Finally, almost as if to spite me, a beautiful Saturday arrives that can accept no excuses. A promise must be kept. Lewis & Clark, however long delayed, must now depart for the wild unknown, even if the wild unknown is only 50 feet from the back porch.

Supplies are gathered, coonskin caps are donned, checklists are reviewed. The two intrepid adventurers cut their way into the dense wilderness – St. Augustine grass cutting viciously at their ankles – as they find the perfect spot to make camp. A site is selected and the tent is pitched, with only minor confusion and sorting of poles, rods, & ropes.

Soon, our meager supplies are safely stored inside; our one sleeping bag for David, a few threadbare blankets for me, and what little food we have left. We take our minds off of the peril of our situation by playing some video games on the 12" color TV that I rigged up. By sheer luck more than anything else, I had rescued the 100' orange extension cord from my pack just before it had plunged over the cliff earlier in the day. As more sheer luck would have it (what can I say, I'm a pretty lucky guy), we had located a natural 110v 3-prong power source nearby.

Finding Liberty

In preparation for the next day, Lewis patiently instructed the older Clark how to play a wide variety of video games. Lewis' favorite teaching method seemed to involve trouncing Clark into oblivion over and over, but to his credit, the elder Clark was an attentive student, and soon learned methods & skills that allowed him to get trounced not quite so badly.

Midnight came and went. Finally, the two weary explorers, facing dawn in only a few hours, secure from the day's instruction, take a quick walk of the perimeter, and then lock down the tent to keep the savage forest creatures at bay. As they lay there in the darkness, with only the nighttime sounds of insects, animals, and people driving around way past their bedtimes, the ever inquisitive Lewis begs to be regaled by some of the more perilous stories of Clark's past. Namely, he wants to hear some ghost stories (*"but not too scary, Daddy"*).

And so passes the night.

In the morning, the two adventurers are abruptly awakened by a beautiful Indian squaw, who had thoughtfully prepared both men breakfast in a nearby tepee. The young Lewis was up almost instantly and bounded off, without even a glancing thought for his own safety. The older Clark, however, took a little more time shaking off the effects of the night; somewhere in the past 30 years, the ground had apparently gotten a little harder, and wounds once ancient and forgotten had been reawakened.

Two things entered into Clark's mind as the morning sun bathed the stiffness in his body. The first were the words of another great adventurer, Indiana Jones, who once said *"It ain't the years, it's the mileage."* The second was a Far Side cartoon where a settler lay beside his wagon, his body pierced with a dozen arrows even as the Indians still circled, who looked up to his partner and said, *"Yeah, Clem, I hurt. But it's a good hurt."*

The expedition was a success.

After breakfast, I came out to the back porch with a cup of coffee to enjoy the peace of the morning with Catherine. David had returned to the tent and was just lying there inside, looking up at the top of the dome with his hands behind his head, a smile on his face. When we asked him what he was doing, he stated that he was just trying to make the campout with his dad last a little bit longer. Suddenly, I realized for the first time how truly important this had been for David. This had not been a silly campout in the backyard at all, but a chance instead for a young boy to get the attention & affection of his father that he so desperately wanted.

I made a decision: Lewis & Clark *would* travel again. And if a brave little air mattress happens to make the next journey with them, well, so much the better.

3

Breaking the Chain

My wife and I were in our late twenties by the time we finally met. I was always partial to short blondes, so I really wasn't that surprised to find my heart captured by a tall, lovely brunette. What did I know? Not too much.

Our first date was a football game between Tampa Bay (my favorite team) and San Francisco. I won't tell you who won the game; suffice to say that we had end zone seats and I got the chance to see Jerry Rice up close & personal about 5 times. It didn't matter. It was a wonderful day. We were married 6 months later.

Catherine and I had both been previously married. She had 2 kids already, so I was entering into one of those "instant families" that some people joke about. But it wasn't a joke to me. I went from "easy going single guy" to "married with children" overnight.

The kids were great though. Lillian was still a baby, only 2 years old. Christopher was 8, which could have been a problem if he was anyone other than who he was. The first time I met Chris, he ran up to me with a smile as big as sunshine and hugged me. Just some guy he'd never seen before, come to take his mom out on a date. That's the kind of kid he was.

The first few years of our marriage were a challenge, but we did pretty good. Like most young families we struggled financially, but were eventually able to hop through several apartments on our way to a small house. We didn't have a lot and the ride wasn't always smooth, but we had each other. And along the way Sarah was born. Then David.

We got a dog. We got another dog. Our little family was growing.

Being an instant father brought it's own challenges, but it wasn't too bad. I'd been introduced into Lillian's life early enough so that she was used to me being around. And Christopher, as I said before, was a great kid; he made it easy. All I really had to do was take what my mom & dad had done with me and apply it to my kids. Things my parents had done that I agreed with I used myself. Things I didn't agree with I changed (I never force my kids to eat something that they really hate).

All in all, this "dad thing" didn't seem too tough, and the years went by with relative ease. Then Christopher turned 13, and suddenly I didn't know what to do anymore. My playbook was blank.

I was 13 when my parents got divorced. On a beautiful sunny morning, my brother and I were informed of what our sisters had already been told; that the safety of our nuclear family had disintegrated. Shortly thereafter, my dad was gone, only to be seen in fits and starts on selected weekends. My mom was left with trying to finish raising 4 kids by herself, 3 of which were teenagers.

We only had 1 car, so my mom began working the night shift at the hospital so that we could have the car in the day to go to school. She did that with the best of intentions, but in retrospect, she should have made us ride the bus. Because 6 nights a week she left for work at 10:15, not to return until 7:30 the next morning. And during that time the inmates were running the asylum. We could do anything we wanted. And we did.

So when Christopher turned 13, I had a big problem. I knew he wasn't going to do what *I* had been doing in my teenage years, but I had no idea what he was *supposed* to do. Even what should have been the simplest of things were instead huge problems: What do you talk about with a teenage boy? How much time do you spend with them? And doing what? When do you talk to them about sex? *How* do you talk to them about sex? Heck, forget the easy stuff, *what time are they supposed to go to bed?* I just didn't know. I had nothing to work from anymore.

I made it up as I went along, of course, but for the most part, I just stayed away from him altogether. Catherine was looking to me to be the father, to do those things that fathers do – that was my job after all – but I didn't know how, so I didn't really try. It was easier to just do as little as possible, because I had no confidence in what I was doing and it felt better to do *nothing* than to do something *wrong*.

When I did get involved it was *always* in a critical way. I went straight to measuring him to a perfect standard. Christopher could do nothing right in my eyes, nothing good enough. I thought I was teaching him, being a wise counsel. But Christopher could probably count the number of times I said "good job" on his thumb. How wise was that? The result was that this kid, this great kid, got shutout by his own family, and I was leading the charge. We were there, but we weren't *there*, and he had a rough time.

By the time he turned 16, Christopher was an alien to us. He was consumed by all things fantasy: fiction, video games, Dungeons & Dragons. He stayed in his room a lot. Mumbled and shuffled when he did come out. Most times he wore either an angry look of rebellion on his face or, even worse, total apathy. He wasn't fun to be around, so we stayed away, counting down the days to when we would be able to get him out of the house. What did he have to be so angry about anyway?

I would try to intervene sometimes, to step up and do the "manly" thing. I'd sit him down and explain to him "how things were". What was acceptable and what wasn't. And then I'd run away again.

There were very few times during his teenage years that we actually made real contact with each other, but I remember one night on the back porch when I was actually trying to be a little understanding for once. We had reached critical mass and something had to give.

I can't recall the entire conversation, but I was trying to get a grip on his obsession with fantasy and the occult. He looked at me and said that he was happier in the fantasy worlds he created than in the real one he lived in. That made me angry. But it made me angrier when I realized he was right. I had given Chris everything except what he really needed: a *father*. And it didn't have to be that way. And it was my fault.

Things got a little better after that. I tried to be more involved, more supporting and understanding. And when I would do that, when I would just *talk* to my son with real love and genuine caring, he would respond. Amazing. He turned out to be a fine young man, but that had more to do with his own character than anything I did for him. And I wonder what wounds he may still carry unhealed. It could have been so much better. So much better.

Whether we like it or not, being a parent is a powerful thing, and how we use or don't use that power has more impact than we can possibly imagine. Everything we do – *everything* – has an impact on our children. Just because we may not want that power doesn't make it go away. We're not affecting stock prices, we're affecting lives, and the decisions we make not only affect our children directly, but also everyone they'll touch, everything they'll do, and everything they'll feel for the rest of their lives. That's not something to be trifled with. It's not something to walk away from, figuratively or literally.

Some people like to think that it takes "a village" to raise children. That it's okay to "share" the burden with others. That it's socially acceptable to disregard our commitments if we just don't want them anymore. That school teachers and daycare workers should do a "better job" with our kids. That the icky things can be hired out to a 3rd party.

What an unbelievable collection of cop-outs. *Parents* raise children. It's *our* responsibility. It's hard, it's uncomfortable, it's frightening, and it requires sacrifice. And it never ends. There is no finish line. Coming up with cheap dime store rationalizations to absolve ourselves of responsibility may make us feel better, but they don't change anything.

When we dam a river, the river doesn't flow; but rivers are *meant* to flow, so they continue to try. When we stop teaching our children, our children stop learning; but children are *meant* to learn, so like the river, they'll also continue to try. Unlike the river, however, they'll probably be more successful. But what will they learn? Who will they learn it from? Will it be enough? Will it help them or hurt them? Do we even want to know?

I try not to be too judgmental, but anyone who says that parenting is easy is either stupid or not doing their job. *Having* kids is easy; *raising* them – raising them *right* – is the most difficult thing we will ever do. It's also the most important. Our kids will forgive us when we mess things up, but will they forgive us if we don't even try?

Let the river flow. And don't be afraid to get wet.

4

The Husband's Side of Submission

Last night at church our pastor was reading selected verses from Colossians 3. When he had finished, someone (a man) piped up and noted that he had skipped verse 18.

"Wives, submit yourselves unto your own husbands, as it is fit in the Lord." - Colossians 3:18

Obviously he wasn't the only one who noticed, because his comment brought about a round of good natured laughter from the entire congregation. Our pastor laughed as well and played it off by saying that he "wasn't going to touch that one".

In his defense, it was neither the time nor the place to discuss that particular verse, as he was making a point about a completely different topic, and the subject of "submission" is a topic unto itself. A rather *big* topic I might add, and one that carries with it a lot of strong and varied opinions. Just take a look at the definition:

Submit: To yield or surrender (oneself) to the will or authority of another. To give in to the authority, power, or desires of another.

To *yield*. To *surrender*. To *give in*. Whoa! It's no wonder that this is a touchy subject. I mean, who wants to do *that*? It's tough enough to submit to God, but at least we can understand that directive, even if we don't always do it. And though God also *specifically* commands wives to submit to their husbands (and Colossians 3:18 is only one of many passages in the Bible where that is very clearly stated), even women who are otherwise very devout Christians sometimes have a tough time accepting *that*, to say nothing of the non-Christian women in our society.

But why?

Well, to begin with, it just doesn't seem fair. The word "submission" carries with it a lot of negative connotation. Merely thinking of the word brings about visions of weakness, pliancy, feebleness, meekness - even deviant sexual preferences - that all point to one thing: lack of control. When it comes to submission, it is *control* - whether we have it or don't have it - that is the underlying issue.

But without realizing it, we are all submitting, and giving up that control, to *something* every single day. By paying taxes we are submitting to the government. When we drive our cars we are submitting to the petroleum industry. Even by sitting down to watch TV, we are submitting ourselves – our minds & our time – to whatever that magical little box has to show us. You may think that that's not the same thing, and you may be right. After all, when we do all of those things we are getting something in return, whether it's social protection & welfare, the ability to travel, or entertainment.

We are taught from childhood that control is something that we need & want and should aspire to have. We are taught that control is *good*, and we should strive to control everything in our lives, from our behavior & language to our education & careers. We need to control our children, our environment, our employees, our tempers, our time – even that crabgrass in the backyard. And don't even get started on control of the *remote* control.

Control is king. It shows that we are "on top of things" and "have our act together". It shows that we're strong, independent, confident, and intelligent. Let's be serious, who in their right mind would want to give up those things? Nobody!

The interesting thing though, is that nobody has to give those up. In fact, in my opinion, no one ever really has, because no one has ever had *real* control over anything in the first place.

Control is an illusion. It simply doesn't exist. If you don't believe that, think about it for awhile and see if you can come up with *one single thing* that you have *absolute* control over. Your health? Your home? Your cash-flow? Your children? Your car? True, we can have more control over some things than others, but do any of us have total control of anything?

By the very nature of it's definition, control is the ability *"to exercise authoritative or dominating influence over"*, and therein is the key to what control really is: *influence.* I can provide a good influence for my children; teach them well, lead by example, discipline fairly, but I cannot *control* what they will do or say. In the end, they determine that for themselves.

I can influence my health by exercising regularly, watching my diet, and refraining from any sort of risky endeavor whatsoever, and still be struck down dead – at *any* age, at *any* time, for *any* reason. Regardless of how much we may want to, we can't really control *anything.* All we can really do is have some degree of influence on a particular outcome. Ultimately, the only one who has any *real* control is also the only one who actually has the wisdom to be able to wield it properly; God.

So what does all of this have to do with submission? Well, when we submit ourselves to someone else, on the surface it looks like we're giving up control, but what we're really doing is giving up our influence. But this is where things get weird, because are we really?

Although it may not make any sense at all, I would suggest to you that when you submit yourself to your husband, your influence actually *increases.* On top of that, despite what you may think, just like when you submitted yourself to Uncle Sam, "big oil", or Hollywood, when you submit yourself to your husband, you will *get something back.*

How can that be? Well, let's back up a minute and take a look at something much bigger than all of us. God tells us that we are to submit ourselves to Him, and that we are to put Him as the #1 priority in our lives.

God is the ultimate authority. In commanding us not to put any other gods before Him, He is making it clear to us that He – *and He alone* – is in charge. He *does not* and *will not* "share" that responsibility with anyone else. It doesn't matter whether we like that or not; it's not up for discussion or a vote, it's just the way it is. He is in charge, and we as Christians must submit ourselves to Him.

On the surface, that doesn't seem to be fair either. In fact, it could seem kind of presumptuous and arrogant of God to demand that we put Him first. Nice job if you can get it, right? But when we put away our selfishness and do just that – submit to Him – what happens? Does God jump around waving a big foam finger yelling "*I'm number 1! I'm number 1!*" and fleece us for everything we've got?

Of course not. On the contrary, he provides a stable foundation for our lives, clears the way before us, protects our sides from attack, provides air cover from above, and guards our flank. All we have to do is trust and follow. It's a curious thing that by submitting ourselves to Him and putting Him first, we are the ones who actually benefit, not Him. *We get something back.*

God tells us to trust in Him, to put Him first. He tells us that in the Bible – *commands* it in fact – and as it turns out, it's pretty good advice. Then God tells wives to submit to their husbands. If that were not for the benefit of us all – including the wives – why would He direct it? Does He give bad advice? Would He lie to us, hurt us, or make us do something that would have a bad result? No way. Those things we do for ourselves.

So, if you submit yourself to another, you can actually come out *better* than if you didn't. At least, in the case of submitting to God. But what about people? Will the same thing happen? From what I've witnessed and experienced in life, not always. The key, I think, is how the person you're submitting to feels about you. Do they *love* you? Do they *care* about you? If not, they will probably use your submission for their own gain, but if they *do* love and care about you, they will use the power that you have relinquished to them to make things better for you. Why does that happen?

Well, flip the coin for a minute and look what happens to the person that you have submitted to. For the first several years of our marriage, I treated Catherine as an "equal partner". We shared decision making responsibility and ran our home, our marriage, and our lives as a 50-50 partnership. One day, she told me that she was relinquishing her end of that partnership, and that I was completely in charge of everything. I had ultimate decision making authority, and what I said was the law of the house.

She put me 100% in charge, and suddenly, I was . . . . well, *in charge*. I no longer shared that responsibility with her. I made all decisions and I was responsible for *everything*, from the important to the mundane. I picked when & where we would go on vacation. I could approve or veto any purchase. The doctrine of discipline in my home was mine to write. My family would look to me – *and me alone* – to chart the course that our family took. In short, my wife would submit to me and she would obey me, regardless of what my "command" was.

Yahoo! Take *that* Women's Liberation! You may think that the first thing I did was jump around waving a big foam finger yelling *"I'm number 1! I'm number 1!"* and fleece my family for everything they had.

In actuality, the first thing I did was have an anxiety attack, because I suddenly found myself completely and solely responsible for the welfare of my wife & family. *In charge? Me? All by myself? Solely responsible? What if I make a bad decision? What if I make a mistake?* No longer was there anyone to "share" the blame if something went wrong. It was all on me.

If submission seems to run counter to everything that modern society tells us from a women's perspective, realize that it does the same thing from a man's point of view as well. For my entire life, I too have been told that women and men should share authority. TV shows and commercials have bombarded me with the same message over and over: men are bumbling idiots who can't seem to do anything right.

The women – and in some cases, even the *children* – are the ones who know the answers, but never the father. The ship I had been traveling on my whole life had sailed many miles away from the port of "Father Knows Best". But whether I liked it or not, I was "all alone at the top." And a funny thing happened. All of my decisions – all of them – suddenly centered not on anything that I wanted, but instead on what my wife and family wanted. What was good for *them* and what was in *their* best interests.

By submitting herself to me, my wife had given me an incredible gift. She was allowing me to be what God intended me to be: a man. A leader, a teacher, a provider, and a protector for my family. A man of strength and conviction – *and* love and compassion – that would stand firm and think for himself. A man who whose actions would be dictated by what was *right,* not what was politically correct or acceptable to mainstream society. My wife was asking me to be a *man*. It was time for me to start acting like one, instead of the milk-toast that I had allowed myself to become.

Up to that point, Catherine & I were often at odds with each other as we both tried to take credit for the good and point our fingers at the bad. By submitting herself to me, the element of competition had been completely removed from our marriage, and I no longer felt that I had to fight to make my views be heard or to secure "my own" things. It was *all* mine now, and what I found was that I didn't want to keep everything to myself. I wanted to give it back. From that point on, the happiness of my wife and my family was paramount. If anyone in my family would suffer want, it would be me.

As an example of how this plays out, consider a night out to a restaurant. In my "old" marriage, where my wife and I were "equal" partners, conflicts would frequently result. Maybe she wanted Chinese, whereas I wanted a good steak. Maybe she wanted a quiet, dark atmosphere, when I wanted a noisy sportsbar. Whatever the reason, with an equal partnership, conflict is *automatic* as soon as there is a disagreement, and because two people are sharing the leadership role, neither has the authority to make a final call.

Usually when this type of conflict came up, I would wind up submitting to her, rather than taking the risk of future silence, cold shoulders, and disdain for intimacy for days or weeks to come. But even though I would submit, I wouldn't be happy about it, and part of me would hold it against her, resenting her for it, feeling that she was using leverage to get her way.

The end result was that for the dinner to continue, *someone* had submit to the other, and regardless of who it was, the evening would be at least unsatisfactory, if not altogether ruined, for one of us. And if one of us was unhappy, you can bet that whoever it was would make sure that the other one felt the same way too. We were equals after all.

Worse than the immediate effect was the long term outcome. Because this type of conflict is never resolved, it doesn't go away. It gets held inside to fester and become part of an internal "stockpile" of ammunition to be brought up during future conflicts. A long term "cold war" develops between husband & wife that neither can win.

Now look at the same situation in our "new" marriage, where I know that the decision of where to eat is mine and mine alone. Guess which restaurant I choose to go to? If you guessed *"Wherever she wants to go"*, you're dead on. Because she has empowered me with the gift of submission, my gift back to her is to do whatever I can to make her happy. And whatever that happens to be, it makes *me* happy.

It may not seem like a big difference on the surface. After all, in both the "before" and "after" illustrations above, we would usually wind up going to where *she* wanted to go. But while that is true, the difference lies in *why* we would do that, and how we both would feel about it. In a 50/50 partnership, we would both frequently lose. Now that I have sole authority, both of us always win.

An amazing thing. By submitting herself to me, Catherine didn't lose a thing. As strange as it may seem, she actually gets "her way" more now than ever before. Her influence has actually *increased,* and not only that, it's perfectly okay with me.

My wife is still my closest confidant, and I still always seek her counsel. And though there are some rare times when we don't agree on something and I feel that I have to make a decision counter to her wishes, I always make sure that she understands exactly why I'm making that decision. To understand that it is in the best interests of her and our family, never my own selfish desires. I have no reason to be selfish anymore.

In closing, there's something else that I'd like to mention. Although this entire discussion has been centered on one little verse – Colossians 3:18 – you should know that there's also a little verse immediately *following* Colossians 3:18 that has nothing at all to do with a wife's submission. It's another command from God – this time directed at husbands – that I now find I am able to obey without any effort at all:

Husbands, love your wives, and do not be embittered against them.   - Colossians 3:19

And He began speaking a parable to the invited guests when He noticed how they had been picking out the places of honor at the table; saying to them, "When you are invited by someone to a wedding feast, do not take the place of honor, lest someone more distinguished than you may have been invited by him, and he who invited you both shall come and say to you, 'Give place to this man,' and then in disgrace you proceed to occupy the last place. But when you are invited, go and recline at the last place, so that when the one who has invited you comes, he may say to you, 'Friend, move up higher'; then you will have honor in the sight of all who are at the table with you. For everyone who exalts himself shall be humbled, and he who humbles himself shall be exalted."
Luke 14:7-11

5

Raising a Walton's Family in a Simpson's World

Within weeks of our marriage Catherine got pregnant with what would turn out to be a beautiful little girl named Sarah. With 2 children already, we made the decision for Cat to quit work and stay at home.

We took a look at how this would impact us financially, and after deducting the costs that it took to allow her to work in the first place (clothes, lunch, gas, daycare, etc.), we realized that only about 10% of what she earned was actually hitting the checkbook as extra income.

Though that made the decision easier, we were soon to fully realize how little it was that I was making on my own, and we watched our credit card balance climb at an alarming – and oh, so consistent – rate each month. We felt ourselves sinking, and started looking for every way we could to stop what little money there was from slipping through our fingers.

We cancelled the newspaper, we stopped ordering pizza, we cut up our ATM cards (still don't have them to this day). We even turned off the A/C, and I can still remember those muggy October nights with windows open and fan blowing, where my 5 month pregnant wife & I would lay on top of the sheets – unmoving – as we waited for the relentless Florida heat to abate enough for us to drift off to sleep while the never ending traffic on the turnpike sang us our lullaby.

But as drastic as some of these measures were, the real "shot heard 'round the world" was when we cancelled cable TV.

If you think lepers in the street get strange looks, try telling people that you don't have cable.

The interesting thing was that we didn't really mind. With only 7 or so stations (a couple of which were suffering so much from perpetually blinding snowstorms that they really didn't count), channel surfing was a quick exercise. It now took us only seconds to realize that there wasn't anything worth watching rather than the ½ hour that it used to take. We spent our time savings playing games together, reading, going for walks, or volunteering at church. Months slipped into years and as our income gradually grew we added some of the things we had given up back into our lives (A/C being #1 on *that* list!), but the continued absence of having hundreds of channels at our fingertips didn't bother us at all.

Six years into our marriage we gained some elbow room and moved into an elegant home in a beautiful neighborhood that somehow had been constructed without having every tree mown down or setting each house so close together that they could have been mistaken for apartments. But the huge trees that shaded us also caused a problem: our TV reception was terrible. We could only get 1 or 2 stations, and even then not very well. It was time for a change. Fitting cable TV into our budget was no longer a concern, and soon all of those long lost friends were visiting us again. You know who they are; the History Channel, the Discovery Channel, the Cartoon Channel, and all their acronymic friends: TNT, HGTV, TLC, ESPN, and the rest. And all in crisp, clear, digital clarity! We were finally back in the 21st Century and we were cooking with gas, baby!

It was great! For a while.

Though we enjoyed having all of these new windows of the world to look through, our time spent doing things together as a family diminished. Not as many books were being read anymore. Games lay unmolested and lonely on the closet shelf. Repairs and projects around the house began to pile up. But while that might have been a little disturbing, our fresh new friends with so much to tell quickly made us forget about it. We were too busy being entertained to worry about such things.

After a couple of years, however, I noticed a change. While we were still ignoring a lot of the things we used to do in favor of watching TV, our fresh friends weren't so fresh anymore. The kids seemed to have narrowed their focus down exclusively to the Cartoon Channel. Catherine started having a hard time distinguishing the new shows on HGTV & TLC from the old ones. Even me, a die-hard History Channel purist, began wondering how many different ways of looking at Hitler's rise & fall were necessary for one person to have. Nevertheless, its addictive nature continued to keep us coming back for more.

But in addition to everyone's waning interest in what we were watching, other factors started to come into play: The quality of the programming. The continuous and increasingly frequent stream of commercials. And the cost. We were paying almost $60 a month for this, and we had no "premium" stations. When the cable company suddenly decided to raise our rates by another $7 a month (for no particular reason that I could tell), we decided to switch to satellite. That got us back to about $40 a month, but we had even fewer channels than before. Then we started having reception problems.

I was sitting on the couch one night with the phone to my ear yet again as I waited on hold for tech support, when the insanity of the situation finally came home. Alienation of my family from each other, programs that ran the gamut from boring to shocking (with very little interesting in between), an endless barrage of commercials telling me and my children how to buy happiness, my non-refundable life ticking away as I wait on the phone for tech support, and my building frustration with all of it. *And I was <u>paying</u> for the privilege of this experience!*

We had a quick family meeting. Actually, it wasn't really a meeting at all. I simply told Cat and the kids that I was canceling the service. To my surprise, there was no big backlash, crying, or gnashing of teeth. They all just shrugged and said "okay". That settled, a quick trip to the store and $26 for a good set of rabbit ears and we had our 7 or so stations – and our peace of mind – back. I considered the $500 a year we began saving as a self inflicted raise.

We still watch TV, but not nearly as much. I've become quite fond of the "mute" button, and will often do my own voiceovers on the commercials, much to the delight of the kids. Usually though, we'll watch movies on our bottom of the line $60 combo VCR/DVD player. We don't rent much; it seems that the public library now has as large a selection of movies, educational programs, and TV series as most video stores. Oh, and they also have books. Lots of them. We usually pick up a few of those too.

When I was in the 3rd grade or so, back when dinosaurs ruled the earth (or so my kids would tell you), I had a strict bedtime of 8:00 on school nights. Except on Thursdays. On Thursdays my parents let me stay up an extra hour to watch *The Waltons*.

I don't know whether it was the show I enjoyed or the fact that I didn't have to go to bed for an extra hour, but I always looked forward to it. Imagine my surprise when, 30 years later, I saw the series on DVD while perusing the library shelves. I checked out the disc of the first 6 episodes from the first season. Figured I'd see if my kids would like it.

They did.

I know it's just a TV show, but it's a good one. A couple of nights a week we'll sit down as a family and watch a "new" episode. It's a big production; David will run through the house like Paul Revere informing everyone that *The Waltons* are coming, and Sarah will then make sure every light in the house is off to avoid those annoying reflections on the screen. By the time the trumpet starts playing, we're all in our places.

I'm thrilled that my kids enjoy it. Seeing a world where values still existed, the pace was slower, hard work & sweat were valued, friendliness was the norm rather than the exception, and family was paramount; the strength of which could weather almost any storm. It was also very noticeable to me that none of the eight kids on the show ever looked John Walton in the face and said "*Don't have a cow, man*". That's the type of family I want to raise. That's the kind of legacy I want to leave.

So, in our own way, we continue to turn our backs to the 21st Century and what it tells us we should hold important. We try to find other pursuits, things we can do together. We sit down for dinner. We read one of Aesop's fables during desert and let the kids discuss what they think it means. Catherine homeschools during the day. I read classics to the kids at night (We just finished *Treasure Island*; a good thing too because the pirate voices were killing me). When we do watch TV now, we make sure that we are in control of it, rather than letting it control us. I like that.

All that being said, I do admit that I was disappointed when Monday Night Football moved to ESPN. But as it turned out, it didn't really hurt at all.

I simply found something else to do.

6

Understanding What We Can't Comprehend

I was watching a show not long ago where scientists & experts were analyzing some of the better known events in the Bible. I've heard these types of discussions before:

"Could there really have been a man of Goliath's size among the Philistines?"

"Was there a rational scientific explanation for the 'fire & brimstone' that supposedly rained down on Sodom and Gomorrah?"

"Is it possible for a man to spend a night with lions and not get torn to pieces without divine intervention?"

I love science almost as much as history, and regardless of whether or not I agree with what is being said, I always keep my mind open to listen to the new ideas, theories, speculation, and educated guesses that come about. However, I always take these explanations with a grain of salt, realizing that just because I read something (or hear it), doesn't make it true.

Since man began exploring his world, scientists of one sort or the other have always existed, and they have always been making new discoveries, issuing new facts, and coming up with new explanations for what they see and hear. I have no issue with science at all, even as it compares to religion. What I do take issue with, though, is when scientists take their speculation or discoveries and push them out as absolute fact, with no further discussion allowed. At least, no further discussion until the scientists themselves decide to change it.

By balancing science with history, I know that science is, and has always been, a work in progress. It is constantly changing, redefining, and correcting itself as our knowledge of ourselves and the world around us increases. Because it's in a state of perpetual change, many of the theories and known facts throughout the ages have been modified, updated, or completely replaced as new information is gained that shows that we didn't have it quite right the first time.

Even today, this is still happening. Just as one example, twenty years ago, scientists "knew" that the universe was 18 billion years old. Today, they now "know", based on further scientific examination, that the universe is only 14 billion years old.

I find it interesting that people rarely question these "modifications" that are constantly occurring. If challenged on it, the scientific community defends itself by saying that they were only providing an estimate, or the best guess based on the information at hand. I wonder why they don't make more of an effort to provide that clarification upfront? Because from what I've seen, more often than not, whatever information is presented is usually given in the format of "this is what happened", or "this is the explanation". That is, at least, until the next revision.

And our society, much like sheep, simply accepts these continuous changes to "known fact" as they occur, much like taking a pill. No questions, just "Oh, okay".

Gulp.

I don't know about you, but the last time I checked, the difference between 14 and 18 billion years was *4 billion*. That's a pretty big error. Don't think so? Try counting to 4 billion. And don't be surprised at all if it turns out that sometime in the future there's an adjustment or two to the 14 billion estimate. I'm pretty sure there will be.

I don't blame scientists for revising what they know. After all, we're constantly learning new things about the world around us. But I do blame them, for whatever reasons they may have, for their vanity in not admitting even the possibility that many (possibly most) of the scientific facts, truths, and explanations that we have today will most assuredly change in some way in the future.

When science comes to bear arms against theology, the Bible must seem a pretty easy mark. Whether you believe what the Bible says or not, it has been around for thousands of years, and though it has been retranslated several times as our language has evolved, it doesn't have the luxury of being able to constantly redefine itself. In the end, the information it contains is static, making a pretty easy target for those who wish to attack it.

So with that background in place, let's return to our program, or rather, the program I was watching. In this particular show, Noah was taking a beating from several experts. One in particular was making a point – very strongly – that there was no way that Noah could have built a boat in the size and dimensions that were stated in the Bible:

"Make for yourself an ark of gopher wood; you shall make the ark with rooms, and shall cover it inside and out with pitch. And this is how you shall make it; the length of the ark three hundred cubits, its breadth fifty cubits, and its height thirty cubits" - Genesis 6:14-15

A cubit is a form of linear measurement from a man's elbow to the tip of his longest finger, which converts to roughly 18 inches. With that conversion factor, the ark would have been about 450 feet long, by 75 feet wide, by 45 feet high. The expert on the show was very adamant that there was no possible way Noah could have built a boat that size using wood & the technology of his day. It was simply *not possible*. He wasn't leaving any room for argument. At most, he stated, Noah could have built a ship about 280 feet long. Yes, it was quite possible that he could have done that.

After making his very clear point that the construction of the ark as described was simply impossible (swallow the pill – *gulp*), he and the other experts then moved right along to discuss the possibility of Noah fitting 2 of every animal on a ship of that size, where he would have gotten them from, etc., etc., etc., and how ridiculous all of that nonsense was. They could have saved their breath, because I wasn't following along anymore. I was still stuck on the boat.

There were a couple of things that I found odd with his determination. One, was that he was using an example of a double-brow boat in his analysis, the classical example of a boat which curves up to a point on both ends. Maybe his assertion regarding the size was correct about a boat of that type, but why was he assuming that that's the type of boat that Noah built? Was it simply because that's the type of boat people have been building in recent history?

The Bible doesn't say anything about pointy ends or a curved hull. It's pretty basic in its description: 300 x 50 x 30 cubits.

I found it odd that the possibility of a rectangular, flat-bottomed ship was given no consideration, especially since I have heard many other experts in past years say – and show in computer simulations – that not only could a "barge" type vessel of those dimensions have been built, but also that from an engineering perspective, those dimensions were well proportioned to a ship of that size, and it would have been the very type of boat that Noah would have needed, providing maximum room, ease of construction, and good stability.

I also questioned the expert's pronouncement regarding the technology that Noah had available, specifically, that the tools & engineering to construct an ark of that size did not yet exist. I think this is a very arrogant assumption, based purely on what technology has been available to us over the past few hundred years and how it has advanced during that time.

Again, taking a look at history, we know that the Romans had the technology & knowledge to build roads, aqueducts, sewers, bridges, and cities out of stone over 2000 years ago. What we automatically assume though, is that our tools, technology, and engineering expertise have continually increased from that point, and that is blatantly not true.

In the time of the 1st millennium, *centuries* after the fall of Rome, the English, who were surrounded by the legacy of what Rome had constructed, didn't have the knowledge to even *repair* these structures as they decayed, much less improve on them or build something better. Crumbled stone walls were replaced with wood, fallen bridges that had spanned wide rivers were abandoned, and sewer systems ceased to exist at all, simply because they didn't know how the Romans had built these in the first place.

Huh. So centuries *after* the fall of the Roman Empire, and we knew *less* than they did? So much for continual advancement. And if that could happen once, is it possible that it might have happened more than once? The answer, of course, is "yes", because we have seen it happen numerous times in history. The bottom line is that we have no idea what Noah did or did not have available to him. We *assume* that what he had to work with, both in knowledge and tools, was pretty rudimentary. But based on history, if we choose to consider it, I think that's a wickedly dangerous assumption.

The last problem I have with whether or not the ark was actually built is another arrogant assumption. Basically, that because there is no evidence of it, it never existed, or if it did exist, it couldn't possibly have been like it was described.

I know that scientists are always looking to prove things, and that they want concrete evidence to back it up, but it bothers me terribly when, simply because there is no evidence that we know of, things we may find incredible are completely discounted as mere silliness and myth.

Think about the pyramids of Egypt. Although we've come up with a lot of good possible explanations as to how they were built, what tools might have been used, and how the dimensions could be so precise, we really don't know. Even by today's standards, they are an engineering marvel, one that would certainly compare with – if not surpass – an ark built to the dimensions stated in the Bible. But of all of the questions that we still have about the pyramids, there is one thing we know for sure: they exist. Of that, there is no doubt. We can see them, and climb on them, and measure them. Even if we might not know exactly *how* they were built, we know that they *were*.

But what if they *didn't* exist? What if they had already long since crumbled to dust or been swallowed up by sand? What if the only evidence we had of the pyramids were some ancient documents – and maybe a few sketches – showing their size and dimensions? Would we believe then that they had actually been built? If we approached them with the same assumptions and attitude that these particular scientists were approaching the ark, I would have to believe that the idea would be absolutely ridiculed.

But that's the catch, isn't it? Because they _were_ built. And even with all of the knowledge and technology available to us today, we still don't know how.

For me, in my quest towards faith, these are the conversations that go through my head. The idea of an all powerful, all knowing God who created the world, who created us, and who can keep track of *everything* that the billions of people on this earth have ever done and ever thought, is beyond human comprehension. Couple that with the lack of concrete scientific evidence of His existence, the fact of which is so continually impressed upon us these days, and it's easy to see why people might have trouble believing in God. Our minds simply cannot comprehend a being of that magnitude and power, and there is no proof of His existence, ergo, He must not exist.

The problem with that is that we live in a world of things that we do not understand and cannot comprehend, but accept anyway without much thought. Here's a question: How big is the universe? Think about that for a few minutes and try to fathom it's true size. Pretty big by all accounts, sure, by *how* big? If we can determine its size, it must be able to be measured, and if we can measure it, it must have boundaries of some sort. But if it has boundaries, what's beyond those boundaries? After all, if something has an end, it also has to be the beginning for something else. But then, how big is whatever it is that exists beyond the ends of the universe? And what's on the other side of *that*?

Maybe the universe doesn't end, maybe it goes on forever. But how could that be? The universe isn't something theoretical, like time or numbers, it's very real and full of real stuff like planets and stars. How could something we can see and touch and cruise around in have no ending? It *must* have an end somewhere. But if it has an end . . .

If we are truthful with ourselves, we can only admit that our minds can't really comprehend the concept, magnitude, and scope of the universe. Theoretical infinity (numbers, time, etc.) is something we can at least grasp, but *spatial* infinity, if we really stop to think about it, is beyond our ability to comprehend. In fact, if the only evidence we had of the universe were some ancient documents - and maybe a few sketches - describing it's size and dimensions, I doubt we would believe it could exist.

But that's the catch, isn't it? Because it *does* exist. And somehow we exist right in the middle of it. And we accept that, even if we can't comprehend it and don't understand it. Why then, I wonder, should the existence of a God that we cannot truly comprehend be that much more difficult to accept?

In the final analysis, I don't believe that science will ever prove or disprove God. I think our Creator set it up that way on purpose. If He intended, He could provide proof to us easily, but to prove Himself to us would also deny us all of one of the greatest gifts that He gave us: the ability to freely make our own choices, even if one of those choices is to deny Him completely. God wants us to believe in Him by faith, and faith, by definition, is belief *without* proof.

That I can at least comprehend, even if I don't necessarily understand.

7

The Prodigal Son's Brother

If you were to ask people to name any 3 parables in the Bible, the story of the Prodigal Son would probably be on most of the lists. It's one of the better known parables that Jesus related, and almost everyone is familiar with it. In addition to having read it several times myself, I've also heard it taught in Sunday school, preached from the pulpit, and discussed in small groups on numerous occasions going back to when I was a little boy. And every time I walked away feeling stupid.

If you've ever found yourself in a position where everyone else seems to understand something that you don't, something that is apparently very basic & very fundamental, you can maybe get an appreciation of how I felt.

Whenever the Prodigal Son came up as the topic of discussion, my ears would prick up and I would wait in anticipation as I hoped to hear someone finally address what I did not understand. The question that no one other than me seemed to have, and the one that I had long since become too embarrassed to ask.

I would look around to see – as always – everyone nodding their heads in agreement, and then the discussion would end and we would all walk away.

The whole story is found in Luke 15:11-32, but to loosely paraphrase it in the interests of space: there were 2 brothers, the younger of which asked his father to give him his share of his inheritance. He then went off and proceeded to blow everything on wine, women, and song, and soon found himself destitute, starving, and far from home. He went back to his father with true repentance in his heart, and his father not only accepted him back, but made a really big deal out of it.

I always understood the basic message of this parable. It serves to illustrate that no matter how badly we mess up our lives, no matter what we may do or how low we may stoop, God will always accept us back if we come to Him with true repentance in our hearts. And not only will God not be angry with us or hold a grudge, He'll make a really big deal out of it. It's truly a great thing.

A great thing, it seemed to me, if you happened to be the prodigal son. But what if you're not? What if you're the prodigal son's brother? Because he *did* have a brother, and his brother was not quite as excited about the prodigal son's return or how he was being treated:

But he became angry, and was not willing to go in; and his father came out and began entreating him. But he answered and said to his father, 'Look! For so many years I have been serving you, and I have never neglected a command of yours; and yet you have never given me a kid that I might be merry with my friends; but when this son of yours came, who has devoured your wealth with harlots, you killed the fattened calf for him.'
- Luke 15:28-30

And *that* was the core of my angst about this parable, because didn't the prodigal son's brother have a *reason* to be a little bit upset?

I mean, here he's been the whole time, being faithful to his father, doing *exactly* as he should, *never* failing in his duties, doing *everything* right. And yet, little brother goes out and makes a complete fool of himself, squanders everything, sins like it's going out of style, does *nothing* right, and then comes crawling back a pathetic mess and – well, well, well – stop the presses 'cause look who's back in town. Oh, and let's not only welcome him back, but let's also just conveniently forget everything he's done, and – Oh! I got it, I got it! – let's *reward* him. You know, treat him like a king and throw a great big party and all that. And don't worry about me. After all, I'm just the son who's been here the whole time doing everything you've ever asked of me. No, no, no, I don't feel slighted at all. My feelings aren't hurt one bit. I'm just happy that Mr. Screw-up gets the love & attention he so obviously deserves.

Okay, maybe that's a little over the top, but then again, maybe not. Don't you think that's probably how the prodigal son's brother felt? And that's what bothered me for so many years about this story, because I would have felt the same way.

The focus of the teaching, preaching, and discussion always seems to be on the first part of the parable; the prodigal son's return. But this is a long parable, and the second part of it – almost *half* of the entire story – isn't about the prodigal son at all; it's solely about the prodigal son's *brother*; how *he* felt and how *he* reacted, and no one in my life ever did a very good job of explaining to me why he *shouldn't* have been hurt & angry. That part of the story always seemed to get glossed over. "*Well, he should have been happy*", I would be told. Okay, got it. He *should have* been. But he wasn't. And to be honest, I kind of have to side with him; it does seem a little unfair.

The parable ends with the father talking to the prodigal son's brother:

"And he said to him, 'My child, you have always been with me, and all that is mine is yours. But we had to be merry and rejoice, for this brother of yours was dead and has begun to live, and was lost and has been found.'"   – Luke 15:31-32

Once again, I understood these final words of the parable, but they still didn't seem to address why the prodigal son's brother shouldn't have been hurt. They didn't take the sting out of the situation. Here the prodigal son goes out and parties to his heart's desire, and then comes home and it's yet *another* party. Meanwhile, his brother gets nothing for his diligence and loyalty? Nothing?

I struggled with this for *years*. It ate at me, because *Jesus* was the one who told this parable, these were *His* words, and for a long time I felt that there had to be a flaw with the story, because no matter how I looked at it, all I could conclude was that the prodigal son's brother had a legitimate beef. And it seemed to me that Jesus just kind of left that hanging.

It even occurred to me to wonder why Jesus thought it necessary to mention a brother at all. I mean, couldn't He have made the same point about "God taking us back no matter what" if the prodigal son had been an only child? But He didn't. Instead He devoted the entire second half of the story to talk *specifically* about the prodigal son's brother. Why would Jesus go to all the trouble of telling us about the brother, especially if that part of the story was flawed in some way? He had to have a reason, and if I was to believe that Jesus was without flaw, then the flaw had to be with *me* and the way *I* was thinking about the story. There was something here that I just didn't get, something that I was too blind to see.

One of the things that I love about the Bible is not necessarily what it tells us, but what it *doesn't* tell us. It *forces* us to think about what is left unsaid and come up with the answers ourselves. If we do that with a skeptical mind, what we see are "holes" and flaws. But when we do it with a pure heart, a true desire to understand, and (sometimes) an unyielding persistence, the answers – no matter how elusive – will eventually become clear to us. And it's amazing to me how they *always* make sense.

When the answer finally came to me, what I discovered is that there was actually more than one. The mental block that had kept the wisdom of this story from me for so long was that *I* was looking at it from a human perspective, how I think things should be. We may all be created in God's image, but when it comes to our minds, we often *think* very much like the human beings we are. And humans by nature are selfish creatures.

One possibility is that as soon as the prodigal son's father explained to him that "*you have always been with me, and all that is mine is yours*", the brother understood what his father was saying and his anger simply faded away. We don't know what his reaction was to these words, but maybe they were something like, "*Oh, I never thought about it that way. You're right; let's go celebrate*". All he needed was a little reminder.

It's also possible that the brother's anger stemmed from the fact that he didn't know that the prodigal son had returned to his father *repentant*. All the brother knew at that point was that he was back and being treated royally. It could be that he thought the prodigal son hadn't changed his spots and was simply back to see what else he could glean from papa, and he was upset that his father was being so stupid as to cast more pearls to swine rather than show favor to someone who would make much better use of that generosity. If that were the case, then as soon as his father informed him that the prodigal son was in fact a changed man ("*for this brother of yours was dead and has begun to live*") his anger would also have dissipated.

A third possibility – and the most probable in my mind – is that neither of the above happened. The prodigal son's brother was just plain mad, and his father's explanation didn't do much to make him feel any better. As I've already mentioned, if this was the case, it's also how *I* would have felt. And I would have felt justified in that anger.

And I would have been wrong.

The prodigal son's brother *did* do everything right and followed his father's every command, but if he felt anger at his brother that was not appeased by his father's words, it shows that though he may have been perfect in his *actions*, he was not perfect in his *thoughts*. His outward appearance reflected his father's wishes, but inside he was obviously not quite so righteous. He harbored selfish desires, wanted to know what was in it for him, and perhaps even had a hidden agenda for the life that he led. The law was being followed, but not the spirit.

If he was *truly* like his father, he would have *thought* like his father, had the same *love & compassion* as his father, and felt the same *pain* as his father. And if that was the case, like his father, he would have rejoiced at his brother's return. The servants, having seen for years the real grief that he carried in his heart for the loss of his brother, would have made sure that he was *immediately* informed upon his brother's return – maybe even before they told his father. His young legs would have carried him to his brother *first*, and he would have been the first to embrace him, to cover him with the robe from his own back, and to open his home and all that he had to him. And you have to wonder, what would their father have thought had he seen *that* when he finally arrived on the scene?

Who knows? If he was really like his father, maybe he wouldn't have waited in the first place. Maybe he would have risked sacrificing everything to go out and *find* his brother and bring him home, rather than just waiting around to let history play out.

I'm sure there are other possibilities, but all I needed was one to satisfy me. It just had to make sense, that's all.

On a spiritual level, of course, the story isn't about a farmer and his two sons at all. It's about God and *all* of his children; those that are already saved, and those that are yet to be found. What Jesus took the time to do with this parable was to give a message not only to all of the potential prodigal son's of the world, but also a message to all of the *brothers* of those prodigal children. To make sure that those who have already been saved understand that when a child is brought back to God – when a prodigal son returns – he is getting nothing more than what they themselves have already received. And if we don't feel that same excitement as the Father, if we do not see the reason to celebrate, and if we in fact get upset like the prodigal son's brother did, then maybe we need to re-examine where our hearts really are. Are we just Christians on the surface, or does the love of Christ run to our very core?

And *that* was the real epiphany for me with this entire parable. Not the parable itself; not that I had finally "figured it out". But that if *I* had truly been like my Father all along, if *I* had already been with Him, I would never have been confused about it in the first place. The fact that I can make sense of it now gives me no small amount of comfort as I continue in my quest towards faith, because I know that even if I'm not quite where I should be yet, I'm definitely headed in the right direction.

Several years ago I ran the first (and probably only) 5k in my life. As I struggled towards the finish line, I was greeted by friends and other runners who had already completed the race. They yelled words of encouragement to me as I plodded across those last few yards, and then clapped and cheered me when I finally broke the finish line. They were cheering for *me*, not for themselves. There was no need for them to cheer for themselves; they were already there.

8

The Art of the Catch

In the movie *Field of Dreams*, a remote Iowa farmer is compelled to mow down a substantial portion of his cropland to build a baseball field, even though he doesn't understand why and knows that it is financially irresponsible. Soon, long dead baseball legends of the past begin to regularly show up to play baseball on his pristine field. As the movie progresses, we discover that there had been some bad blood between the farmer and his father – a baseball player himself – that had never been resolved. Now, with his father long dead and the possibility of resolution impossible, a part of the farmer is tortured by the grief that he carries with him for words left unsaid.

As the movie nears it's end, we see various other characters in the film get closure on certain aspects of their lives, but the farmer is still left trying to understand what all of this has to do with him. Finally, it's the farmer's father who arrives on the field, back in his glory days as a young ball player, and the farmer suddenly understands the gift that has been laid at his feet: a second chance. The movie closes with the father and son just beginning the process of healing their wounds, by playing catch.

There was a time when playing catch was a pretty commonplace thing in America. It doesn't take a lot of fancy equipment, there are no monthly contracts, and you never need tech support. There's no setup time, pieces to put together, or instructions to read. You don't have to learn which buttons to push on the controller, and you don't have to dedicate a specific amount of time to play.

Two people, two gloves, and a baseball. Just pick them up and walk outside.

I missed a lot of opportunities to spend time with my oldest son Chris as he was growing up. Like many men, even the *thought* of "bonding" can make me feel uncomfortable. In our quest to be brave leaders, wise visionaries, bold conquerors, and captains of industry, showing a display of our affection – especially to another man – could too easily be seen as something less than the strong alpha male that we wish to present to the world. But therein lies the forgotten beauty of playing catch.

On the surface it's a display of masculinity, a recreation of a time-honored and celebrated pastime. And yet, beneath that facade of manliness, it's simply a wonderful way for two men to spend time with each other – one-on-one – with only the other to think about.

It's something fathers can do with their sons at any age, from the moment the child can pick up a ball, through grade school, high school, and beyond. Watching their sons grow and develop, seeing over time how the pendulum shifts from the child dropping almost everything to catching nearly anything. Noticing the accuracy sharpen as the years pass, witnessing the strength of the young arm increasing, and feeling the bite of the ball hitting your glove harder with each passing season. Bit by bit, stepping further and further away from each other as the throws get longer and the boy turns into a man – mimicking the natural course of life itself – and yet at the same time, providing the ability to always stay connected.

Unlike playing a video game, watching TV, or even working on a project together, the beauty of playing catch is that it's personal; you must pay attention *solely* to your partner. Talking is optional, but concentration is not. To get distracted is to risk an errant throw, or worse, to be hit by the ball. And yet imaginations are somehow still free to run wild, opportunities to give praise & encouragement present themselves in a continuous stream, and the air itself seems charged with joy, optimism, and endless possibilities.

There are many things that we can do with our sons, but there are none so pure and easy as simply throwing a little leather ball back and forth. I missed the chance to do that with Chris, and I don't want to make the same mistake again. So when I see the blue skies beckoning with their siren song, I invite my younger son David to pick up his glove and step outside to play catch with his old man, and suddenly, the backyard is transformed into our own personal field of dreams.

In my dream, Chris is there too.

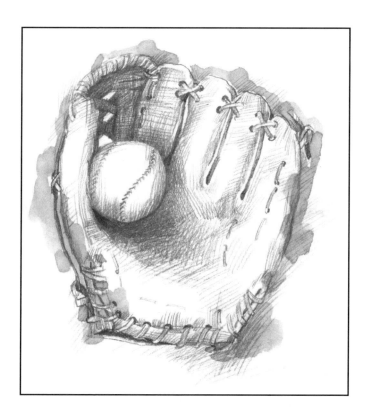

9

The Power of Prayer

Oldest joke in the world: A nervous paratrooper is about to make his first jump. He hears the gravelly voice of the jumpmaster going over the procedure one last time with his men: *"When you exit the aircraft, count to 3 and then pull your main ripcord. If for any reason your main chute does not deploy, pull your emergency ripcord to deploy your backup chute. When you reach the ground, a truck will be waiting to take you back to base."* The soldier jumps from the plane, counts to 3, and pulls his ripcord. Nothing happens. He pulls his emergency ripcord. Nothing happens. *"Oh, this is just great,"* he thinks as he falls through the air, *"I'll bet that stupid truck won't be down there waiting for me either."*

Silly I know, but there is a message underneath the silliness. Our friend the paratrooper felt that he'd been lied to a couple of times, so he lost faith in the rest of what he'd been told. Consequently, if he felt that he'd been told the truth on the first two things, I'd bet that he'd also believe that the truck would be waiting for him just as he'd been promised.

Belief in God, belief in the Bible, belief in the death & resurrection of Jesus Christ, belief in salvation and heaven; belief in all of these things comes through faith, and faith alone. We are told that God hears our prayers. Matthew 7:7 tells us: *"Ask, and it shall be given to you; seek, and you shall find; knock, and it shall be opened to you."* What would happen to our faith if we asked, sought, or knocked, and nothing happened? Conversely, what would happen to our faith if something did happen?

Just as I believe that actions speak louder than words, I also believe that experiences illustrate better than explanations. For instance, I could tell you about the power of prayer, I could preach to you about how it makes a difference, and I could assure you that prayers are indeed answered. But why would I do that? It's nothing that we all haven't already heard before.

What I find much more fascinating – and convincing for that matter – are "real life" examples of how prayer has had an effect on someone's life. The only experiences that I can share are my own, and they may or may not be of interest to you, but just in case, here are some of my experiences with prayer.

The first prayer I can ever remember was in the 4th grade. I was a pretty good student, and almost never got into trouble, but on this particular day I had a lapse of judgment in Mrs. Laney's Social Studies class. There were few places worse than Mrs. Laney's classroom to behave in "conduct unbecoming"; her reputation for having an extreme lack of tolerance towards errant little boys was well known.

I don't remember what it was that I did, but I suddenly found myself standing in the hall with my cohorts in crime, waiting for Mrs. Laney to get the class settled before she escorted us down to the principal's office. Our principal was another person with a well known reputation; his being a "swift and non-negotiable" approach to discipline. It was rumored that even parents were required to grab their ankles when they visited his office.

I was petrified, and though God rarely ever had occasion to hear from me, He heard from me that day. Even though I was stone-cold guilty as charged, standing in that hall on the verge of tears, I apologized, I begged, I promised, and I pleaded.

Five minutes passed. Ten minutes. Then twenty. I don't know whether God made Mrs. Laney lose track of time or if He simply softened her heart, but eventually the door opened and she scolded us all back into the classroom.

Now, you may think that was just coincidence or luck of the draw, and it's possible that it might be at that, but I can also tell you that that was the only time all year that Mrs. Laney *ever* failed to take anyone to the principal's office once they had been sent outside in the hall.

Several years ago I came home on a Monday afternoon after meeting with a new boss that had been placed over my department. During our meeting, she had looked at me and said "*I can't believe* (with your background and experience) *that you were able to get a job here. You would never be able to get a job here now.*" I was shocked at her bluntness, to say the least. I went home that day certain that I was on the verge of being fired, but prayer intervened. Not even my own prayers, but someone else's. Shamefully, while I personally didn't pray about the situation, my mother did. Not only did I not lose my job, but four days later, on Friday afternoon, I got a promotion from the same woman who had just told me I had no right to be working there in the first place. Huh.

A couple years ago I was searching for a new printer for *Making It Home*, a Christian Women's magazine that my wife & I used to publish (realize that what I knew about the printing industry at the time could fit into a thimble and have room left over for some iced tea.) Over the course of a few weeks, I had requested & received quotes from several companies – all of them looking pretty much the same to me – and was feeling increasingly anxious about who I should work with and entrust with the printing of the magazine. Finally, as I stood on my back porch, I looked up into the afternoon sky and simply asked the Lord for help. "*I don't know what to do,*" I said. "*Just tell me who You want me to work with, and I will.*"

About 2 hours later a quote hit my mailbox. It was so *unlike* all of the other quotes I had received (in a very good way) that I knew I had my answer. As it turned out, it was also the last quote that would come in. Which kind of makes sense if you think about it; I already had the only one I needed.

There are a lot of "quick & simple" prayers like that which have been answered in my life. And like the outcomes to the prayers above, it's very easy to look at them and just write them off to coincidence. Skeptics would say "*Well, you only remember it because it just happened to turn out the way you wanted. You just aren't remembering all of the times that it didn't.*" They probably have a scientific diagnosis for it as well, something along the lines of "selective memory disorder" or the like.

I have to admit, if it were only "quick & simple" prayers with an "either/or" type outcome, I might even buy into that. But there are some other prayers I have had answered that were just a little more complicated. I'm not a big believer in coincidence, and when I see an entire series of "coincidences" tied together, any skepticism I may have about prayer swings 180 degrees in the opposite direction.

I've mentioned earlier about our move to Kentucky. How, even as I was sitting in my boss' office resigning my job (unbeknownst to my wife), she in turn had found a house for sale on the internet that had gotten her so excited she had already called the owner to ask questions (unbeknownst to me). I've mentioned that we took that to be, I don't know, maybe "divine providence"; that that was where God wanted us to be. But that's not actually the whole story.

While we did drive up to Kentucky with the thought firmly in our minds that we were going to move there, our initial reaction upon arriving was not so optimistic. We were going to meet with the owners on a Tuesday morning, but we arrived early enough the day before to drive by and take a look. As we got deeper into the heart of Casey County, I started feeling a deep unease. This was farm country. Cows, horses, hay, rolling hills, barns; it was almost like being in a foreign land. When we reached Liberty, the idyllic vision of the house and the town that we had already painted for ourselves in our minds suddenly fell rudely to the ground. The house was, well, *not new.* It seemed to *lean* a little in places. And the picturesque street with stately old homes and maple trees that I had created in my mind's eye didn't exist. There was a funeral home across the street. A church on one side, a phone company building & cell phone tower on the other. And the town – the town was *tiny!* Even though that's what I had told myself I wanted, now that I had it in my sights I was recoiling from it.

We sat in the car – my wife & kids & I – just kind of staring at the house for a few minutes. It was absolutely silent in that car, and from that silence I could tell that everyone felt the same thing I did. And what I felt was a great big emphatic "*No*". What were we doing here? This wasn't our "home turf". We had no family here, no friends, no nothing. What were we thinking?

We drove back to Somerset in almost total silence. Back at the hotel, Cat & I talked in private; we both shared the same misgivings. In fact, we were so sure that this had been a mistake, we weren't even going to bother to go see the house the next morning. We already knew we weren't going to buy it.

Catherine called a realtor & friend of ours in Blue Ridge, GA to see what might be available there. Georgia was closer to what we thought of as "home", and we at least knew a little bit about the area. But Nancy didn't have a whole lot of optimistic news for us. In fact, the impression she gave Catherine was that she didn't really want to talk to us at all.

Oh, wonderful. If I felt like I had a bowling ball in my gut before, I was now completely beside myself. I had quit my job, our house was already sold, we had about 5 weeks to move out, and I had no place to move my family. What had I done?

I sat in the darkness behind the Holiday Inn while Catherine went to get something for the kids to eat. I wasn't hungry. Finally, I looked up into the sky and just laid it out at His feet. My prayer went something like this: "*Dear God, I need help. I thought this was where you wanted me to be, but it doesn't feel that way. Just tell me where you want me to go, and I'll go, but please, please don't let me make a mistake. If it were just me, I wouldn't care, but please don't let me move my family someplace where they won't be happy. Please don't let me make a mistake.*"

It took less than 10 minutes to start getting His answer.

My mom was driving up from Charlotte to join us, but had gotten lost and had been subsequently delayed. Actually, she had driven to the wrong town completely (you'd have to know my mom), but I wonder if her mental error wasn't also part of some "divine providence", because within minutes of my prayer, she finally pulled up to the hotel, right in front of where I was sitting. She got out of the car talking; she was going to move to Kentucky too, she already had 2 people interested in buying her house, etc., etc. I had never seen her so animated or excited, and it made me sick to finally interrupt and tell her that we weren't going to be moving to Kentucky, that this had all been a big mistake.

She understood our feelings, but also convinced us to at least keep our appointment the next morning to see the house. We were already up here anyway. It couldn't hurt to look.

As it turned out, once we walked into the house, our perception of it changed completely. It felt comfortable, warm, & inviting. It had charm and character. It felt *lived* in. Catherine liked it. I liked it. The kids were putting dibs on bedrooms.

We spent the rest of the morning looking around the town and exploring a bit, and as the morning progressed, I kept noticing things. I found out from some of the people I talked to that many of the residents had lived in Liberty all of their lives. I learned that many people had also moved away, but had then come back. *Why would they come back?* At the realtor's office we parked next to a new truck that had the windows down and the *keys in the ignition*! Just sitting there, like there was no fear at all of someone stealing it. Was this the kind of place where you could do that?

I noticed the Ten Commandments boldly posted in business offices and restaurants. When we commented our amazement to a proprietor we were told, *"Well, if some people don't like it, I guess they can do their business somewhere else."* No malice, but no apologies either.

I noticed a store called "Goose Creek Gifts", and I thought how odd that there would be a store with that particular name in this tiny little town. I had lived in Goose Creek, SC for years while in the Navy. It had been my home.

I started thinking, *Blaine, God's trying to tell you something. Are you listening?*

The final "straw", if you will, was at lunch. We went to eat at the Bread of Life Cafe. After lunch I walked outside and saw a sign on the outside of the restaurant – a literal sign – that almost made my jaw drop. The sign was round, with a picture of a rooster over a black background, and the word "Willkom" underneath. It was significant to me in that I had only seen that sign in one other place in my entire life; on the door to my garage back in Orlando where it had been hanging for 5 years. My home.

And right then, I knew. This was where God wanted me after all. In *this* town, in *that* house. From the moment I had asked for help, He had been guiding me, putting things in front of me that I could see & hear that would ease my anxiety, quell my fear, and show me that – for whatever reason, even if I didn't understand why – *this* was where he wanted me to be.

That prayer and the answer I received stands out in my mind for several reasons. For one, it was a little more involved than most "simple prayers". Secondly, it was answered very quickly (as it needed to be). And thirdly, I realized what was happening *as the prayer was being answered.* God was *talking* to me, and I *understood* that He was talking to me, even as He was doing it. Following His will on that was one of the best decisions I've ever made.

If you're still interested, I have one other story to tell. This prayer and the answer to it was a little more complicated yet, involved even more "coincidences", took significantly longer to unfold, and resulted in the absolute best thing that ever happened to me. I didn't understand how it was being answered. In fact, I didn't realize until years later that anything was happening at all. And I didn't even have to make a decision. On this one, God wasn't giving me that option.

When I was 24 I got married to a girl I had dated for 4 years. The relationship should not have lasted that long, and certainly should never have resulted in marriage, but I was dug in like an Alabama tick and wouldn't let it end. I just couldn't face the thought of "starting all over again". I had reached the ripe old age of 24, after all. So despite all of the warning signs, the marriage went through. Three months after the wedding, however, my new bride went on a date with someone other than myself. As you might imagine, this didn't really fit into my view of what a monogamous marriage should be. (In the years since, I've not only been able to forgive her, I've actually come to be *thankful* that she did that. But that's certainly not how I felt at the time.)

I was absolutely devastated. Anger, humiliation, hate, betrayal, and every other negative emotion there is took turns that year coursing through my veins. It was bad enough when I only had to deal with them one by one, but the worst was when I could feel them all at the same time, making me feel like a washing machine churning with negative emotions. As bad as the days were, the nights were far worse. I got drunk every night just to get to sleep. Going to bed sober would only allow my imagination to run uncontrolled in the quiet darkness, and I have a vivid imagination.

It was one of the lowest points of my life, but during it, and most certainly because of it, I started doing something that I had never done seriously before. I began to pray. Consistently. Regularly. Every single day. At first it was simply because I didn't know what else to do, but it soon became a habit that continued even after the emotional trauma of the failed marriage wore away. I can't remember my prayers exactly, but I was hurt and lonely. I wanted someone to love me. I wanted a wife. God heard my prayer, and He did answer it, but it took awhile. Much longer than I would have liked, but in retrospect, also as soon as He could.

Three years after the collapse of my marriage, in April of 1993, the phone rang. I couldn't know it at the time, but that phone call would alter the course of my life in the most wonderful way I could ever imagine.

The call was from a man named Robert who I had served with for several years in the Navy. He was calling to invite me down to Orlando to have a job interview with the company that he worked for. The fact that I got the call at all was both surprising and puzzling. It's important to know that although we worked with each other in the service, we were not what you would call close friends. Robert was a rather loud and arrogant guy (one of his nicknames was "Bobnoxious"), and one of those people who always felt the need to "one-up" you in any conversation. Whatever you had done, he had done something bigger and better. On top of that, I hadn't seen or spoken to Bob in almost 5 years. Why would it suddenly come into his mind to think of me? And how did he track me down? Because it had to have taken some work. Very few people even knew where I was or how to reach me. I had been staying in Charlotte with my mom (who had a different last name) and going to school since I had been discharged 7 months before. I didn't have a permanent address or phone number anywhere.

So it was odd. Nevertheless, my savings were being depleted at a rapid rate, and the prospect of employment sounded just fine to me, so I drove down after the spring quarter and interviewed. And nothing happened. So I enrolled for classes in the summer quarter and kept going to school.

Three more months went by and the summer quarter was almost over. I now had no more money to continue my education; I *had* to get a job. I went to interview with a man in Charlotte, and I guess I impressed him because he called me 3 days later to offer me the job. But I had to turn him down, because the day before – *one day before*, after hearing *nothing* for almost 4 months – I got a phone call from that company in Orlando offering me a job, and I had already accepted. If that call had come just one day later, my life would have taken a completely different course. Random chance?

I think it's important to know that Orlando just happened to be the one place that I really wanted to live. I had gone to school there in the Navy and had really like the city. It's also interesting that my best friend just happened to be living in Orlando at that time, so I wouldn't be all alone in this new city. And what about Robert? Well, that was interesting too. Once I had the job, Robert and I really didn't have a whole lot to do with each other. We never hung out together, we never went to lunch; we didn't even talk to each other at work very much. It was almost like he had done what he was supposed to do, and now that he had done it, he was going on with his own life.

Looking back, I think that's exactly what happened. That all of these things were just pieces of a puzzle that were all working together with the intent to get me to Orlando at a certain time. Because as it turned out, I wasn't there to get a job, or to live in a favorite city, or to reunite with an old friend. I was there because that's where my future wife was, the woman that God had picked out for me, and the time had finally come to put us together. Even though I had long since forgotten my own original prayer, God hadn't. He had been working on it ever since, and was about to deliver on it in a big way.

Catherine & I met that August.

We went on our first date in November.

We were married in May.

Okay, you may say, that's a real sweet story, and there are some aspects to it that maybe seem a little odd and coincidental, but it doesn't prove anything. Sooner or later you were bound to meet someone that you'd fall in love with. After all, 3 years had gone by.

True, but the 3 years isn't coincidental either, it's *important*. I had been absolutely demoralized by the failure of my first marriage. My self-esteem, self-worth, self-*everything* had been absolutely crushed. I needed time to heal from that, and healing takes time. I also needed time to clear my head, and to think about & understand all of the things about that relationship that had been so very wrong. I needed time to make some decisions about the kind of man I wanted to be. I needed time to mature. And all of that doesn't happen overnight; it takes time, a lot of time. It wouldn't have made any sense at all for God to introduce me to the woman that He'd picked out specifically for me before I was ready. I would have just blown it.

In the interim, I dated a few girls. But all of my relationships during this time had a finite ending from the very start. One girl was moving back home in 3 months when we started seeing each other. With another, we had 4 months to pal around before I transferred to Guam. Like that. In retrospect, I think God was keeping me going without giving me the opportunity to get in too deep. I'd had my shot at picking a wife; He wasn't going to let me make another mess like that again. This time it was going to be His call, not mine.

There's also another reason why God waited 3 years; He *had* to. I had left Him no choice. Because during this whole time I was still legally married. Over the years – for one reason or another – there had been several delays in getting my divorce finalized. I wonder now if some of those "delays" might not have been so accidental; after all, it's not as if Catherine was just sitting around waiting for me to show up. God was busy working in her life too. There were some timelines to deal with and a little bit of coordination required.

The final "coincidence" of God's work here is also the piece of the puzzle that brings everything together full circle. Because I finally became legally divorced in April of 1993. In that month I was no longer bound by the commitment of my failed marriage. And in that same month I would receive an odd phone call out of the blue from a man named Robert that would change my life forever. I was ready, Catherine was ready, and God's hand moved.

I have to tell you that when I read back over the words I've used to explain what happened here, it all looks so plain. I feel like I've completely failed to relate how incredible and intricate these events really were. Maybe the only way you could understand it fully is if you had lived it. If you had, you would know – you would *feel* – just as I do; none of this was random coincidence.

No way.

To me, the most amazing thing about prayer is that we all have it available to us. Think about that! All of us – every single person – has *unlimited* access to the most powerful and loving being in the universe, and we can call on Him anytime, anywhere, 24 x 7. No lines. No phone trees. No waiting.

God *will* hear our prayers, and He *will* answer them. We may not understand what He's doing, we may not like the answer He gives us, and we may not even notice that He's doing anything at all, but it happens just the same. And I'll be honest with you, being able to see how the hand of God has already been at work in my life sure makes me feel pretty good about whether or not that truck will actually be there waiting for me when I finally hit the ground.

10

Easy Money

ATTENTION!!

$$ EASY MONEY $$

Tired of wasting your life away by working for your money? Who said that making money should require work anyway? Wouldn't it be nice if someone would just **give** you money every month for doing nothing? Well, I'm here to tell you that I will do just that.

That's right. I will give you **CASH MONEY** for nothing! Sound too good to be true? Well, it's not. In fact, I will send you money **EVERY MONTH** for the next 10 years! **NO** gimmicks, **NO** tricks. All you have to do is give me 1 hour of your time and a minimal investment of $40.00 upfront, and then watch the money **ROLL IN**! How much? How about **$1,000.00** paid out in **GUARANTEED** monthly installments for the next **10 YEARS**!

Don't Delay! Act Now!

"Get rich quick" schemes and tantalizing offers of "easy money" have been around for a long time. There have been occasions when I've actually been tempted to respond to a few; not in the hopes that they would be true, but just out of curiosity to see what I would get if I sent in my $30 to get "all of the secrets." I suspect that I would have received *something*, probably along the lines of a flimsy pamphlet telling me that the "secret" was to send out an advertisement to prompt thousands of schmucks to send me $30.

The above ad, however, was real – there were no tricks or gimmicks – and I've been collecting my check every month since I responded. Okay, okay, it didn't happen *exactly* like that. There was no ad, but there *could* have been. What really happened was this:

The bathtub in our downstairs bathroom had a small leak when we moved in. Nothing alarming, just a steady *drip . . . drip . . . drip*. I made a mental note to fix it sometime, but it wasn't a big priority. Over the next few months I started to get an idea of how much it was going to cost to live in our new home, slowly finding the answers to the "unknowns" that every new house offers until you see what you can expect your monthly utilities to be.

It was in this way that I was able to determine how much we paid for our water. It wasn't that much, but we're also on city sewer, and the cost of that is in direct proportion to the amount of water that we consume, since it assumes that most of it goes down the drain. Still, even counting water & sewer together, the cost was pretty reasonable, or at least, it *should have* been.

To my dismay, however, in addition to finding out how much everything was going to cost, I also was finding out how much of everything we were actually *using*, and I was *shocked* to see that we were averaging almost 250 gallons of water per day! 250 gallons! That's almost five 55 gallon drums of water, every single day! How could we *possibly* be using that much?

I called a little family meeting to make everyone aware of the problem, and to discuss ways we could all be a little less wasteful. I also decided it was time to investigate my leaky bathtub faucet a little further.

I'm not sure if it was my imagination, but it seemed that the *drip . . .drip . . . drip* had now become *drip, drip, drip.* How much water was this thing leaking anyway? I decided to figure it out, and collected the leakage for 10 minutes, measured it, then multiplied by 6 to figure out how much it was leaking per hour. It came out to almost exactly 1 gallon. That was a lot, sure, but it wasn't that much. Or was it? 1 gallon an hour, every hour, 24 hours a day, 365 days a year. The leaky faucet wasn't the source of our entire problem, but it accounted for fully 10% of our daily water usage all by itself.

Looking at our monthly water usage compared with our water & sewer bill, I was able to figure out how much that leak was going to cost us if left uncorrected; $70 over the course of one year. Seeing that number suddenly moved the job of fixing the leak up a few notches on the priority list.

A trip to the hardware store, $40 for a repair kit (I know, that seemed a little rich to me too; they must be pretty proud of them), and an hour of my time later, and the leak was fixed. I started to think of the money I would save and suddenly I found myself grinning as my imagination conjured up the fictional voice of a slick salesman pitching me the "easy money" scheme.

You may be saying, *Wait a minute, you said a total of $1,000 over 10 years, but you're only saving $70 a year. That doesn't add up.*

Well, there are 3 other things to consider. First, that $70 a year that I'm *not* spending anymore is *post tax.* To pay that $70 dollars, I would actually have to earn about 20% more, because Uncle Sam takes that out upfront in income tax. That bumps the total up to $840 over 10 years. (By the way, and this has nothing to do with anything, but doesn't it seem odd that our post tax dollars should be referred to as our "disposable income"? It sure isn't disposable to me. I wonder if that term originated from some government accountants; that they defined it as "disposable" because they don't get to spend it themselves and thereby "dispose" of it to us? Hmmm.).

Secondly, I assumed that the leak would have gotten progressively worse over that 10 years. And thirdly, what are the odds that my utility rates would not increase over that same time span? I added a little more to account for both. As far as the 10 years goes, I figure that that's about how long it will be before the faucet starts leaking again.

I know it's not a king's ransom, and it will take 10 years to pay off in full, but if it would seem unconscionable for any of us to throw away $1,000 *right now*, why would it somehow be acceptable to do it over the course of a decade? Plus, in addition to the savings in money, it's also something that I can feel good about, because though I'm not an extreme environmentalist, neither am I gratuitously wasteful, and if a whale or two has been saved by my actions, I'm perfectly okay with it.

I've fixed a few other "leaky faucets" as well.

Many years ago I almost cried as I cut up my ATM card. How could I *possibly* live without it? What if I needed money? How would I get it? As it turns out, I was able to live without it just fine. In fact, it's interesting to me now that something that I once thought of as an absolutely indispensable part of my life – as that ATM card seemed to be – now seems like nothing more than an amusing foreign concept.

I wonder how much I have saved over the years by not having immediate access to my money – either from a nearby ATM machine or by having the cash already in my wallet – for frivolous and wasteful impulse buys? How much have I saved by not having to pay ATM transaction fees? Or by not having to pay the service fees for all of the checks I used to bounce as a result of never knowing how much money was really in my account because of my constant unrecorded visits to the ATM machine? I'll never know for sure, but I imagine that if someone wrote me a check for the total amount, I'd be pretty happy to see it.

When Catherine & I had cell phones, it seemed amazing to me that the human race could have ever survived before their existence. Now that they're in the trash, I suddenly remember. It really wasn't that difficult after all. And it certainly wasn't as annoying. Figuring out how much I *won't* be spending each month for those things will be much easier to figure out than the ATM cards; in case you're wondering, it comes out to well over $10,000 over 10 years. And as a pleasant side effect, now that I'm not incessantly yapping on the phone in my car, I've started to notice things again that I had forgotten about; things like traffic signals, pedestrians, and other cars.

I need to point out that I am no financial guru. In fact, even though I know what I *should* do all the time, I am still very sporadic about it. For instance, I will spend 5 minutes comparing different brands & sizes of peanut butter to figure out which is the best value in order to save a few pennies, and then turn around and blow $30 on something completely ridiculous without even *thinking* about it. But I'm getting better.

The first step in getting some amount of control isn't even deciding to fix these "leaky faucets" that we have in our lives. First, we have to figure out what's leaking in the first place, and that can be a lot more difficult than we might imagine, because in the business of living our lives, we don't always even know what is actually going on.

To see what I mean, let's take a look at a fictional man named "George". George is just your average guy who's trying to make a living. He's married, has some kids, and takes his responsibilities seriously. He works hard, and as the years pass, his hard work pays off and he finds that he has a little more wiggle room financially. To celebrate, George decides to give himself a gift that will make his life a little easier and remove some of the burden that he carries. So instead of spending several hours every Saturday morning mowing the grass, he hires a lawn service to do it for him. He can certainly afford it, and it's nice to be able to enjoy the good life a little more by having a few extra hours of leisure to spend with his family. That is, after all, what he's been working so hard for, isn't it?

A few years pass. George notices that he's gained a little weight, and decides to do something about it. He's doing even better financially, and decides that a membership to a health club can easily fit into his budget. So now, in his free time on Saturday mornings, he hops into his car and heads off to run the treadmill at Bally's.

Overall, George is fairly happy with his life and the progress he's made, except that it seems he doesn't have any more time to spend with his family than he used to, and even though he is making a *lot* more money, it still seems like he's living paycheck to paycheck. Where is his money going? And his time? He can't figure it out.

Most people have a fair amount of common sense, and the thought of paying someone to do a job for us, and then turning around and doing the same job for someone else, only now paying *them* for the opportunity to do it, would seem ludicrous. But isn't that what George is doing? Leaking at both ends?

He used to spend his Saturday mornings mowing the lawn, now he spends them at the gym. From a time perspective, it's a zero-sum game at best. He's gained nothing. But from a financial perspective, look what's going on: not only is he spending money to pay the lawn service to mow his grass for him, but since he's out of shape, he's now paying *more* money to someone else for the privilege of getting the exercise that he used to get mowing his own lawn in the first place! On top of that, he has to spend more money to have some coolie-coolie clothes to work out in, pay for the gas he'll burn in the car to commute back & forth from the fitness center, and, of course, buy a few bottles of water to take with him (at a rate of over $5 a gallon if you care to figure it out), as well as spending a few more minutes each month mailing out those extra 2 checks to the lawn service & health club. All that for the opportunity to sit in traffic and then stare at a wall as he runs nowhere on a machine? This time, it's *not* a zero-sum game. He comes out a *huge* loser on this – to the tune of *thousands* of dollars a year – and what's even more incredible is that *he doesn't even realize it*!

Oh, and by the way, this is just *one thing* in his life. He's involved in more. So is his wife. So are his kids. The good life that he's worked so hard for is somehow not as good as the one he had. For all his hard work and progress, he has nothing more than he did before, and in fact, in most things, he has less.

I would think that none of us would willingly walk into a situation like that, but then again, neither did George. It happened *gradually*, as a slow, progressive sequence of events. He started by treating a disease that was uncomfortable to him, but then found that he had to get another treatment to take care of the side effects that the first treatment caused, which in turn created *more* side effects that required *more* treatment – and so on, and so on – never realizing that these new diseases were all of his own making, because his life had now gotten so complicated that he didn't have time to dwell on what started it all in the first place.

I think this is where I'm supposed to say *"Surprise! I'm George!"*, but in all truth, I'm not, though George, and the predicament he found himself in, are indeed based on a real life example. But while I myself never wound up in that *particular* situation, I did get into others that were just as crazy, if not a little more complicated, and all the while never realizing that my life wasn't getting any better; just busier, more stressful, and costlier in both time and money.

It takes me about 3 hours to mow my yard. I have a little less than an acre of grass to cut, use a plain old push mower, and figure that I walk 6 or 7 miles before it's all said and done. When I'm finished, I like to sit on the porch with a glass of cold lemonade and survey the work that I've accomplished with my own hands as the smell of fresh cut grass floats on the breeze. It's a good feeling. True, sometimes it can get to be a chore, but then I think of the money I'm saving, the exercise I get, the simplicity of my life, and the intangible pleasure of a job well done. Sometimes I even take off my shirt and throw in a free trip to the tanning salon as I push the mower around and try to think of other ways I can earn more of the money that I've already earned.

Next winter, instead of having the temperature warm enough for me to watch TV in shorts and a T-shirt, I might turn the thermostat down a couple of degrees and snuggle with my wife and/or kids under a blanket. Wouldn't that be more fun anyway? I'm also going to replace the weather stripping on the front door to stop that cold air from sweeping in under the bottom. I just got a quote from a different auto insurance company that will save me $220 a year, so I'll be doing that. I wonder how much water each load of laundry uses, and what would happen if we could cut-out one or two loads a week? Oh, and that reminds me, right now I can . . .

As it turns out, it looks like I'm going to be paying myself a *lot* more than just $1,000 over the next 10 years. And other than a "minor investment" of time and/or money upfront, I won't be doing a thing to earn it. It's all easy money.

11

The Little Yellow Boots
That Could

My mom lived almost 10 hours away, which put her on the outer fringe of our realistic "travel range". Had she been closer, we would have made the trek more often, I guess, but as it was, it was a once a year event that happened on Thanksgiving week. We would load up the mini-van with a week's worth of clothes, toys, & supplies, and then wedge the children in wherever we could, knowing that over 500 daunting miles stood between us and our objective.

Nine and a half hours of close confinement later (and much to the relief of everyone), the headlights would at last illuminate our destination: Grandma's house. There was something about finally piling out of the car and making our way to her front door – with the chill of the crisp November air and the crunch of the fallen leaves under our feet – that seemed almost magical.

In a way, it *was* magic. We were in a land far, far away, with exciting discoveries to be made and interesting histories to explore. It was a place where my kids could peruse the books of their father's youth, where they could open a toy chest decades old and unearth the same toys – in various states of repair – that I had played with as a child. There were interesting crannies to investigate, a huge backyard to explore, and priceless treasures to secure.

But of all the memories made, odysseys taken, and gifts bestowed, none is more remarkable to me than a pair of little yellow boots.

The edges of Grandma's kingdom were bordered by a mystical river, wild & unexplored. To a less vigilant eye, it might closer resemble a ditch, but my children were under no such fantasies. Once discovered, this mysterious waterway begged to be explored, and, with Grandma accompanying them as the King's emissary, my intrepid young explorers would venture out to brave the perils of the unknown. They would spend hours blazing paths, damming waters, and living adventures others could only dream about. And then they would return, exhausted & triumphant; and covered with mud.

The shoes were the real problem, because they simply could not take the abuse of these frequent excursions and be relied upon to escort the children with any dignity whatsoever to the simpler, less dangerous, locales of the region. So the wise and resourceful Grandma bestowed upon her grandchildren a special gift to aid them in these most noble of expeditions: rubber boots.

My little adventurers could now explore to their heart's content, and upon returning from the ravages of the wilderness, could retire their accoutrements safely away until the opportunity for the next death-defying journey presented itself. But one little warrior named David would have none of it. *His* boots were different. They were possessed of a mystical power that none of us could realize, and he had no intention of limiting them to occasional excursions into the unknown.

On the surface, there didn't seem to be anything special about them. To me, they looked like an ordinary pair of rubber boots. They were bright yellow, quite small, with rubber loops extending above the tops to aid in pulling them on. A half inch blue stripe encircled the base of each just above the sole, and two smaller blue strips adorned the upper edges. They were made in China.

None of that, however, seemed to have any meaning to David. He loved those boots, and would wear them whenever he saw fit, which was most of the time. Under normal circumstances, David shares a trait with his father that was no doubt given to him by me; one of caution and even outright anxiety regarding things & places unknown. But in his boots, he was fearless.

He wore them everywhere, and would do anything in them. Whether swinging in the backyard, riding his bike down the street, or running over homemade obstacle courses he setup for himself (*I'm getting into shape, Dad. I need to build up my muscles*), his face would set with determination against whatever opponents his imagination could muster, and he would vanquish them all.

To my shame, there were times when I would try to intervene and separate my young superhero from his source of power:

David, if you want to go to the store with me, maybe you should put on a regular pair of shoes.

But why, Daddy? He would ask with genuine curiosity and puzzlement. *What's wrong with these?*

"What's wrong" indeed. Was it *him* that I was concerned about, this little boy who could so boldly confront the world in his little yellow boots without a second thought, or was it me, an aging man who might possibly be embarrassed to be seen in public with a child so ridiculously attired? Did I want to be the Lex Luthor of my son's childhood, stealing away his power only to shackle him instead with the kryptonite of public opinion to carry with him throughout his life?

Why, I guess now that I think about it, there's nothing wrong at all, I would say with a smile, and we would then bound off to the store together with the father basking in the courage of the son.

Years have passed, and regardless of whatever mystical energy those little yellow boots contain, there is one nemesis that even they are powerless to defeat: a little boy who is furiously growing into a young man. David still loves his boots, and he still wears them with the same reckless abandon that he always has, but I know it is coming to an end. Even if I can pretend that they are not the worse for wear, the proclamation from David himself that his toes get *"a little scrunched up"* when he wears them now is a clear signal that they will soon lose their animation entirely, only to find themselves pushed aside and forgotten. The time is coming when they will retire as partners in adventure to become instead collectors of dust.

When that sad day comes, however, there will be some salvation for those little yellow boots that have served my son so well. They will not be discarded; how dishonorable that would be! Instead, they will be rescued, and moved to a place of safety as they join an elite group of treasures that have a worth to me beyond comprehension. There they will remain; quiet, patient, and without complaint.

And maybe one day, years distant, a small young boy bearing a striking resemblance to David will make a trip to his grandparents house for Thanksgiving. And maybe that young boy in his exploration might come across a chest, hidden and obscure in the corner of a closet, and open it to find a fascinating pair of worn & scuffed little yellow boots.

And maybe he'll ask his Grandpa if he knows anything about them.

12

The Optimistic Thermometer

As I've bumped my way along through my 40 odd years I have also bumped into, quite by accident, little pearls of wisdom that have helped me to understand things better. There is wisdom to be found in the world, sometimes in places that you would least expect, and if that wisdom does not conflict with God's word, if it in fact makes God's word a little easier for me to understand, I don't have a problem with latching on to those things and storing them away. However, it's something that I try to be careful with.

I recently read an article that talked about the danger of what it termed as "bible illiteracy". There are many ways to get perspective on Christianity; study books, daily devotionals, TV shows, magazines, and more, but although all of these can be good companions, none of them should ever take the place of the Bible. It is the all-inclusive, unabridged, official operators manual of life.

The danger is that if we don't study that source guide, if we instead take what others say as the truth without checking for ourselves, we can soon find ourselves to be "bible illiterate", and wind up believing in things that simply aren't true. About 50 years ago, the term "separation of church and state" was first used in connection with the U.S. Constitution. Over the decades, that phrase has been repeated over & over so often that the vast majority of Americans now believe that somewhere in the Constitution it actually says "separation of church and state". It does not.

In fact, it doesn't say anything close to that.

So as you continue reading, just realize that what is to follow comes from the world, not the Bible, and although I think that these things reflect biblical concepts, that is only my interpretation. Yours may differ, and as with everything else that you may see, hear, or read, I would encourage you to test them against the source guide itself.

These little "golden nuggets" that I find run the gamut of well known clichés, lessons learned from my own experiences, even jokes with an underlying moral. A lot of them are quotes, many of which are well known to everyone. For instance, there is the quote *"Whether you think you can do something, or you think you can't, either way you're right."* That quote is currently credited to Jack Welch, the former CEO of General Electric, but I'm pretty sure it was said earlier by Henry Ford. (For all I know, Henry Ford was simply repeating it from someone else 100 years before his own time). It doesn't matter. What *does* matter is the truth of that statement, because I've seen it at work in myself.

Throughout my life, I have walked into many situations & tasks unsure about the details and requirements of what it would take to successfully complete them, but with an uncompromising will to succeed. In those situations, ones where I did not allow myself the option of failure, I have always been successful, at least to some degree. On the other hand, whenever I have approached a task with doubt, where failure is not only an option, but an expected outcome, I've pretty much gotten exactly what I bargained for.

I also know that God has given me certain skills and abilities, and that, through Him, all things are possible. So I don't see any harm in embracing that statement as long as I keep it in context with where my abilities came from in the first place, and who my success should ultimately be attributed to.

Many of the things in my little book of wisdom are from movies, which is no surprise because I love watching movies and have seen quite a few. In the movie "Rudy" for instance, there is a scene where the title character, who is desperately trying to get accepted at Notre Dame, asks one of the priests if he knows of anything that can help him get into the university. The priest replies, *"Rudy, I've been in the church for over 40 years, and there are only two things I know for sure; there is a God, and I'm not Him."*

As soon as I heard that I thought, *Oh, that is so good! "There is a God, and I'm not Him".* What a grounding statement! Talk about something that will bring you back down to earth in a hurry if you get a little too big for your britches. Short, sweet, to the point. Nice.

But a movie doesn't even have to be a particularly good one for me to find something in it that I can use. One of my favorite golden nuggets is from the Arnold Schwarzenegger movie "Predator" which came out back in the 80's. Even in my younger days, when gory battles with aliens ranked up pretty high on my appetite of Hollywood fare, I didn't think this movie was that great. But there was one line in it that I loved. It took place just after Arnold and his band of merry men are leaving the scene of a battle. One of the soldiers in the helicopter is wounded, and a fellow soldier points this out to him, telling him that he's bleeding. The wounded soldier looks back at his friend, and in a very macho, gravelly voice – complete with the big chaw of tobacco in his cheek – tells him *"I ain't got time to bleed."*

Again, I thought, *Oh! I love that! "I ain't got time to bleed."* Doesn't that just *reek* of urgency, and shouldn't that be something that we should apply in our lives everyday on this earth? I would imagine that none of us would feel particularly cheated if we lived to be 90 years old. That seems like a pretty long time. But even if we do live to be 90, the first thing we need to do is carve 30 years right off the top, because that's how much of that time we spent sleeping.

Suddenly, we're looking at only 60 years of actual conscious interaction with the world, which may still seem like a lot, but keep that knife handy, because of that remaining 60 years, how much did we use up in the bathroom? Commuting to and from work? Washing dishes? Or any of the many other necessary but time consuming duties that we must carry out just to get through each day? All of a sudden, that great, big long life doesn't look so long anymore.

As if that isn't enough, *Hey! Life isn't easy!* We are all going to take some shots and feel our fair share of pain. We *will* be wounded – again and again; we know that. The question then, is how do we react when we do get wounded, be it physically, emotionally, or spiritually? Do we retreat to the safety of our homes, feel sorry for ourselves, and tend to our wounds until we are 100% better? Or do we slap a bandage on our arm, pick up battle standard, and head back out to the fight? The bottom line is that life is short, we've got things to do, and the clock is ticking. Do any of us have time to bleed?

I'm an avid reader, and the subject matter of my reading has always been less important to me than whether or not the author knows how to write. One author that I used to read quite often years ago was Lawrence Block. Mr. Block has about 60 titles to his credit, and though he isn't the best writer I've ever read, he can spin a yarn better than most. Before you head to the bookstore, please note that most of his novels are murder mysteries, and can be quite disturbing. Not only are the murders depicted very graphically, but also the series of events that lead up to solving those murders. The bad guys in these stories are not nice men. To be honest, the good guys aren't all that nice either.

Be that as it may, one of my favorite golden nuggets happened to come from one of these novels, however unlikely that may seem. As I was reading this particular book (cheerfully titled "Hope to Die"), I came across a couple of sentences that stopped me in my tracks: *"You can go to the ocean with a bucket or a spoon. The ocean does not care."* I don't remember how that thought fit in with the story (in fact, I don't remember the story at all), but I've never forgotten it, and have, over the years, given it much thought as a philosophy regarding the part that I play in this great big world.

There are 3 things that strike me about it right away. First, *what's my tool of choice; a bucket or a spoon*? In other words, how big of an impact do I intend to make in my life? Secondly, *what am I carrying in my selected tool of choice*? Assuming that I want to make a big impact in my life and have chosen the bucket, what have I filled it with? Is it full of hope, optimism, enthusiasm, dedication, encouragement, and love? Or is it instead full of grief, hate, anger, pessimism, apathy, selfishness, and fear? Thirdly, *which direction am I going*? Am I taking these things to the beach (i.e., into the world) with the intention of pouring them out? Or am I returning from the beach, having scooped these things up and taken them away to horde for myself?

There's a lot more to think about than first meets the eye, especially when you consider the possibilities that can occur depending on how each of those 3 questions are answered. The choices, however, are all ours to make, and regardless of what we choose, the earth will just keep spinning along it's merry way. It does not care.

Finally, if you're still there, I wanted to share the story of my optimistic thermometer. When I lived in Florida, I wasn't that concerned about what the temperature was, primarily because it didn't change a whole lot. Hot & humid was generally to be expected, and I was very familiar with what it felt like. Now that I live further North, however, I've been introduced to temperatures that I'm not at all familiar with, namely cold ones. And as silly as it must sound, I'm fascinated with them. At what temperature do your ears start to hurt? What does 15 degrees feel like? If I walk outside and my first inhalation freezes the mucus lining on the inside of my nose, how cold is that? I know I must sound like a total nut job, but this is all new to me. I just don't know.

To aid in my scientific analysis of these newfound cold temperatures, I thought it a prudent idea to purchase a thermometer. There's nothing special about the one that I got; it's round, about 4" in diameter, and has a nice big dial on the front that's easy to read. And I found the perfect spot for it: right outside my kitchen window, positioned so that I can see it whether I'm in the house fixing a cup of coffee, or outside standing on the back steps. Had everything gone as planned, the story would end right there, but there turned out to be a problem.

The whole essence of the problem, was that my perfect spot for the thermometer happened to be on the southeast corner of the house, and every morning, as the sun would first peak up over the hills and then slowly crawl it's way into the sky, my little thermometer would sit there in the radiant light of the sun and get very happy.

I noticed this for the first time shortly after I bought it. I walked outside one morning at about 10:30 into brisk – but sunny – 40 degree weather. I knew it was about 40 degrees because, well, it was *cold*, and even though I'm still a novice, I do have a general feel of what 40 degrees feels like. I also knew it was 40 because I had just seen the local weather update on TV. Even so, I like to check all my data points, and since I now had my very own thermometer, I fully intended to put it to task.

So after taking a brief survey of the backyard and noting that the frost had not yet melted from the grass, I gave a casual glance to my thermometer. Hanging out there on the side of the house, basking in the rays of the sun with his little thermometer RayBans on, he very boldly and very confidently informed me, *"Blaine, it's 75 degrees out here."*

I was like, *"WHAT?! 75 Degrees? Little buddy, that's WAY off. You're not even close!"*

After the initial shock wore off, I got a little upset. I mean, we can put a man on the moon, I can pick up my telephone right now and call someone in Tokyo, I can find my exact position anywhere on the face of the planet with a little handheld gizmo, but I can't tell the temperature in my own backyard any closer than 35 *degrees*? You've got to be *kidding* me.

I then graduated straight to "man-think" mode and started contemplating the various ways I might fix the problem. I could move the thermometer someplace else where the sun wouldn't shine on it, but I liked where it was. I could put some sort of sunshade around it, but would that really work, did I feel like doing it, and how much junk do I want to hang on the side of my house anyway? I was considering the option of having to spend $50 for some "high-end" thermometer that was impervious to sunshine, when a thought suddenly hit me. That's right, my silly little thermometer, apparently sensing my struggle, had just clocked me in the head with yet another golden nugget of wisdom.

Because you have to know that during the night, when it's overcast, or in the late afternoon when the sun has passed over the house, my little buddy keeps pretty accurate temperature. It's only when he's basking in the rays of the sun that he gets a little loopy. When that happens – as far as he's concerned – it's a whole lot nicer outside than it really is, and nobody's going to tell him otherwise.

As a Christian, that's something that I need to remember. Because when I allow myself to bask in the light of the Lord, when I keep him near me during the day and feel that radiant warmth & light shining on my life, suddenly all of those issues that I have to deal with every day – from the minor annoyances to the great big messy cat-hairball problems – don't seem so bad. It's only when I step out of that light, or when I allow something to obstruct that light, that I feel the weight of the world start to bear down on me. And I don't have to let that happen.

So after some thought, I've decided that I'm going to keep my little thermometer right where it is. No modifications. No sunshades. And if I ever feel the trials of life start to creep in and blunt my spirits, I know I can count on my little thermometer to be there to remind me of what I should be doing. To take a step back if need be and get myself back into the light of the Lord, or to move whatever is blocking it from shining on me out of the way. Because I know that as long as I do that, when I keep myself in the unfailing light of Jesus Christ, not only are the current conditions a whole lot nicer, but the future forecast . . . well, that's just unreal.

13

My Second Choice

The box was 23" long, 10" wide, and 6" tall. I kind of guessed at the dimensions I would need when I cut the pieces out, but I figured it would be fine for its purpose.

It had been raining for the past day and the wood was still wet; not ideal for woodworking, but the skies had been holding their peace for a few hours and I thought I should take advantage of the break in the weather. It wasn't something that I wanted to do, but as I sat on the stoop and nailed the pieces together, the sun suddenly came out and stayed with me for a few minutes, as if to encourage me and tell me that everything would be okay. As I was finishing, my daughter walked up and asked me what I was doing.

Sometimes it's very hard to tell the truth.

The first time I saw her, she was in a cage with a cement floor, just one chain-link stall among a row of others. The noise was deafening; the kind of racket that makes it hard to think clearly. The kind of racket that makes you want to leave as soon as possible. I intended to do just that, but first I had to find a dog. I squatted down to look into the back of this particular cage and saw a little black dog come forward from the shadows up to the door. She licked my fingers through the cyclone fence and let me scratch the back of her head. Her fur was long and curly and black as jet – more like hair really – and though she had some of the looks of a Cocker Spaniel, it was plain that she was just a mutt. The look in her little brown eyes told me that she would rather be anywhere else in the world but here.

Finding Liberty

We had gotten Rusty a year earlier. Rusty was a medium sized dog – about 50 pounds or so – who had some of the color & temperament of a lab. He was also a mutt through & through, but I've always been partial to mutts. I think they're just so spastically happy that someone would want them that they don't really care about anything else except pleasing their masters. You take a mutt out of the shelter and their loyalty is yours forever.

Even so, aside from brief moments of attention and activity, I think it must be pretty lonely to be a dog, especially in a house with little children and busy parents who sometimes just don't have the time or energy to spend with the family pet beyond what is absolutely required. We didn't want Rusty to be lonely, so we were going to get a pal for him.

The dog that I really wanted looked a lot like Rusty. She was a little smaller in stature, but had his same coloring and overall build. Unlike Rusty's stiff hair, her fur was really, really soft. She was a beautiful dog. The problem was, she *knew* she was a beautiful dog.

Catherine and the kids had joined me at the shelter during my lunch hour. We had brought Rusty along too, to see how he would get along with the "possible" dogs I had picked out the day before. This beautiful golden female with the soft fur acted like, well, like a beautiful golden female with soft fur. There was an attitude about her, almost as if she were saying, "*You may now bask in my glorious presence, o' lowly humans*". Hmmm.

Rusty didn't seem to mind the attitude, though. He liked her. Boy, did he like her. In fact, he tried to like her several times just in the 5 minutes that we had her out of her pen. I had visions of uncomfortable conversations that I would have to have with my little children in the very near future about certain birds and certain bees if this dog were to come home with us.

Um . . . maybe not.

We then fell back to my second choice, the little black dog. It didn't take long to know that this would be the one, because everyone fell in love with her on the spot. She was sweet,

80

cuddly, and completely without malice or pretentiousness towards us or the kids. This was a dog who desperately wanted us to take her home. Even better, Rusty didn't seem to notice her at all; if apathy were a dagger, he would have dealt her a mortal blow that afternoon. We made our decision, and picked her up the next day after she had been spayed (and you just know that if she hadn't wanted to get out of there before, she certainly did now!). Rusty displayed his maturity by pouting all the way back home.

Despite his initial disgust with how the whole "dog selection process" had turned out, Rusty and our new little dog, which we named "Rosie", soon learned to make the best of things together. While true that from a romantic perspective Rosie seemed to have the same effect on Rusty as a cold shower, he discovered that there were other things to life than just perpetuation of the species, and soon they became good friends and inseparable companions, whether scouring the kitchen floor after mealtime (pretty good pickings when there are four small children around!) or patiently grooming each other.

I think Rosie had been abused by her former owners. During the first year she was with us, she would often cower down when I approached and relieve herself all over the floor. It took a long time for her to realize that I didn't intend her any harm. It made me wonder about who she may have encountered earlier in her life that did. Eventually, she came to trust us completely.

Rosie was always an incorrigible beggar. Anytime the door to the refrigerator was opened, the clink of silverware was heard, or the electric can opener hummed, she would suddenly be at your feet in the kitchen.

Much skilled in the art of being pitiful, Rosie would wait quietly near your feet while you were eating until you noticed her. Once eye contact was made, she would turn her head away as if she were ashamed for being so brazen, and then a second later, with her head still turned away, she would lift her eyes to see if you were still looking at her. If you were, she would quickly look away again, in obvious shame, of course.

Catherine & I enjoyed no end of laughter as we played this game with her again and again.

I would always shoo her out of the kitchen during meals, and she would slink away (with much pitifulness and shame) until she was just outside. And I do mean "just outside". You would often see just her head peeking around the corner (sometimes just her nose), with her paws just barely extending into the kitchen doorway. *I'm not reeeeeaaaaally in the kitchen, 'cause remember when you told me that you didn't want me in the kitchen?*

Despite my best efforts to break her of begging, I know that Cat would frequently reward her efforts when I wasn't around. I really didn't care.

When we lived in Florida, our house had a privacy fence around the backyard. This was nice because it allowed us to let the dogs outside without having to constantly supervise them or keep them chained to a post, but it posed other problems. I don't know whether the phases of the moon had anything to do with it, but every now and then our dogs would decide that a little field trip was in order, and they would disappear into that strange world beyond the fence. Rosie was always the instigator on these missions. She would start a hole, and then when she had cleared the walls of Alcatraz, Rusty would take over and dig until the hole was big enough for him to fit through as well.

I never knew where they went on these midnight excursions, but I can imagine them in my mind's eye galloping happy and carefree through the neighborhood, their souls running wild in reckless abandon. They would always show up the next morning, filthy and wet and tired. They knew I wasn't going to be happy, but I could tell that deep down they didn't care. Whatever they did on these random jaunts was obviously well worth whatever price they would have to pay me. They would always accept their scolding with due humility, and then retreat to cool, dark quarters to sleep it off.

I can't remember how many holes under that fence I filled in, how many flower beds I reconstructed, or how many hours I worked to make the backyard "escape-proof". No matter what I did, Rosie the opportunist would find another way. But she never left her pal behind.

As the years passed, Rusty started to show his age. Now, on those mornings after one of their infamous escapes from the backyard, I would see only Rosie walking back to the house on the sidewalk. Behind her, maybe 100 feet or so, would be Rusty, out of breath and barely shuffling along. Rosie would stop every now and then to let him catch up a little, never letting him get too far behind. Through all the years and all of their romps, she never came home without him.

I have been preparing myself for Rusty's death for some time now. We've had him for almost 11 years, and we don't know for sure how old he was when we got him. For the past several years, it's been very noticeable that he doesn't move around quite like he used to, prefers sleep over activity any day of the week, and just seems & acts old. Rosie, on the other hand, could fly up and down the stairs with ease, and was always ready to play. I had comforted myself with the fact that as hard as it would be to lose good ole' Rusty, at least we would still have Rosie around for a few more years to keep us company. It simply never occurred to me that she would die before he did.

It's still a little hard to believe. One day she was bounding around like she always had, and the next day we noticed that she seemed a little tired. We just figured she had a little flu bug or something – it had happened before – but then she started losing her appetite too. We got some dog food that we knew she liked and started being a little more liberal on some of her favorite table scraps: meat & cheese. For a few days she seemed to be getting better, getting some of her old energy back, but maybe that was just optimistic thinking, because soon it was obvious that she was getting worse.

She didn't seem to be in any pain; she just looked tired, like she had given up. Just to be sure that there wasn't some ridiculously easy cure for whatever she had, we finally took her to the vet. I don't like vets in general; I know that there are some good ones out there, but my experience with them is that most are just in business to make money off of our guilt about our pets.

I took both Rusty & Rosie in for an annual rabies booster years ago and got handed a bill for almost $400; they had taken the liberty to do a few "extra" tests that they deemed necessary. A few years later on my way home from work, I picked up a kitten that had been hit by a car. It was in the middle of the road, dragging it's leg, scared and confused by all of the traffic; I couldn't stand the thought of just leaving her there to wait for another car to come by and finish her off. I took her to a vet (a different one) in the hopes that maybe she just had a broken leg. They took her in the back room, watched her die for 10 minutes, and then told me that they were very, very sorry and that would be $85 please.

All the vet could tell us about Rosie is that her red blood cell count was very low, but they didn't know why. They recommended a blood transfusion. A transfusion? All I could think of was a bathtub that had been full of water for years and was now almost drained; did it make any sense to put more water in it without at least knowing why it had drained out in the first place?

They also offered heartworm preventative medicine. Does she have heartworms? *Well no, but . . .* So my dog is dying and you don't know why, but even though she's 10 years old and has somehow made it this far without ever getting heartworms I should start her on a heartworm medication right now?

Transfusions, heartworm medication . . . I was in sales long enough to recognize up-sells when I saw them. I paid them the $300 I had already racked up and took Rosie home, no more impressed with veterinary care than I was when I went in. Sometimes, it's just time. They would have done better just to tell me that.

Rosie slipped away quietly on a Saturday night, just a few hours after I had finished her little casket. Earlier in the day I had looked up into the cloudy sky and said, *"Lord, if it's Your will to take her, if she isn't going to get better, then please just take her.*" A few hours later, He did. We buried her that night in our flower garden. There was just enough room in her little coffin to include her favorite toys and a few letters that my children wrote. The marker on her grave has these words: *God's love is seen in a single rose.* I know that to be true.

I don't really know what my point is here. Maybe it's that we shouldn't take for granted the things that we have today, as there's no guarantee that they'll be here tomorrow. Maybe it's to live our lives with urgency, because all living things will eventually fade away. Maybe it's to love with everything we've got *right now*, because we may not get another chance. Or maybe there is no point. Maybe I just needed to write about a little black dog who will be missed very much on this earth.

I'm glad she got to see snow at least once.

14

Standing Before the Spear

The January 30, 1956 edition of *Life* magazine featured a story about 5 missionaries that were brutally murdered in the jungles of Ecuador by people of a primitive and extremely violent tribe called the Waodani. What follows is a brief (and very incomplete) summary.

The missionaries, along with their wives and young children, had already been living in isolated areas of Ecuador for several years ministering to the local population, and they were well aware of the Waodani's existence and their reputation. Far from limiting themselves to just indiscriminately killing anyone who would trespass into their territory, the Waodani's violent behavior permeated even their own culture. To the Waodani, life was simple; if you were offended for any reason – no matter how big or small – you killed the one who offended you. Usually their wives and children and anyone else in their family too, lest you leave anyone who may later return to take retribution on you. Their culture had been described as the most violent of any people ever discovered; 3 out of every 5 adult Waodani deaths were homicides, brought about by the hand of their own people. Even without the threat of an outside world crowding in on them, the Waodani were in danger of killing themselves into extinction.

The missionaries knew all of this, and wanted to help them. So when chance, luck, or fate intervened and enabled the missionaries to discover where a segment of the tribe lived, they felt compelled to make contact with these people, well aware of the danger involved.

They flew to a sandbar on the Amazon river near a Waodani village and made contact with 2 women and 1 man who ventured out to meet them at their encampment. These initial meetings were an exciting success to the men; they even gave the Waodani man a ride in their plane.

Unknown to them, however, their lives were being held in a fragile balance, and the scales were about to tip.

The man who had visited them wanted to marry one of the 2 women that had also come along, but there were some in the tribe who didn't want that to happen (the 3rd woman who was part of those initial meetings was essentially a chaperone for the other two). At some point, the young man & woman showed up back at the tribe without their chaperone, and when confronted about why they were alone together, they told the tribe that the foreigners had tried to kill them, and that they had had to flee for their lives.

In that moment, with that simple self-serving but oh so understandable lie, the death sentence for the 5 men was sealed. The tribe went to the sandbar and, as was the nature of their culture, brutally killed all 5 of the young missionaries with spears and machetes.

Not long after the massacre, Rachel Saint, a sister of one of the murdered missionaries, and Elizabeth Elliot, the widow of another, reestablished contact with the Waodani and went to live with them in the jungle and bring them the word of God. After only a few short years, they were able to slowly overcome the inherent suspicion and violent nature of the tribe and change them forever.

Although this all happened 60 years ago and is well known to many, I knew none of it until just recently, when I read the book *End of the Spear* and watched the movie of the same name, as well as a companion film entitled *Beyond the Gates of Splendor*, a documentary of the event.

As I've reflected on all I've learned, there are several things that stand out in my mind that not only leave me in awe with sheer amazement, but also force me to ask myself some hard questions that I may not want honestly answered.

First, is the men themselves. These 5 men, in all of the vitality & potential of their youth, decide not to pursue "the American Dream", but instead give up the creature comforts that they've known all of their lives and take themselves, their young wives, and their babies into a remote and isolated land so that they can minister the word of God. These were smart, good looking, educated, strapping young men with their whole lives ahead of them. They could have been successful in any profession they chose. And they chose, in the prime of their youth, to serve God.

I have never known a culture that breeds young men into their twenties with that kind of integrity, conviction, and depth of character. It's hard for me to believe that one ever existed. The culture that I was brought up in, just a few short decades after these men, left me at the same age with almost none of those same qualities. Even today, I am still struggling to achieve them.

It was told that one of the 5 men, Jim Elliot, didn't have time for girls during his college years. Although he was good looking and extremely popular, he was also celibate, and *proud* of it. He considered it to be one of the highest callings of God. *What?*

In contrast, the culture of my formative years in the late 70's and early 80's *ridiculed* celibacy. Virginity was an affliction to rid yourself of as soon as possible, and that mentality was so strongly enforced upon me that I would make up *lies* about my sexual exploits rather than expose the truth of my virginity. And this was in *High School*! How twisted had things become that not only would I not look at the purity of my body as a gift, but would also so thoughtlessly break one of the 10 Commandments to prevent anyone else from knowing that I possessed that gift?

Jim Elliot championed his virginity. I bore mine with shame. These men chose to dedicate their lives to serving God. I chose to make money for myself. They willingly gave their lives for something they believed was more important than themselves. I've only been interested in making my own life better. It's a difficult mirror to gaze into, because the stature of the man I see reflected back at me is much smaller that I had previously thought.

Another thing that struck me about the story was the act that would be the catalyst for driving the Waodani tribe to kill the missionaries: a simple lie. A lie told for the same reasons that we see so often today; to deflect responsibility for our own actions onto someone else in order to save ourselves from being held accountable. Should it be any surprise that our words have the power to kill? Not really; it's not like we haven't been warned:

"Their tongue is a deadly arrow; it speaks deceit; With his mouth one speaks peace to his neighbor, but inwardly he sets an ambush for him." - Jeremiah 9:8

"Your tongue devises destruction, like a sharp razor, O worker of deceit." - Psalms 52:2

"By forbearance a ruler may be persuaded, and a soft tongue breaks the bone." - Proverbs 25:15

"Thou shalt not bear false witness against thy neighbour." - Exodus 20:16

Even so, I still don't think we fully grasp the power of our own words, and the damage & destruction that they can cause. The Waodani people didn't know this, of course, but we do. What's our excuse for continuing to do it?

It's ironic to me how, in our culture today, even as battles continue to rage about whether or not it's "acceptable" to post the 10 Commandments in our halls of justice, the vast majority of our laws today are all in some way derived from those original 10.

We have *hundreds* of laws written in the floweriest of languages spanning a vast realm of different areas of deceit that, in the end, are all simply embellishments of something that God was able to put into such simple and succinct terms: *Do not lie.* Have you ever stopped to think about what life would be like if everyone were able to follow *just that one* commandment? It's difficult to imagine.

Speaking of "difficult to imagine", the next thing that hit me about this story definitely falls into that category, and was also the one that bothered me the most, because the questions about myself that it unearthed were unsettling for me to think about.

To put it simply: *they had guns.*

I've thought about that a lot since learning what happened. These 5 men had weapons that they could have used to defend themselves with, but they didn't use them. And it wasn't because they didn't have time to use them either; they knew before they ever went out to meet the Waodani that they wouldn't. They had told their families before they left that regardless of what happened, they would not shoot the Waodani. Their reason? Get this: *"because they aren't ready for Heaven; we are."*

Can you imagine?

I close my eyes and put myself on that sandbar with those men that day, deep in the Amazon jungle, alone & isolated from the rest of the world. Suddenly, after such successful first meetings with these people, we are being attacked, and I don't know why. All I know for certain in these frantic, fearful seconds is the realization that my life is about to be violently ended. I see the spears. I see the machetes. I see the intent.

I am a young man, and I have something to live for; my wife, my children, and all of the memories of a lifetime yet to be lived. And I possess the means to secure my own deliverance. What would I do?

Although I can try to deceive myself by saying that I can't really know for sure, in my heart I know very well what I would have done.

And it's that particular standard – that bar – that these men in their actions set, that bothers me the most, because I feel that I fall so miserably short of it. Five young mortal men – boys, really – did something that I know I myself could not. They saw their fate coming towards them, knew what it meant, and they did not even *try* to kill their attackers. They tried to fire warning shots, they tried to get to the radio in the plane, they tried to physically grab and hold the Waodani, and they tried talking to them; *but they did not shoot them.* In the end, they all accepted the thrusts of the spears and the blows from the machetes rather than defend themselves and cause harm to these people who didn't know Jesus Christ.

What kind of a society breeds men like that? And where does that leave me?

I like to think that I'm getting to be a pretty good Christian, that I walk a fairly straight path, and that, while certainly not perfect, I can generally feel good about who I am. But although all of those things may even be true, is all of it just the manner in which I live my life, or is it, to me, life itself? I *understand* what the Bible says, I *agree* with it, but do I really *believe* it to the center of my being? Enough to die for it?

It's sobering to get yet another reminder that your faith is not what it should be. To see that, for all of the good that you may have done and the progress you might have made, you are still nowhere close to your destination. With everything that I have found out about these men, and all of the thoughts I have had about them, that is the one thing that they have made crystal clear to me even 60 years after their own deaths.

As a last point of thought, it's not lost on me that the actions of these men were very Christ-like in nature. I know that they were not perfect, and I certainly do not want to dietize them in any way, but the similarities are obvious. Like Jesus, they were trying to teach the word of God. Like Jesus, they were betrayed. Like Jesus, their lives were sacrificed. And most importantly, like Jesus, they accomplished more in their deaths than they ever could have with their lives.

As I look off into the distance past the hills that surround my safe little existence, I wonder what would have happened if those 5 men had *not* been killed. I think the best that they could have hoped for would have been to successfully bring the word of God to the Waodani people. That would have been a great thing, of course, and that *was* the mission that they were trying to accomplish, but if that *had* happened, who today would even know about it? Or care? The story, the message, and the feelings & thoughts that they provoke would have been buried right where they began; deep in the heart of the Ecuadorian jungle.

In sacrificing their lives for God, however, not only did they accomplish their original mission of building a bridge to the Waodani people, but in the decades since, tens of thousands of other lives around the world – including my own – have now also been influenced by what happened so long ago on a remote sandbar in the Amazon river.

I don't know what my future holds, what events I will be faced with, how I will react, what I will accomplish, or how my own life will end. Maybe something will happen to me that will change me in an instant. Maybe I will get to where I want to be by the sheer persistence of never giving up or losing sight of my goal. I don't know. But I do know this: I know the kind of man I want to be. I want to be the kind of man who has such faith & conviction that he will have the courage to stand before the spear for his God and not waver.

In Memory

Jim Elliot
Nate Saint
Roger Youderian
Pete Fleming
Ed McCully

"If it be so, our God whom we serve is able to deliver us from the furnace of blazing fire; and He will deliver us out of your hand, O king. But even if He does not, let it be known to you O king, that we are not going to serve your gods or worship the golden image that you have set up." - Daniel 3:17-18

15

Saturdays With Sarah

When my daughter Sarah was a baby, she had just enough energy to make it to lunchtime. There was no "gentle warning tone" when her gas gauge neared empty, just a predictable yet sudden moment – somewhere between noon and 1 o'clock – when her eyes would screw shut, her mouth would open wide, and a piercing wail of fatigue would start to vent from deep within her.

On Saturdays, this was my call to action. I would dutifully scoop up my baby girl into my arms, retire to the darkened bedroom, and begin the ritual of her nap.

Holding her little body to my chest, I would pace the confines of the bedroom with a slow, rocking gait. I would quietly sing her a lullaby – usually the same one over and over – until her insistent crying gradually abated to the gentle hitches of soft, muffled sobs. As the fight continued to leave her body, I would stop singing the lullaby and begin humming it instead, the vibrations from my chest adding their own chorus to an already sleepy symphony.

When I sensed that she was all but played out, I would lay her on the bed. She would wake up, of course, but that was expected, so just as soon as her head was on the pillow I would quickly lie down beside her. At this point, she would no longer have the energy to actively contest the inevitable, but her droopy eyelids would continue to battle gravity and resist the siren song of sleep for as long as they were able.

I knew from experience that if I just remained there with her, she would be fast asleep in 10 or 15 minutes. I also knew that after those same 10 or 15 minutes of lying next to her warm little body and breathing in her sweet baby perfume, I would be asleep too, and my Saturday would suddenly have a great big hole in it.

I really couldn't complain. For 5 days each week I was not there at all to assist my wife with the children, and during *every* night of the week I simply was not endowed with the necessary equipment to help out even if I had wanted to (and I can promise you that during those nights I had absolutely no desire to be of *any* assistance whatsoever). So if the weekend gave me the opportunity to provide my wife with a little relief, it should not have bothered me at all. But it still did. Especially on Saturdays.

Sundays were already kind of a "scratch" anyway. Church in the morning, lunch, maybe a football game in the afternoon; then dinner, baths, and everyone to bed early in preparation for Monday morning. But *Saturdays* . . . well, those hurt a little.

Saturday was the one day that was open to all possibilities, and it was the one day that I had available to get accomplished whatever it was that I needed to do. And there was always *so much* to do. The grass needed to be cut. The cars needed to be washed. I needed to make some headway into the pile of things that had broken during the week. Half a dozen unfinished projects begged for attention. The list seemed almost endless, and that was just the "preventive maintenance" I needed to do to keep from falling behind further than I already was. New projects? Something just for fun?

Forget it.

So when I would hear Sarah get fussy on Saturday afternoon I would almost always feel a touch of frustration coupled with a vague sense of loss. I would think of those things that I would not be able to do simply because my daughter needed to take a nap, and who, in doing so, would inadvertently pull her daddy into the same land of blissful slumber regardless of how hard he tried not to go.

Once again, a Saturday with almost unlimited potential would be gutted.

Some things will always be, but some things will never be again. 10 years have now passed. The grass still needs to be cut, the cars still need to be washed, and I still have a half dozen projects that need my attention, but my little girl doesn't take naps with her daddy anymore.

Sarah is 11 now, and the vague sense of loss that I feel at this point in my life is one of knowing that my baby girl will never be a baby again. She has girlfriends that occupy her time now. She has private talks with her mother that I am not privy to. She still loves her daddy, but she isn't quite as dependent on him as she used to be.

My little girl plays softball now, and through some twist of fate I somehow got roped into being an assistant coach for her team, even though I know nothing about coaching. It's been a rude awakening for me to learn how much time being a coach will carve out of each week. For 3 months now we've had practice after practice and game after game in a seemingly endless buffet of sweat, dust, sunburn, bruises, and sore muscles. Sometimes it seems as if every time I turn around I'm getting ready to head back out to the ballpark. I admit, it's been a little frustrating at times.

But then I look at my daughter; so excited as she runs out onto the field, so determined as she stands in the batter's box, so happy as she chants with her teammates in the dugout. And I am here with her.

Suddenly, my heart swells with joy as any & all regrets of what will *not be* are washed away by the realization of what *is*, and I am able to fully appreciate these fleeting moments in time simply for what they are. There are some things I can no longer do with my daughter, but this is something that I *can* do with her – *today* – and I intend to soak up every single minute of it while I still have the chance.

Because some things will never be again.

16

Countdown to 1984

In 1945, George Orwell's *Animal Farm* gave a simple yet realistic account of Stalinist communism, including an eerily accurate description of what its condition would degenerate to by the time of its collapse more than 40 years later. Not only did Orwell get more right than not with his depiction, but many of the examples of the slow & systematic governmental decay that he used to illustrate the novel can be seen with glaring clarity in institutions of government all over the world, including our own.

One year before his death in 1950, Orwell's *1984* was first published. Like *Animal Farm*, it also dealt with a totalitarian government, but in this novel, we do not see the steady decay over time. Instead, total corruption is shown to have already reached its apex, except that in this instance, the government is not about to allow itself to lose its power. *1984* depicted a nightmarish world where war was constant, thought was an arrestable offense, love was outlawed, individuality did not exist, and Big Brother watched your every move. If *Animal Farm* showed *how* a government corrupts itself, *1984* showed what that corrupted government can create.

In it's day, *1984*'s depiction of the future was the topic of much discussion, and there was a good deal of speculation as to how correct Orwell's vision of the future might really be, regardless of how impossible it seemed at the time. As the real year 1984 came and went, it was generally concluded by all – myself included – that Orwell had missed the mark quite badly. 23 years later, I'm not so sure. In fact, today I think it is much more likely that the only thing he really "missed" badly was the year itself.

As I reread *1984* again last month, I was struck by something that was mentioned near the very beginning of the book, something that I would never have noticed upon my first reading a generation ago; flat-screen TV's that hang on the wall. *We didn't have flat-screen TV's that hung on the wall in 1984*, I thought. No, we didn't. But we do now. Granted, unlike the novel, we have the ability to turn ours off if we so choose, but I have to wonder, will that always be the case?

My curiosity sparked, I started looking for other things in the novel that didn't exist 23 years ago, and as I continued to read, my list grew alarmingly long. To make matters worse, most of the things that I stumbled across were not even mere physical devices, but instead were things that were much more vague and disturbing. Things that fell into the categories of "guideline", "policy", and "practice". And all of them not only seem to be universally *expected* in today's world, but also *accepted* as well.

One of the first "unthinkable" premises presented in *1984* is the one in which everyone is being watched. "Big Brother", while an invented imaginary head of state, has the very real ability to see and hear everything that you are doing. Anytime, anywhere. At the time of its publication in 1949, I imagine this idea had to appear almost laughable. In the year 1984, perhaps not so laughable as far-fetched. Today, even the most ardent skeptic would have to admit to a certain amount of truth to the concept, albeit maybe at present still in a more limited, primitive capacity.

But when was the last time you stopped to really think about the *level* at which we are being watched today?

It's well known that if you have a TiVo, all forms of data on your viewing habits can be collected. If you have a satellite dish receiver connected to a phone jack, customer service technicians can access it. And if you have internet access, any educated hacker has a free pass into every file on your computer. Even with firewalls, how can we prevent access into our homes if those wanting access are the very ones who created the firewalls for us? TiVo's, dish receivers, internet . . . none of those things or the potential capabilities they provide existed in 1984. But they do now.

We are being videotaped on the highway, in stores, at bank ATM's, in parking lots, and at many other times when we might least expect it and possibly never know it. Today, not only can we be photographed, videotaped, and/or recorded with a discreet cell phone, but that information can then be sent anywhere in the world with the touch of a button.

E-mails, credit card transactions, internet surfing, electronic purchases, toll-road speed passes – just to name a few – all leave traceable paths of our whereabouts and habits. We now have GPS trackable computer chips that are being encouraged for implanting into our pets, that have been *mandated* for use with farm animals Note 1, and in some cases voluntarily used in people. As far back as 2001, the U.S. government has been floating the idea of using computer chips as part of a universal ID card program for all U.S. citizens, and the option of physically *inserting* trackable computer chips into the bodies of military personnel is already on the drawing board. I wonder, should that experiment come to pass and be "successful", how long until it does not seem like a good idea to do with *everyone*?

And don't be too quick to brush this off with the notion that most of the above "data collection" is taken in by private companies or disparate organizations. As we continue to see more and more separate corporations merge into near monolithic entities, along with their influence & power over government agencies increasing in proportion to the wealth they have available, how long before most of those "non-government" companies become little more than a branch of government itself, in action if not in name? Is it unreasonable to assume that many are in bed with each other already, and have been for some time?

Most of the above abilities to "watch" people did not exist in the year 1984. It makes me wonder then to what level this continuous erosion of privacy by means of technology will reach 23 years from now.

Another major tenet in *1984* is the need for a perpetual state of war, an endeavor which in Orwell's world is no longer used to conquer other peoples, but has become instead a tool to *control your own*. War is a means to use up all surplus of production so that the citizens become more dependent on the government. It is used to incite unquestioning patriotism to frenzied levels, to prohibit travel so that interaction with other peoples is prevented, to grant supreme governmental authority to enact whatever it deems necessary for the "protection" of it's citizens, and ultimately to provide a distraction for every citizen to keep them from thinking about anything else.

Of course, a government entering into a perpetual state of war is a ludicrous concept. Surely the now 6 year old "war on terror" will ultimately come to a successful conclusion, won't it? It's unconscionable to think that anyone would think of using it as a tool for any of the above purposes, isn't it? And certainly we would place strict limits on any intrusions that might be requested of our own freedoms and constitutional rights, wouldn't we?

A third reality of Orwell's *1984* world is the existence of the "Thought Police", a clandestine government organization whose sole purpose is to seek out those who are having thoughts – *any thoughts* – that go against party doctrine. I admit, even the name "Thought Police" sounds ridiculous, much less the concept, and I can only imagine what people must have thought in 1949. After all, even today, how could anyone be caught, much less punished, simply for what they were *thinking*? I would guess that several hundred potential terrorists being held captive at Guantanamo Bay on the grounds of what they were thinking might not agree that it is so outlandish a notion.

I know, I know – *that's different*. Of course it is, and in all honesty, I have to agree. But that's how it happens: with a first step. A first *justified* step. But is it really implausible to foresee that envelope of premeditation expanding over time to include other offenses? If, for example, sometime in the future I make some anti-government statements on a phone call that is being monitored by the NSA, and I also have a gun registered in my name, and my electronic trail shows definite movement towards Washington D.C., can anyone guarantee that I won't be arrested on the premise that I might possibly intend to perform an act of terrorism against the government?

Because ultimately, all of these things that are mentioned in *1984* work together for one purpose: *control*. Those who have the power want to keep the power, and they *will* keep that power as long as they can control the masses, and therefore they will take any and all steps necessary to accomplish that task. While that may sound paranoid, I think we would all be better off not to underestimate how strong the lure of power really is. As a motivator, power trumps even money. After all, if you have power, who needs money?

There is a lot more to *1984* than I can effectively translate here; the similarities between the story's "Newspeak" language and the vernacular that has evolved out of our own instant messaging & email, the subtle (and sometimes not so subtle) twisting of historical events, the bombardment of our senses with media messages at every turn . . . there are so many parallels it would take another book to adequately compare them all. In Orwell's world, all of these things intertwine together to create a beast against which there is no power on earth big enough to conquer. I have to wonder why I should believe that these things would create anything different in our own.

So, knowing that the world of *1984* isn't something that anyone wants (other than those who would be in power), why do we allow movement in that general direction to continue? There are at least 4 reasons.

First is that the movement is too slow, and the various interlocking pieces too unconnected, to really notice. It's a simple case of letting the camel get his nose in the tent. The initial intrusion isn't very bothersome, and a good excuse for allowing it can always be made. Later, when a hoof makes an inevitable appearance, this new intrusion by itself still isn't anything to get all worked up about, and again we are provided with a reasonable justification for it. In addition, there is nothing to make us automatically associate the hoof with the nose; we treat them independently as different things in different places at different times. Finally, as time continues to march onward, we simply forget how things used to be.

There was a time, for instance, when income tax did not exist. In fact, for over half of our country's existence, we were somehow able to survive without it. It was not until the passing of the 16th amendment in 1913 that a permanent tax on personal income was imposed, and then at only 1% Note 2. Anyone still paying 1%? I have never known a world without income tax, or what life might have been like before it. And since there has always been income tax in my lifetime, as far as I'm concerned, *there has always been income tax*. How could I really see it any other way? The truth of the past does not change the reality of the present, so is the truth even really true anymore?

Secondly, we sometimes allow these things to happen because we actually want them, and in some cases even initiate the demand ourselves. The convenience that they provide us *today* outweighs any potential negative consequences that the future might hold. Sure, a cell phone can be tracked with GPS, but I can live with that as long as I can talk to someone whenever I want right now. Yes, letting an unseen technician access my home through my TV receiver might be a little unsettling if I thought about it, but I don't feel like trying to fix it myself, and I'm so happy that I don't have to fix it myself that my mind is too occupied with how happy I am to ponder the ramifications very much.

Third, we are lulled into allowing these erosions of privacy and freedom because they are pronounced as *"for our own good"*. Like carrots they are dangled in front of us under the auspices of our own protection, personal safety, or health, and like piglets to the sow, we accept them willingly because we have in many cases already forgotten how to think for ourselves.

And finally – and probably most disturbing – there is plain old apathy. We see what is going on and fully realize the significance of it, but we simply turn a blind eye and go about our own business, usually with the justification that there is "nothing I can do about it". Perhaps more realistic might be "nothing I *want* to do about it".

Well Gee, Blaine, thanks a lot for killing my buzz. I was actually having a pretty good day until I read this. Not so fast! This isn't a doom & gloom article, it's simply a perspective of a future that might possibly happen. It certainly doesn't need to.

When I think about all of the truly great changes that have occurred in our history – whether they be physical inventions, policies, practices, laws, or whatever – I can't help but notice that all of them almost overwhelmingly occurred because there was a *problem* that needed to be fixed. After all, if there is nothing wrong, there is nothing to make us think anything needs to be different than what it is.

As much as we might complain about the problems that we have in our lives, problems are the catalysts that inspire change. Those who understand that opportunity almost always comes knocking disguised as a problem are usually the ones who are able to take advantage of it (while the rest of us sit back and bemoan our bad fortune).

So if we *are* headed towards some type of unwanted Orwellian future, all we need to do is first recognize that there actually is a problem. Second, we need to realize that problems have solutions, and finding the solution is actually an opportunity to make things better. And third, we need to take some action to make the solution a reality. If those 4 reasons that I mentioned are in fact how we got into the problem, we simply cannot allow them to continue to happen. We have to start *noticing* what is happening around us, we have to *stop accepting* (or even asking for!) things that lead us away from God's word, we have to start *questioning for ourselves* what is "for our own good" and what is not, and we have to be unafraid – and willing – to *do* something about it.

The *good* news is that that is already happening, and has been for several years. The "silent majority", tolerant to a fault for so long, has begun to push back. Resistance – *peaceful* but *firm* resistance – is taking place all over America.

Regarding education, for instance, if you are homeschooling your children, you have already taken action in joining a growing group of millions of other parents who have politely but firmly said "No, thank you", and have become part of an even larger group of people who, though they may not homeschool, are in full agreement that our educational system is broken and are also taking action of their own. Like so many things, it may seem like the process is excruciatingly slow, but history will undoubtedly show that it "all happened within a few short decades".

Women that have left the workforce to be homemakers – a group that is also continually growing – have quietly made *their* position known to a befuddled and increasingly agitated establishment that they do not wish to participate in someone else's version of what life should be.

In doing so, they have become role models to other women in that they are leading by example; showing that it is not only possible, but also absolutely acceptable, to move in a direction that your heart compels you to, rather than to be badgered into going down another road by a deafening but ultimately powerless group of people who will tell you with their mouths that they have your best interests at heart even as their hands are busy pushing their own agendas.

Those are just two examples of things – *many* things – that are already beginning to turn us away from a path that would otherwise lead us into a future similar to the fictional but possible world of *1984*. And not to be overly optimistic, but why shouldn't we think that we can be entirely successful? After all, Jesus told us that with God, all things are possible. In the face of that, Orwell simply doesn't stand a chance.

Note 1: for more information, go to www.usda.gov/nais/. Additionally, please refer also to stopanimalid.org and NoNAIS.org for alternative viewpoints.

Note 2: only for individuals making more than $3,000 annually. Additional surcharges from 2% to 7% were levied on incomes over $20,000.

17

It's Nothing Personal

In March of 2004, my new boss of 2 months called me into his office and proceeded to rip me apart for 45 minutes.

John (my boss) had held an impromptu after-hours meeting earlier in the week with all of his managers. It was an informal affair, and we had just been talking about different things that were going on. At one point, John asked me what my opinion was of a project that we had been working on for the past 2 months. I said that I thought we had made it too complicated and that it was taking too long to complete, and that I had learned in my life that it is usually better to keep things simple if at all possible. He nodded, the conversation shifted to other things, and I took the opportunity to walk out and go to the bathroom. Since this was more of a "get together" and it was already almost 7 o'clock, I decided that rather than elbow my way back into his office, I'd just go home for the day.

Now I was again in his office, only this time he was furious. He was pacing back and forth, glaring at me, jabbing his finger at me, asking me to give him one reason why he shouldn't fire me right then. I think he used the words "fire you" about 20 times. In all my years – including 9 in the military – I had *never* been verbally dressed down like I was then. This was my 3rd strike; and in only 2 months! This 3rd one, like the previous 2, were completely unintentional. In all 3, I didn't even realize or understand that I had done something wrong until it had been explained to me afterwards. But as much as I told myself that maybe I could see how I could have avoided the first two, this 3rd one was a complete baffler.

He asked me if I remembered the meeting and what I had said. I told him yes, and I reiterated my words. He said, *"Blaine, that may be what you remember, but I'll tell you what really happened"*.

According to him, what I had done was to tell my commander-in-chief to his face – in front of all his lieutenants, and halfway up this "hill" we had been trying to climb for the past 2 months – that the course of action he had taken was a complete waste of time, that I knew a better way, and if anyone had only asked me beforehand I would have told them what we *should have* done and we would already be finished by now. Then, to make sure there was no doubt about how I really felt, I took to my heel and walked out on them all.

I was aghast. The blood drained from my face. I could see what he meant, and how what I had said & did *could* have been taken in that context, but I argued my innocence on the grounds that that was *not* what I was *trying* to do. He had absolutely no sympathy. Couldn't have cared less. He told me to think it over during the weekend and let him know on Monday if I wanted to keep my job, and that, regardless of what my answer was, the next mistake would be my last.

I went home in shock. I didn't know what to think. My head was on the chopping block and I couldn't even understand why. *Fired?* I've never been fired in my life; had never been even close to being fired. I was his *best manager*, and he was going to fire *me*? He had asked for my opinion and I had given it! How could that be wrong? Was I supposed to degrade myself into nothing more than a fawning "Yes" man? What was his problem? And, how could I avoid making another mistake when I didn't even understand how or why I was making them in the first place?

The next morning I woke up and literally had an epiphany. Without any prelude whatsoever, I suddenly knew *exactly* what was going on; not only what I was doing wrong, but more importantly, *why* it was happening.

Since John had walked in our doors he had stressed "teamwork". He had said that we (his management team) were all brothers in arms. We'd work together, win together, and fail together. All stuff I had heard before. What I didn't understand at the time was that he really meant it.

In the years preceding John's arrival, our department had been run by a boss who was primarily concerned with himself and his own career, and his attitude had been driven down into all of his managers.

All, that is, except me.

I didn't like what he did, or what was going on, so while I worked with them by necessity, I also tried to keep myself apart and at least do the right thing by those who worked under me. I didn't have a lot of respect for my peers, and for some of them, I had nothing but downright contempt.

So under my new boss – whose values I shared – I finally felt like I was going to be vindicated for my past efforts, and as a result, I was more or less waiting for the "incompetence" of my fellow managers to be discovered; excited even at the prospect that they were soon going to get what they deserved, and all the while not noticing that regardless of what had happened in the past, my peers were now all making every effort to work together for a common goal while I continued to keep myself apart and do my own thing.

Football coach Lou Holtz once told a story about one of his offensive lineman at Notre Dame who was giving only a half-hearted effort during a practice. Frustrated that this player was not responding to any of his instruction, he pulled him out completely and, much to the bewilderment of his team, made the offense run plays without him. After running 4 or 5 plays with a gaping hole where this lineman would normally play – and getting mauled by the defense each time – the quarterback finally got so frustrated that he went over to his coach and told him that this was crazy!

Lou asked him why.

"Because we don't have a left guard!" the quarterback yelled in frustration.

Holtz replied, "You haven't had a left guard all day. When did you notice?"

And that was my realization. *I* was the left guard! Yes, I was wearing the uniform, yes, I came to the practices and games, but I was keeping myself apart from the rest of my teammates, distancing myself from them so that it would be obvious to John that my abilities were not to be confused with theirs, and in doing so I had become the very thing that I despised!

In order to keep myself at the same distance from them as I had in the past, it was necessary for me to change too, and because they were all now moving in a positive direction, the only way for me to do that was to head the other way. The result is that instead of being one of John's best resources, I had turned myself into his biggest problem; a cancer that had to be removed if the body was to continue living

It was a very liberating feeling to suddenly understand what I had been doing. I felt at once not only immense relief at finding the solution to what was going on, but also a towering wave of shame at my own behavior. All of my problems had been rooted in one thing: *selfishness.* And it was no surprise to me that once I choked down my rather large slice of humble pie and started working with my peers in a selfless manner – caring about them, defending them, and helping them – everything changed. I didn't make any more "mistakes". In fact, with this new mindset of "selflessness", making those kinds of mistakes wasn't even possible. But not only that, I found that it made working so much more enjoyable, and ironically, also eventually led me to leave the job completely.

It all comes back to one thing: *selflessness.*

I've come to believe that all great truths share two common characteristics: They are all brutally simple, and they are all rooted in Biblical concepts. As complicated as my little story above may be, and regardless of all the factors involved in it (the vast majority of which I was not able to elaborate on), the root of it all, the key that unlocked the solution, was (of course) brutally simple. And though the word "selfless" does not itself appear in any Bible translation that I have searched through, the *concept* of it runs rampant throughout.

Finding Liberty

I've heard it said that man is inherently evil, but I don't think so. I think we are inherently *selfish*, and that is what leads us to do evil things. Think about all of the stories and parables in the Bible that you know of, and all of the sins and errors that are illustrated in them, and ask yourself this question: Is there a single sin that was not rooted in selfishness?

Were Abraham's lies concerning the status of Sarah as his wife told because he wished to protect her, or himself? Was Jacob's deception of Isaac performed because he was concerned about Esau? Did Peter deny Christ 3 times because he was worried about Jesus? What about Herodius? She held a grudge against John the Baptist that ultimately led to his beheading, but why did she hold a grudge against him? Was it because she gave a hoot about whether or not he dunked a bunch of people in the Jordan river, or was it instead because John had Herod's ear and was possibly going to ruin her sweet gig as the king's wife if Herod ever started listening to what he said?

What about Eve?

What about Cain?

What about Joseph's brothers?

What about any of them? Is there a single sin in the Bible – or in our own lives – that was not committed out of some type of selfishness? And if not, that begs another question: Would it even be *possible* to commit a sin if we lived our lives in a completely selfless manner?

I don't think so. When I look at the only man ever to set foot on this earth who was able to go through life without ever committing a sin, I see a picture of utter selflessness. Everything Jesus did in His life, not only what He taught and what He did, but even His very life itself – and death – was not for Himself. It was for us. *All* of it.

I don't know whether Jesus was without sin because He was selfless, or whether He was selfless because He was without sin, but I do know that there is a definite connection between the two.

As Christians, we aspire to be like Jesus, even though we know that we will never be able to. But do we go about it the right way? I think that sometimes we get caught up in trying "not to sin" and fail miserably because, like "Blaine the Cancerous Manager", we are looking at the individual symptoms (sins) and not understanding that regardless of what they are or how diverse in nature they may be, the real problem is that they are all emanating from a deeper underlying disease (selfishness).

In Matthew 19:23, Jesus tells us that it will be hard for a rich man to enter the kingdom of Heaven. So hard in fact, that having a camel go through the eye of a needle will seem easy by comparison. It's interesting to me that Jesus does not say it's *impossible* for a rich man to enter Heaven, nor does He condemn wealth in general, He just says that for the rich it's going to be very difficult. But why would that be? If the only difference between me and someone else is that I'm financially wealthy and they aren't, why would it be harder for me to enter Heaven? The only explanation that makes sense to me is that I would never be able to accumulate wealth in the first place if I was a selfless man, and if I am primarily selfless in my actions I am inherently less prone to commit sins against God.

In 1 Corinthians 13:11, we can find these words: *"When I was a child, I used to speak as a child, think as a child, reason as a child; when I became a man, I did away with childish things."* There's a definite transition that takes place here; a transformation of a child to a man. But what differentiates the child from the man? What are these "childish things" that we are supposed to do away with?

When we say that someone is acting childish, what do we mean? We mean that they are acting selfishly, because that's simply how children think. All a child cares about is himself, because when you are a child, "yourself" is as big a world as you can handle. A child doesn't understand that everyone else around them also has needs, desires, and feelings; those realizations don't come until much later. And since all they can comprehend is themselves, everything that they say or think is *about* themselves. How could it be any other way?

And if "childish" is the same as "selfish", wouldn't it make sense that the opposite of childish – "mature" – should mean the opposite of selfish? I think that's what Paul is saying; that when we were children we were selfish (and that was okay because that's just how it is), but when we made the transition to becoming an adult, we stopped being selfish and became self*less*. Wouldn't that be a more accurate measure of what it means to be an "adult" instead of just pronouncing that we are all grown up when we reach some arbitrary age? I know I didn't feel like "a man" when I turned 18. Or 21 or 30 for that matter. Looking back over my life thus far, I don't think I actually became a man (at least not by Paul's definition) until I hit my late 30's.

(As a side note, it's interesting to me that in the dictionaries that I've checked, the definitions of "childish" and "mature" do not mention anything about selfishness or selflessness. Also interesting to me is that while many grownups don't get overly offended by being called selfish, don't you dare call their behavior childish! And yet, when you look around at people in the world today, what do you see?)

Go 2 more verses in 1 Corinthians to 13:13 and you'll see this well known verse: *"But now abide faith, hope, love, these three; but the greatest of these is love."* I've learned in my life (the hard way, of course) that love requires sacrifice. It doesn't matter if it's love of your spouse, your children, your friends, your coworkers, or God Himself. True love requires sacrifice, and sacrificing of yourself for another is again a reflection of selfless behavior.

Take a look at marriages that fail and you will see that the selfish desires of one (and sometimes both) were the instruments that pulled the marriage apart. The sores of the disease may appear as financial problems, infidelity, verbal or physical abuse, or anything else, but I promise you, the root cause was a selfish desire of some type.

Even though the Bible does not specifically mention the word "selfless" or any of it's derivations, it sure seems to be an underlying current that runs throughout. Maybe I'm reading too much between the lines, but I don't think so. It sure *feels* right, and I've learned to trust what my heart tells me more than my head. At any rate, in this case, the feelings of my heart don't seem to be in any conflict with the logic of my mind.

There's still so much more that I don't understand. There are whole books in the Bible that I have yet to read, and others that I have read that I've mostly forgotten. My walk as a Christian, like my growth as a man, is still a work in progress. But I am convinced that even though I am still hopelessly inept at it, selflessness is one of the lessons – one of the great truths – that we are supposed to learn in this life.

And it's an amazing thing. Because not only does being more selfless of heart bring me closer to what God would have me to be, not only does it reduce the quantity and magnitude of the sin I commit in my life, but it makes something else happen that is completely unexpected and totally wonderful.

I mentioned earlier that my "discovery" about selflessness made my job much more satisfying in the short term, but also that it eventually led me to leave it. The reason is that everything that I had been working for up to that point was about me; my whole life to that point had been about getting the "good things" in life and reaching that pinnacle of financial independence that is "the American Dream". But it wasn't working.

The more I tried to make myself happy, the more miserable I got. It made no difference how much money I made, what I bought, where I traveled, what house I lived in; no matter what I tried to do to make myself happy, I couldn't do it. Sure, there was temporary pleasure in almost everything, but it always quickly faded away and had to be replaced by "the next thing".

When I started thinking about what truly made me happy in life, I realized that the "hole" I was trying to fill went away when I did something for someone else. Whether my wife, my children, my friends, or neighbors, when I took the focus of my efforts off of *me* and put it on *them*, I found that it made me feel wonderful. And it made no difference whether they even knew who it was that did something for them. It gave me that feeling of contentment that Paul tells us we should have. It was an intoxicating feeling, and what's more, it didn't go away. It was like a foundation for happiness. I found that I was happy even when there wasn't anything in particular to be happy about. There could be absolutely nothing going on in my life, and I *still felt good.*

And, when there *was* something specific to feel good about, be it a celebration, a funny joke, a good dinner – whatever – I felt a much higher state of appreciation and pleasure than those things had ever made me feel before.

I'll close with a story about a man who was expecting a large inheritance from his father. Much to the man's dismay, when his father passed away, all that was given to him was his father's Bible, along with instructions to read it thoroughly. Angry and disgusted, the man threw it on his bedside shelf, where it remained for the rest of his years. Finally – old, bitter, withered, and bent from the hard life he had had to live because of his father's stinginess – he lay on his own deathbed and relived in his mind the misfortune of his life. He noticed the old Bible still laying on the shelf covered with dust and, more out of spite than anything else, he picked it up and opened it to the first page.

A $1,000 bill dropped into his lap.

He turned the page and another $1,000 bill fell out. And another, and another, and another. By the time he had leafed his way all the way through his father's bible, three quarters of million dollars lay heaped in a pile. If only he had done what his father had asked him to do at the very beginning . . .

I think about all of the instructions that God has given us, all of the things that He tells us we need to do. I think about our reluctance and sometimes outright defiance of following those instructions as we go through our lives like rebellious children, putting our faith in ourselves and taking the paths that we wish to follow rather than venturing down the road that we've been instructed to go.

Wouldn't it be funny if, by simply doing what God tells us to do, we actually found the happiness that we were searching for so fruitlessly on our own, a happiness that we could enjoy *now*, in *this* life?

And wouldn't that be just like God not to tell us that that was going to happen?

18

The Eye of the Beholder

It amazes me how women always seem to obsess about their looks: their weight, their hair, their complexion, their thighs, their clothes – if you're a lady you know I'm preaching to the choir; you know the list. And despite my most genuine reassurances, Catherine has a tendency to be overly critical of herself as well. It's amazing, though, that the things she beats herself up over really don't make the slightest bit of difference to me. My wife is beautiful, even if she doesn't understand why.

If beauty truly is in the eye of the beholder, only the beholder can define what beauty is. Not only will this change from person to person, but each definition can wind up covering some pretty strange ground. For instance, take a look at what Solomon thought was beautiful. Here's one description that he gave of his true love:

> *How beautiful you are, my darling.*
> *How beautiful you are!*
> *Your eyes are like doves behind your veil;*
> *Your hair is like a flock of goats*
> *That have descended from Mount Gilead.*
> *Your teeth are like a flock of newly shorn ewes*
> *Which have come up from their washing.*
> - Song of Solomon 4:1-2

Um . . . . . goats? Your hair looks like a bunch of goats? Would you consider that a compliment, or an insult? It may sound strange to us – really strange – but remember, Solomon was absolutely *smitten* with this woman, and to him, these must have been the highest of any compliments that he could give.

Here's a question for the ladies: Are *you* beautiful? Well, I guess it depends on who you would ask. So, who *would* you ask? Whose opinion matters to you? Which "beholder" are you trying to impress?

Hopefully you've put God as the number one priority in your life, but if that's true, then you have to know that God already thinks you're beautiful. He created you after all – just the way you are – and would God create something that was displeasing to His own sight? Do you think that after God created you He stood back and said something like, "*Uh-oh. I kind of flubbed this one*"?

We are all beautiful to God. Of course we are! Do any of your own children look ugly to you? I know, I know, "*That's different*". And you're right, it is. So let's take a look at what people on this earth think, what *their* definition of beauty is. Again, whose opinion matters to you? Which beholder are you trying to impress?

Are you trying to meet the standards of beauty that the fashion industry dictates? I have to ask, why should a group of generally flinty women (and men of less than masculine persuasion) get the right to tell everyone else what beauty looks like? And what do you get if you do meet their standards? Are you going to win some kind of prize?

Maybe you're trying to meet the standards of other women, to impress *them*. If so, why? Would these women not be your friends if you didn't have "the look"? If that's the case, maybe they're not really the friends that you think they are. And if they aren't your friends at all, if they're just the remaining group of nameless women sharing the planet with you, who cares what they think? How does their opinion in any way affect you?

Is it men? Does it matter to you what *they* think? Are you trying to impress the male population at large? It's not that difficult to do. We are a pretty fickle bunch. But if that's what's important to you, there should be flashing red lights and alarm bells going off like crazy, because why would you care if they think you are beautiful? Why are you trying to impress them? And, more importantly, what if you're successful?

If this is what's important to you, not only are you walking a dangerous line yourself, but realize too the thin ice that you are inviting these "other men" to tread upon by trying to meet their definition of beauty: Temptation. Lust. Idolatry. Coveting. Adultery.

I recently read a woman's account of something her mother told her regarding a certain "suggestive" blouse that she owned as a teenager: *"If you don't plan on serving anything stronger than coffee, don't hang out the liquor sign."* I've heard worse advice.

I would suggest that if anyone other than your husband's opinion is important to you – what *his* definition of beauty is – you might want to do some soul searching to find out why. Because if he truly comes second in your life only to God, why should the eye of any other beholder matter?

So what does your husband think is beautiful? Ask him. He'll tell you. Just don't be surprised if what he tells you turns out to be a reflection of the woman that you already are.

Behold My Beautiful Wife

My wife is beautiful.

She is outwardly beautiful. Her clothes are feminine, yet reflect a modest aura of mystery that others can only guess at. She is lovely when she wears her hair down; whether carefully sculpted or carelessly tousled on her pillow as she awakens, it gives her a beauty and grace that defies logic. I feel as though she is teasing me when she wears her hair up, and I'm still amazed that with the simple pull of a comb and a gentle shake of her head, her beauty can be magnified so greatly with so little effort.

She is physically beautiful. I love the softness of her body, the smoothness of her skin, and the warmth of her touch. I love where her waist gently swells out to her hips, and to feel that swell with my hands is to know without a doubt that I am in the presence of a woman. She thinks it's unsightly, but she couldn't be more wrong.

She is inwardly beautiful. The genuine kindness and caring that dwell in her heart is magnificent to witness. She has a playful spirit, and I will go to great lengths to break her composure, and then delight in her tears of laughter. She is beautiful when she smiles. The light in her eyes, the happiness on her face; Her joy is my heart's desire, and when that contented inner beauty shines out in her smile, all is right in my world.

She is spiritually beautiful. What makes her most beautiful to me is something that no one else can experience. She is beautiful because she is my wife. Because she wears my ring. Because in the presence of God she said "I do", and in doing so chose to spend the rest of her life on this earth with such an imperfect man, and to share her beauty with me despite all of my faults. She knows there will be no refunds on her time; there will be no "do-overs". And yet, by my side she remains.

If that's not beautiful to behold, what is?

"Like a lily among the thorns,
so is my darling among the maidens."
Solomon 2:2

19

Poop is a Palindrome

My 9 year old son David and I were on a mini "Boys Only" Double-Secret adventure. Cat & the girls had gone up to Lexington earlier in the day for their own double-secret adventure, but theirs undoubtedly involved shopping malls, things that were clean, and restaurants where you sit down. Oh, somebody get me a cup of coffee; I'm feeling all sleepy just thinking about it.

We, on the other hand, had given ourselves a little treat at that most manly of restaurants, McDonalds – where you eat with your hands as nature intended – and were now on our way out to Grandma's farm to continue other manly pursuits, like walking around on her farm and pretending we actually knew something about farming, and maybe playing with her kittens for a little bit. As a humanitarian gesture only, of course.

On our way over, David and I were critiquing the movie "Cars", which we had seen a few weeks earlier and which had since been the subject of much philosophical thought & discussion. David suddenly noted that "race car" was a palindrome.

I agreed that indeed it was, and immediately offered up "radar" as another. To dazzle him further with my vast store of knowledge that serves no purpose, I also informed him of a few real (if not a little strange) sentences that were palindromes too: "Niagara, O roar again!", "Did I see bees? I did", and the well known "A man, a plan, a canal - Panama!".

We bantered back and forth for awhile, sharing other words we could think of that were also palindromes (and quite a few that were not) when David was suddenly gripped with all of the enthusiasm and excitement that Einstein must have felt when the theory of relativity finally clicked into place.

"*Poop* is a palindrome!" he suddenly exclaimed, and before I could even respond, he left me to my own devices as he wrestled with some maniacal laughter that had attacked him. I just couldn't help but smile.

For something that is such a natural and commonplace part of our everyday lives, adults sure don't seem to talk about poop very much. But while we may try to overlook this ignoble subject, and maybe even pretend that it doesn't even apply to us, children have no such qualms. They are absolutely fascinated with it, and seem to think that anytime is a good time to talk about poop.

The most popular place by far seems to be the dinner table. Hey, we've got everybody together anyway, what better time than this? Company over? Even better. It's about time we got some outside opinions around here.

Maybe it's just my family (oh, please, please tell me it's not), but it seems that during every meal, within only a few minutes of saying grace, the conversation somehow gets steered into the toilet. Catherine will put up her best front and try to regain control, but it's kind of like trying to stop a roller coaster after it crests that first hill. Once it goes over the top, you just have to let the laughter run its course.

She will, of course, point her finger and blame me for this socially unacceptable chaos even as she herself tries to hold in her own laughter and maintain composure. I will, as usual, look shocked and surprised at her judgment and, even as the kids are falling out of their chairs, throw out my never-fail comeback: "*What are you looking at me for?*"

Girls seem to eventually grow out of the "Let's talk about poop" stage. They reach a point in their lives where topics like that are simply not to be mentioned. Instead, their interaction evolves into civilized get-togethers where they daintily share a cup of tea and talk about such scintillating topics as hanging draperies, cutting flowers, and scrapbooking. Snore.

Men, on the other hand, generally see no problem in clinging to those tried & true subjects whose knowledge we have been blessed with from the earliest basic instincts of youth: Sports, food, cars, and – especially when we are in the presence of our young sons – sometimes even, well . . . . you know. Hey, why do you think we're always laughing?

By the way, I don't know if it means anything, but both "Mom" and "Dad" are palindromes too. I'm not real sure how I feel about that.

20

The City Mouse, the Country Mouse, and the Small Town Mouse

I was keeping a careful eye on the lady walking behind my car as I was backing out of the parking place. Once I knew that she was off to my side – and still keeping my eye on her – I continued to back slowly out of my space until . . .

- Thunk! -

Words like "Nice", "Great", and "Wonderful" entered my mind as I pulled forward into my original parking place. There's nothing quite like the feeling of hitting another car, but it's even worse when you know how absolutely avoidable it was, seeing as how you were only moving at a speed of about 1 mph, and the other car wasn't moving at all. And, too, when it happens in the parking lot of your auto insurance agent.

I got out of my car, waved to Kevin (my agent) as he came out of his office with the lady who obviously owned the car I had backed into, and soon found myself inspecting bumpers with them.

It was immediately apparent that there was no damage. My car is a Ford Focus made mostly of plastic, and it was fine; hers was a big mid-80's chunk of Detroit iron that probably would have laughed at me if I'd hit it at 40 mph. Regardless, I gave her my name and number (she already knew who my insurance company was) and told her if anything came up to call me.

60 seconds later – this time after successfully navigating past all 3 cars in the parking lot – I was home (my agent's office is less than a block down the street). Pretty fast, but apparently not fast enough.

Whenever I do something stupid, I try to grease the skids with Catherine before I tell her what it was by saying *"Honey . . . I'm okay!"* This statement is supposed to deflect any anger Catherine might have about my actions off to the side and replace it instead with sincere gratitude that I'm not physically hurt in any way, but experience – and frequency – have shown Catherine that it's nothing more than a preamble for whatever stupid thing I just did. But I didn't even get a chance to tell her; *she already knew!*

WHAT?!

I know that there are no secrets in a small town, but is it too much to ask for at least a slight *delay*?

A friend of ours (who owns the business right next to the insurance company) was getting into her car on her way to visit Catherine and had seen me back into the other car (of course, I now wonder if she was *really* going to see Catherine in the first place or if that's just where she suddenly *decided* to go after seeing me playing bumper-cars in the parking lot next door).

Since she was still there at my house, I decided to have a little fun with her and asked why she hadn't come to my defense as a witness to tell everyone the obvious truth: that the parked car had hit *me*. We stood there talking for a minutes and everyone enjoyed a good laugh at my expense.

Then the phone rang. It was my insurance agent. *"Blaine, we just got the estimate for the repairs on that lady's car. It's going to come in at around $4,000."* That's all the farther he could get before he started cracking up.

Ha, ha, ha. Very funny. Who needs Wally Cleaver and Eddie Haskell around when your own insurance agent takes the time to make a special call just so he can give you "the business"? We laughed, I asked if I still had my safe driver discount, he assured me everything was fine, and the whole incident mercifully ended.

Big cities definitely have their merits. There's simply more of *everything*; people, shopping, leisure activities, entertainment, churches, restaurants, parks, businesses, and the employment opportunities that go along with them. The downside is that, well, there is simply more of *everything*; traffic, crowds, noise, stoplights, prices, crime, and all of the stress that goes with those things as well.

Country living? Well, it offers pretty much the polar opposites of the cities; all of the positives of a city are the negatives of the country, and all the negatives of the city are the positives of country life. If cities occupy one extreme end of the spectrum, the country occupies the extreme opposite.

We're all familiar with the story of the City Mouse & Country Mouse, but somewhere in between is the Small Town Mouse.

Open any atlas of the United States and your eye is usually captivated instantly by the large cities and the crisscrossing network of interstate highways. But look underneath that and you'll see hundreds – *thousands* – of little towns spread out across the landscape: Carthage, IL. Morton, WA. Oakwood, TX. And, of course, one that is now near and dear to my heart, Liberty, KY.

For someone like myself who has lived all of their adult lives in larger cities like Charleston, Charlotte, and Orlando, these places were always something of a mystery. I've driven through hundreds of them over the years – always on my way to a bigger destination – and often wondered who these people are that live in these places? Why do they live there? What do they do for fun? What do they do for *anything*?

In a nutshell, small towns don't have any of the "extremes" – either positive or negative – of either the city or the country. Small towns have people, just not that many. As a result, we have traffic, but there's not too much of that either. And since there's not much traffic, there isn't a need for many stoplights (we have 3). Restaurants? Yes, but not a huge selection. Shopping? Absolutely, just don't be too picky; you won't find the "warehouse" of variety that you might elsewhere.

On the surface, it's exactly what you would think, somewhere in between the city and the country. How close to one or the other simply being dependent on it's size. And yet, somehow there's more to it than that.

There is a lack of anonymity in a small town that you won't find in the city or the country. Out in the country, you can have an anonymous existence by virtue of the fact that you are pretty much isolated to yourself. Any ripple you make goes unnoticed because there simply isn't anyone around to see. On the other hand, in a large city of hundreds of thousands, as odd as it may seem, you're just as anonymous; there's simply too many people already there for any of them to really notice you. The ripple you make there is immediately trounced out by all of the other waves. In either place – city or country – you could disappear off the face of the earth and very few people would really notice.

But in a small town that just isn't true. Your ripple is noticed, and it means something. People know who you are, and not only would they notice if you suddenly disappeared, they would care, because one way or another, whether the impact you made was a good one or a bad one, you *had* an impact.

It seems strange to me that so many people go to places like New York and Los Angeles to "make it big" when, other than a very tiny minority, they actually wind up becoming smaller than they were when they started as they're engulfed by a crippling mass of humanity that makes them insignificant by comparison.

I'm nobody special, and for the 12 years I lived in Orlando, I felt like nobody special. But here, in this little town I now call home, I almost feel like a celebrity. I'm the same guy – still nothing special – but because so many people here know me it makes me *feel* like I'm someone special. Even the mayor knows me. He knows my name, where I live; heck, one day he even stopped and talked to me in my backyard while I was mowing the grass (granted, he was campaigning at the time, but still . . .) To put that into perspective, I didn't even know who the mayor of Orlando was, and you'd be quite correct in thinking that he never came over to my house while I was mowing the grass.

In a small town, people *will* know who you are. They're curious when someone new comes to town – and why not? That's big news! *Who are they? Where did they come from? Why are they coming here? What church do they go to?* Half the town knew more about us before the moving truck left the house than the entire city of Orlando knew after 10 years!

When Kevin called me up after my fender bender, he told me (between laughs) that he was surprised I just didn't take off. "*Kevin*", I said, "*this is Liberty. Half a dozen people saw what happened and most of them know who I am. Where would I go? Where would I hide?*" For a good case in point, just look how fast it took for my wife to find out what had happened.

There's also an accountability in a small town that you just won't find elsewhere. Isolated in the country, you're pretty much accountable to no one by virtue of the fact that there isn't anyone else. In the city, the pendulum swings radically the other way as you become little more than one of a countless horde of businesses and people who hold no accountability to each other due to the sheer numbers involved. An upset customer? Who cares? There's plenty more where they came from. Write a bad check at the grocery store? So what? Just pick another one that doesn't know who you are.

In a small town, it doesn't work that way. People and businesses are not in unlimited supply, and word *does* get around. If my insurance agent, for instance, doesn't do right by me, he knows that it could be the death knell of his business, because a lot of people – his customers and potential customers – are going to find out about it. By the same token, if I were to try to swindle him – say with a false claim – people are going to hear about *that* too, and suddenly Blaine's reputation as someone you would like to know and do business with is gutted. It's a double-edged sword that keeps both of us honest with each other, if for no other reason than we *have* to be honest if we are to survive here.

I like that accountability. It's a built in standard that I am held to all the time. It removes much of the temptation to be unscrupulous, to lie or cheat, or to pretend to be someone I'm not. It builds a loyalty to businesses who do things for me that they didn't have to do. It keeps me from making excuses to not show up in church on Sunday morning. It keeps me from saying something that I might regret.

They say that "locks keep honest people honest". Small towns do the same thing. It simply can't be avoided, but if you don't have anything to hide, you find that you don't want to avoid it anyway.

But the very best thing about small towns is simply the people in them. Small towns are defined by the *people* that make them up, rather than the buildings and houses and streets of the infrastructure. When the isolation of the country and the distractions of a big city aren't there, all you really have left is people. And that's not a bad thing, because people are the only physical things in this world that are really of any importance at all. The skyscrapers, cars, iPods, theme parks, shopping malls, video games, sidewalks, bowling alleys, etc., are all great, but without people, they form only a hollow shell of a world.

In the extreme country, there aren't any people at all. In the big city, there are so many that they degenerate into nothing more than obstacles that keep you from getting to your destination. In a small town, however, people *are* the destination.

I think I'll stay.

21

The Devil is in the Details

As I would suspect is the case throughout all of America, churches here in Casey County, KY have an alarming lack of youth showing up on Sunday mornings. In the fall of 2006, a small group of musicians attempted to counter that trend by sponsoring a Christian rock concert here in our little corner of the world. It was meant as a bridge, a means of reaching out to the youth of our area and connecting with them at the place where they happen to be.

The next week, a scathing letter to the editor appeared in our local paper denouncing the event, saying that there is nothing "Christian" about rock music and that it is instead an instrument of the devil. The writer went on to condemn long hair also; saying that Christian men wear their hair short and neatly trimmed.

This letter touched off a minor firestorm, and letters quickly dominated the editor's page as people voiced their opinions on the topic and argued their case for or against. A scripture was fired off across the bow. A broadside of other scriptures were shot back. The vast majority of letters were written in a kind, loving way, but many were much more opinionated and damning.

This went on for 2 months.

All of the people who sounded off their opinions in this little episode were Christians, none of whom were willing to budge from their own predetermined personal convictions, and who, if anything, now cling to them even more tightly than before. The question I have is not whether you think Christian rock is right or wrong, or whether Christian men should have short hair. The question is this: In what way did all of these Christians move God's kingdom forward by publicly bickering & squabbling amongst themselves – because that was certainly how it appeared – on the pages of a newspaper read by hundreds of people, many of whom *are not* Christians?

Because if I'm a non-Christian reading those letters week after week, I've got to be thinking to myself something along the lines of, "*Are you kidding me? These are the people who say I'm lost? These are the people who tell me how wonderful it is to be a Christian because of all of the love that Jesus Christ has brought into their lives? These are the people who say I'm wrong and they're right? That they know the one true God? They can't even agree on something as insignificant as the length of your hair!*"

The sad part is, they would be wholly justified in thinking those thoughts. I mean, why would *anyone* want to be a part of a group like that, especially when there are plenty of ready alternatives that are so much more appealing.

A year or so ago a very devout Christian woman saw a teenage girl at the mall walking with her mother. The girl was dressed, as dozens of other girls walking around the mall that day were, in the current fashion of the day; a "Britney Spears" ensemble of blue jeans, t-shirt, and bare mid-rift. The exception was that the shirt that this particular girl was wearing also had the letters "WWJD?" emblazoned on the front.

The Christian woman was offended, and proceeded to walk over to the girl and denounce her publicly – in front of her mother, in front of everyone – for not being dressed as a proper Christian should be.

Since this story was related to me, I've often wondered what became of that young girl. A young girl at a very impressionable stage in her life. A time when, consciously or not, she is choosing role models and mentors to guide her, making decisions that, unbeknownst to her, will affect the entire course that her life will take, and in the process, forming for herself a set of opinions and beliefs that she will carry with her for years to come.

However "wrong" this young girl may or may not have been in her "Christian attire", at least she wasn't afraid to associate herself with the name "Jesus". How many teenage girls have the guts to do even that? And if she maybe wasn't a "proper" Christian, at least she had a foot on the right path; a path that over time would have eventually made her realize all by herself that, among other things, perhaps her attire was not appropriate. I have to wonder if Christ is still a part of her life now, or if He instead is closed away forever behind a door that was slammed shut in a shopping mall.

There's a saying I read once that states, *"Don't speak unless you can improve the silence."* Was the silence improved here?

I think that that Christian woman – as well as all of the people who weighed in with their letters to the editor regarding the concert – were well meaning. I'm sure they had good intentions. But the road to hell is paved with good intentions, and if the end result is that a couple miles of interstate was constructed in that direction because of these incidents, does anything change just because "we didn't mean for that to happen"?

We talk a lot about the evil that Satan does in the world, but I'm not so sure Satan is really that busy anymore. I see him more like a Maytag repairman; highly skilled in his art, but not a whole lot to do at the moment. All of us Christians seem to be doing a pretty good job of doing his work for him. Fussing, arguing, judging, and rebuking amongst ourselves. Apparently not content with just keeping non-believers away from God, we take it a step further and slice our fellow Christians to ribbons before throwing the unsightly trash of their being out of our self-righteous front door.

And for what? Oh, that's the kicker! For a *detail*. A detail that we can't even prove is correct, that doesn't even necessarily have anything to do with anything, but one which we have decided to embrace and defend at all costs. We've all heard the old saying, "can't see the forest for the trees", and that's what these individual details are; separate and distinct trees that are part of a much larger whole. But in our obsession over one or two of these details that we feel so strongly about, we will blindly exalt and protect them, and all the while remain blissfully ignorant of the rest of the forest, even as it burns to the ground around us.

That may seem a little harsh. I mean, we're only talking about 2 small instances here, and we are only human after all. We know we will stumble and fall sometimes. But surely we – Christians – do much more good than bad. In the larger scheme of things, these incidents themselves are merely a couple of minor "details" aren't they? Is it possible that I'm simply making a mountain out of a molehill?

Maybe. Each molehill by itself is certainly rather small, but what happens when you pile them all together? Because there sure are a lot of them: How to conduct Baptisms, the rapture, alcohol consumption, head coverings, modest dresses for women, what music to listen to, hair length, body piercings/tattoos, what foods we're supposed to eat, church attendance, anointing with oil, what day is the real Sabbath, speaking in tongues, attire at church, predestination, working on Sunday, laying on of hands . . . folks, I'm just getting started. Pick your poison, identify your detail, and I guarantee you'll find Christians somewhere fighting about it with other Christians.

Note that I'm *not* saying we should relax what we believe in, or water down our faith so that it "feels good" to everybody. I'll talk about that later. But for now, just realize the damage that we do to ourselves – and everyone else – when we allow these individual details to become more important than the larger whole that they are a part of.

United we stand, divided we fall.

You can say whatever you want about the Catholic church, but like it or hate it, one thing is for sure; for the first 1500 years after Christ's death & resurrection, if you were a Christian, you were a Catholic.Note 1   In other words, regardless of what differences of opinion Christians in the Catholic church had with each other, regardless of whether or not the hierarchy of the church was corrupt from power and money, at least all of the Christians in the world were on the *same team*. But from the moment Martin Luther posted his 95 thesis' on the church door, we have allowed our differences of opinion and our varying interpretations of the *same book* to divide us further and further upon ourselves.

I'm not saying that Luther was wrong for doing what he did; far from it. But have things gotten any better since the reformation? It's not as simple as saying "Catholic" and "Protestant", because there isn't just "one" protestant church. You've got the Methodists, the Baptists, the Presbyterians, the Lutherans, and the Episcopalians. Then there's the Jehovah's Witnesses, the Mormons, the Seventh Day Adventists, and the Church of Christ. And don't forget the Quakers, the Puritans, the Shakers, and the Amish.

That's about all, right? Doesn't seem too bad.

But you already know that's not even close. Although that's 13 separate denominations right there, there are plenty more where they came from. And once you get a complete list (if you can), take a closer look at each one. Just in the classification of "Baptist" churches you have Southern Baptist, American Baptist, Primitive Baptist, Full Gospel Baptist, Separate Baptist, Independent Baptist, and so on. Push on to the Presbyterians and you'll see there isn't just one of those either. Ditto for the Lutherans. Ditto for the Methodists. And don't even bother to try to get a headcount of all of the "non-denominational" churches out there. You'll hurt yourself.

How many protestant denominations are there? I have no idea. I've seen estimates ranging from 35 to 23,000 (yes, that was 23 *thousand*). I don't think anybody really knows. Just throw a dart; you're bound to hit something.

Why so many? They're all worshipping the same God, aren't they? They all use the same Bible, don't they? Yes, and yes.   The divisions come from disagreement, and the disagreements are all on varying details. Details of method. Details of style. Details of interpretation.

Who's to say who is right and who is wrong? After all, do any of us actually have the ability to see into the mind of God? To say for sure that "*This is what God meant. Everybody else is wrong*". As with any argument, it soon degenerates into being more about *who* is right than *what* is right. Winner take all.

Details have not just divided the Christian church, but have *splintered* it into hundreds – possibly even *thousands* – of disconnected fragments. Was this done for God's sake or mankind's? Whose kingdom did this fragmentation of the Christian church serve better, God's or Satan's? And does it make a difference whether that's what we intended to do or not?

I go back to what that young girl in the mall had on her shirt; a catch-phrase that was pretty popular a few years ago. WWJD?: *What would Jesus do?* It's a shame that this little question came and went as little more than a fad, because it's a powerful question, one that we would all do better for remembering and continuously asking ourselves.

What *would* Jesus do?

Details? I don't think Jesus cared a whole lot about details. You can see His disdain for meaningless details throughout the gospels: Not enough loaves and fishes to feed the multitude? So what. A minor detail. Too late to heal the little girl because she's already dead? Don't worry about it. Want to get baptized but can't because you're already hanging on a cross? "*Truly I say to you, today you shall be with Me in Paradise.*"

True, Jesus was detailed about *some* things. His entry into Jerusalem, for instance, was very specific regarding his mode of transport and his lodging. I don't know the significance of why He was so specific in that case, but I know He had his reasons, and in some way those details served His purpose. And that's where I think the difference lies; do the details that we embrace serve His purpose, or ours? Are we so focused on the details themselves that we are completely missing the spirit behind them? Have the details become more important to us than God Himself?

Jesus' run-ins with the Pharisees, Sadducees, and scribes are very interesting. These were all people who knew the details of the law, and they held themselves in very high regard. Like vultures they would hover around Jesus, just waiting for Him to slip up so that they could pounce:

Eating with tax collectors and sinners! (Matt 9:11)
Not fasting! (Matt 9:14)
Working on the Sabbath! (Matt 12:2)
Not washing His hands before He eats! (Matt 15:2)
And so on, and so on.

Every confrontation between Jesus and these men was a matter of some detail. When you think about it, Jesus was really quite the maverick. He was constantly crossing over these lines in the sand – these details – and stepping on the toes of those who held them so dear. And I think in His actions He makes it quite clear that it's not the details that matter, but the heart behind them.

Jesus warns us in several of the gospels to beware "the yeast of the Pharisees", and He makes it quite clear how He feels about the Pharisees, Sadducees, and scribes in Matthew 23, the entire chapter of which is devoted to them, albeit probably not in the manner they would have preferred.

"But woe to you, scribes and Pharisees, hypocrites, because you shut off the kingdom of heaven from men; for you do not enter in yourselves, nor do you allow those who are entering to go in." - Matt 23:13

But I think we're making a big mistake if we think that Jesus is simply talking to a bunch of men who all died 2,000 years ago. He's talking to *us*, because every one of us has the potential to become a Pharisee just as soon as we allow the focus of our hearts & minds to slip away from the righteousness of God and become instead centered on the righteousness of ourselves, a condition which quickly leads us to begin judging others on matters of detail. And when our hearts & minds shift away from the Lord, like Peter we suddenly find ourselves sinking into the waves.

I look at Christianity as a mountain to climb. On the mountain are all of those who have accepted Christ as their personal savior. Some have been climbing that mountain for a long time, others have just begun. Some move more quickly up the slopes, while others have a more difficult time. But while we may all be scattered across the face of that mountain, and though some of us have made higher ground, we all have one thing in common: we are all trying to reach the top.

The interesting thing is that none of us can reach the top on our own. In the end, the summit can only be reached through the saving grace of Jesus Christ. What is important is not *where* we are on that mountain, but *that* we are on the mountain. Because as long as we are, it makes no difference to what heights we might ascend to as Christians in this life; as long as we are on that mountain – *anywhere* on it – the hand of the Savior can ultimately reach down to us and pull us to the top when we expire from this earth.

It's interesting that in any other group of people – doctors, lawyers, athletes, soldiers, etc. – we inherently know that there are wide variations of skill and ability within those groups. I've personally known salesmen who were so good they could literally sell you your own shirt and make you think you got a great deal. I've also known others who couldn't give away a glass of water to a man dying of thirst. Yet they both wore the badge of "Salesman". In any group of like minded people, due to knowledge, experience, ethic, mental comprehension – whatever – some are simply better than others.

But have you noticed that that reasoning doesn't seem to apply to those who put on the badge of "Christian"? As soon as someone becomes a Christian, they are immediately held to the same standard by which all other Christians are measured. It's bad enough that secular society holds us in that regard, but to make matters worse, we do the same thing with each other. The problem is that we are all at different levels in our climb up that mountain. Those on the lower slopes need help – not animosity – from those who are higher up. The climb is tough enough as it is without all of us shooting arrows at each other, targeting, judging, & rebuking those who have not reached the point where we happen to be, or maybe more appropriately, where we *think* we happen to be. The first thing we as Christians need to do is to *encourage* those who are on the beginner slopes to *keep climbing*, not give them a reason to turn around and give up.

Once we've got that taken care of, the second thing we need to do is to get the attention of those who are not yet on the mountain at all, and give them a good reason to want to check it out.

Because stretching out below the foot of the mountain are the flat plains of secular living. Lots of people on those plains, and it's pretty easy living there – no mountains to climb, no standards to uphold, no boring accountability to worry about – and there's plenty to keep you occupied. Neon lights, parties, raucous laughter; drugs, booze, sex, & money flow like a never-ending river.

Some of the folks on the plains are firmly rooted; they're staying put. But there are scores more who are asking themselves questions. They're very busy there, they're having loads of fun, but they feel hollow and unfulfilled. They often look over at this mountain and see all of these people climbing it. Why? Sure seems like a lot of work. They get curious and walk over to it's base. What will they see? Will they be greeted with a smiling face and a wave? Will someone say to them, *"Hi there! Join us, won't you? I know it looks hard, but you'll never regret it. C'mon! We'll help you!"* Or will someone look down on them from the heights of self righteousness and say *"Get away! You're filthy and you're dirty and you reek. I know what you've been doing! We don't want your kind here."*

Last Sunday in church there was a young boy – probably 10 or 11 – who was sitting in the pew in front of me. I'd never seen him before and he was sitting there by himself. He had an earring in his ear and a definite look of attitude on his face. His behavior was atrocious; wiggling & squirming, putting his feet up on the pew in front of him, laying down, kicking the hymnals back and forth in their holder. Not only was he not listening to a word being said, but he was disturbing others around him, distracting us from focusing on the sermon.

In all honesty, I didn't like the boy. I wanted to give him a good smack upside his head and tell him to put his feet on the floor, sit still, and show a little respect to God in His own house.

But in a moment of restraint that is unfortunately all too rare in my life, I actually stopped and *thought* about the situation before I acted. I told my inner Pharisee to just shut up for a minute and let me figure out what I should do. I wanted this young boy to behave, yes, but that's only what *I* wanted, and I wasn't even sure if I could say or do anything to accomplish that end. More importantly, I started to think about what *God* wanted for this boy.

True, his behavior was deplorable, he wasn't listening to a thing being said, and he was annoying those around him. *But he was in church.* He was in church because our Youth Minister had somehow convinced him to come, and had taken the time to go pick him up and bring him. So what if he didn't know how to act in church; so what if he didn't know or care what it was all about. He had probably never even been to church before. But he was there now. He was at the foot of the mountain. Was I willing to take the chance of breaking God's tenuous hold of this young boy and send him away from the mountain before he could even find out what it was all about simply because he was annoying me?

In the end, I did nothing. Despite it all, he was at church. Let him come back to church again. And again. Let him realize that church is not a bad place, that the people he sees here will not judge him or hold him to a standard he isn't ready for.

And after he's been there a few times and starts to feel a little more comfortable, maybe someone comes up to him and says something like, "*You know young man, it's great to see you here. We love that we get to spend some time with you. Could*

I ask you a favor, though? I've noticed that during the church service you sometimes put your feet up on the pew in front of you. There are some folks here who get a little distracted by that. Do you think maybe you could help them out and keep your feet on the floor? That would be so great if you could do that. I really appreciate it."

And with a few kind words, a lesson is learned and a young boy takes another step toward the mountain.

I wonder what would have been different if that person who wrote the condemning letter about the Christian rock concert had said instead, *"I just wanted to say "thank you" to all the men and women who took the time to reach out to the youth of our community and hold the Christian rock concert. I don't care for rock music or long hair myself, but it was refreshing to see that someone cared enough to actually <u>do something</u> to fight for these young people. Your efforts have inspired me to get off of my behind and do something myself! Would anyone like to help me?"*

I think the enemy just blinked.

I wonder what would have been different if the Christian woman in the mall had checked her desire to berate that young girl and instead said something along the lines of *"Young lady, I just wanted to tell you how proud I am of you for not being afraid to associate yourself with Jesus Christ. You don't know it, but your actions are making other young women look at you and wonder what it is you know that they don't. I wish you all the best in your walk as a Christian. Please don't ever give up!"*

Oh, my. I do believe Satan just sat up and dropped the remote control.

Note 1: An earlier division in 1054 had already split the Catholic church into "Eastern Orthodox" and "Roman", but the real free-for-all didn't start until 1517. I am also not considering the many unorthodox sects (Gnostics, Ebionites, etc.) that existed during those times.

Author's Note: Several weeks after I wrote "The Devil is in the Details", that young boy I mentioned earlier accepted Christ as his Savior and was baptized.

While I did nothing myself to help bring that about, you have no idea the relief that I feel for not doing anything that might have prevented it from happening. I had an opportunity to finally speak with him a short time later; he seemed surprised that everyone knew his name. I said, "Why shouldn't everyone know your name? You are important."

No big shakes, I know, but how much better for him to hear that instead of the "Shut up and sit still!" that I might have said earlier.

22

The Cat Returns

"Hey Blaine, do you want to go sailing tomorrow?" asked my dad. We had always had a small daysailer in our family when I was a little boy, and our family would often go out on a Saturday afternoon and make a day of it on the lake.

"Okay, sure," I said.

"Great. It'll just be me and you; everyone else is busy tomorrow."

And right then I felt it. A hesitation mingled with a little fear.

Just me and him? By ourselves?

Odd that I should feel unsettled about that. I was 13 years old, loved my dad and certainly didn't have any reason to be afraid of him, and I had been in his company for my whole life. What did I have to be afraid of?

Although he was certainly no stranger to me, most of my time with my dad had always come in short bursts; during the evenings or on weekends, sharing time with two sisters, a brother, a mother, and whatever else happened to be going on. I had spent longer times with him on many occasions sure, but there were always either other people with us – family or friends – or a job to be done that gave a focus to our attention.

This, however, was different. This was *leisure*. There would be no central task dominating our minds and occupying our time, and there would be no one else there but us.

A daysailing trip is pretty much just that; a day of sailing. The drive to the lake was over an hour each way, there was a good half hour on each end of setting up & launching and then recovering & breaking down the boat, and then 3 or 4 hours on the lake itself. That's a long time.

In the face of all that, I was nervous, because even though I had known him my whole life, I didn't really *know* him. Not enough to feel comfortable with him for hours, one-on-one, with nothing else to do. Up to that point, there had always been other factors involved.

I shouldn't have worried; we wound up having a great day. Soon after starting off to the lake my apprehension vanished and never came back. I vividly remember being out on the water, basking in the sun as the sails hung listlessly (the wind having taken a short hiatus) and watching as a butterfly flew past the boat. We laughed about that; we had just been outrun by a butterfly! By the end of the day, the only regret I had was that it couldn't have lasted longer.

But it *didn't* last. Very few things do. All too soon that day was gone, and not long after, so was my dad. I would never get closer to him than I did that day on the lake, and for all the ground we had gained with each other that day, we would do nothing but lose it from then on.

It's hard for a young boy to understand how his father could chose the world over his own son. To leave just when the real work of building a boy into a man is beginning, the effects of which will be carried forward to be felt within the circle of that boy's own family in years to come. Knowledge & instruction never gained cannot be passed on. It must all be relearned.

Twenty five years after a butterfly wins a race, my family is packed up and ready to move.

The house is empty, the papers have been signed, and a beautiful sunny day greets the beginning of a 2 day drive to a new home and a new life. Standing on the driveway, 9 year old David learns for the first time that he will be making the trip in daddy's car. By himself.

And right there, I see it; that slight hesitation, that brief flicker of apprehension in his eyes. He doesn't have to say a word, because I know exactly what's going through his mind. *Just me and dad? All by ourselves? For the whole trip?*

But just like that other boy long ago, he soon learned he had nothing to fear, and warmed up quickly to the fact that he had his dad all to himself, a truly captive audience. We talked about - oh, I can't even remember the things we talked about - but somewhere around Valdosta he discovered that I had never seen the movie *The Cat Returns*, and with great excitement he began to relate it to me.

At length and in minute detail.

Every move by every character explained, every conversation – down to the specific words used – all carefully related. So detailed was his retelling that when we finally stopped for the night in Macon, he wasn't even halfway through (though I wouldn't discover that until the following day). I went to sleep that night amazed at the almost photographic memory of this little boy who called me Daddy.

All told, it took him almost 3 hours to relate a movie that couldn't have been more than 90 minutes long, and the joy that he took in telling me the tale shined through on his face the entire time.

Since those uneventful yet wonderful 2 days, David has repeatedly asked when we'll go on a vacation to some far away place. And I can see very clearly in his eyes that the destination itself does not matter to him in the least; it's the *trip* that he wants. Just another opportunity to spend time – a lot of time – with his father as a captive audience.

He wants another day on the lake with his dad.

23

Dog Days of Winter

My daughter Sarah has always wanted a dog of her own. The requests must have started 6 or 7 years ago, because I distinctly remember her bringing up the subject while walking along the streets of a neighborhood that we had moved out of back in the late 90's.

In the past 2 or 3 years though, her desire and petitions have became stronger and more frequent. The books that she brought home from the library started to include a sprinkling of titles about dogs, but over time came to be *exclusively* about dogs; stories about dogs, training methods for dogs, guides to dog types. The subject soon became the only thing she wanted to read about. And always, always, her soft brown eyes and sweetest demeanor: *"Puhleeeeease, Daddy?"*

My answer, however much I loved my little girl, was always "no". We had 2 dogs already, and I had long since established a 2 dog limit on our home. We had had 3 dogs for a brief period of time years ago, and it was just too much. We had Rusty, we had Rosie, and that would just have to do. On that I would be firm.

But then Rosie died, and a funny thing happened on her passing. As much heartache as her death brought to our family, it also opened the door to a new happiness that we had never known. Because for the first time in over half a decade, I was finally able to tell my daughter "yes". I don't think I have ever seen her so excited.

I learned in Rosie's death that although I may have a strict 2 dog maximum, I also seem to have a 2 dog minimum. While it may seem callous to some that we could "replace" Rosie so soon with another dog, we *needed* another dog; not to replace Rosie, but to help ease the pain of her passing. So within a week, there could be heard the pitter-patter of 4 new little feet roaming our halls.

She came from the animal shelter as all of our dogs do. A little over 2 months old, she had been born in the shelter; it was the only life she had known. Not what you would call the "pick of the litter", she was a little smaller than her siblings, scruffy, lanky, and still recovering from a type of mange which left only a little hair on the top of her head and none at all around her eyes.

The man at the shelter seemed puzzled and a little worried that we were interested in her. He kept asking questions – "You want *this* dog? Are you sure you want *her*?" – almost as if he was trying to talk us out of it. He told Catherine that he wasn't sure about her health. It made no difference. Sarah took one look and it was over. "Muffin" was now part of our family.

As the weeks passed into months, it was amazing to watch my daughter with her newfound love. She took her charge very seriously; dutifully cleaning up "accidents", playing with, caring for, and patiently working to train Muffin on what she was allowed to do and what she was not.

Sarah was an unbelievable "mother". Every morning when I came down the stairs I would find her snuggled under a blanket sleeping on the couch after having taking Muffin out already, and her little dog would be nestled next to her legs. Muffin was an early riser, and when Muffin was up, *you* were up. I worried a little (and felt guilty a lot) that my little girl would have to get up at 6:00 a.m., 5:00 a.m., or even earlier to take her dog outside in any combination of dark, cold, and rain. But Sarah never complained. This was her dog. She had waited years to get her, and she had no intention of failing in her commitment.

During this time we discovered Muffin's tenacious spirit; she would chase, fetch, and return any ball, stick, or frisbee with unending enthusiasm and energy (she would just as tenaciously make you fight for the same ball, stick, or frisbee to get it back from her!). We discovered her playfulness; she would charge across the backyard again and again to jump into a pile of leaves. We discovered her quirks; she would bark & run from the strum of a guitar just as she would from the vacuum cleaner. But more than anything, we discovered her love.

Muffin wants to be *near* us, *always* in our company, tail wagging and begging approval, attention, & affection. If you walk into the next room, she'll follow. If you sit down, she'll sit down next to you. If you hold her in your lap, she'll constantly tilt her head back to look at you and try to lick your face.

Sounds like a lot of dogs, and to be truthful, it is. But this is the first time I ever really *noticed* how absolutely unconditional the love of a dog is.

Whenever we leave our house, we put Muffin & Rusty in the kitchen to keep them out of mischief and then block the doorway with a baby gate. When we return, we'll open the front door, and there at the end of the hallway will be Muffin. Standing up on her hind legs with her front paws on the top of the baby gate, her body stretched out to it's limit, whimpers of delight coming from her throat, and her tail wagging so furiously that it literally lifts her feet up off the floor as it swings from side to side. Sometimes she gets so excited that she'll have an "accident". Imagine that, being *so happy* just to see someone that you lose control of your bodily functions!

It's an amazing reception. You just can't help but feel good knowing that this creature loves you so much that she could get that ecstatically happy just *to see you walk through the front door*! And she does that *every single time*!

People don't treat each other that way. Even with people that we love very much – our spouses, children, parents, siblings, good friends – we don't show that kind of unrestrained happiness just to see someone again. About the closest we come to it is when someone we love is brought back to us from a situation that we didn't think they would survive; a hostage that gets released without harm, a little boy lost in the woods who is found by a rescue party, or a soldier returning from a war zone. In *those* situations, we see a glimpse of what unrestrained love among humans looks like. We see embraces so strong that they crush the air out of our lungs, smiles that split the masks of our faces wide open, eyes that swell and overflow with tears of joy, and mouths that cannot suppress the laughter bursting from our souls.

Maybe that's why Muffin acts the way she does whenever we leave. Maybe, on a much simpler level, she inherently understands that every time we walk out that door, there's no guarantee that she will ever see us again. So when she *does* see us again, whether its been half an hour or half a day, she is so relieved and happy that she simply can't help herself.

It's curious that we don't view things that way. Because we lead a very perilous and uncertain existence on this earth just going about our daily lives. We're fragile beings. We break easily. We know that. And yet, we act as though there will always be "a next time." Even the way we part with each other assumes that we will see each other again:

"See you Monday!"
"I'll talk to you tomorrow."
"We'll be at your house tonight at 6:30."

We assume "a next time" so automatically (and one could argue, arrogantly) that we completely take it for granted that it *will* happen, and in so doing we never take the time to think, "What if this is the *last* time?"

Because we *know* that sooner or later, there *will* be a last time. We know that one day, that friend of ours who sits near us in church every Sunday is suddenly not going to show up anymore. And we know that there will come a day when we ourselves will walk through the church doors for the last time. We know that. We just don't like to *think* about it. But maybe we should.

What would it hurt if I held & kissed my wife each time – *every time* – like it's the last time that I will ever have a chance to do so? Would it be so bad if that friend I spoke with just yesterday saw genuine enthusiasm and excitement in my eyes & voice for no other reason than just the fact that I was seeing him again today? Would my children be upset if I picked them up and hugged them each morning in the same way I would if they had just been returned to me after being lost for days in the woods? And most humbling of all: Does it really take a *dog* to show me how I should be treating the people that I love every single time I am blessed with being in their presence?

Call it "Muffin Life Lesson #1": We need to treat each other like every meeting will be our last, because one of these days, it will be.

That right there should probably be the end of the story, but of course it's not. As if it's not humiliating enough to be taught something by a stupid dog, it's even worse when you realize that the school day is far from over. The more I thought of it, the more I understood that there was even more to learn from this dog than just how we should love each other. I needed to learn how I should be loving my God.

Because if you're a dog, a human being must seem an astonishing and marvelous being indeed. To Muffin, I must seem like a god. I do have very god-like qualities when viewed from a dog's perspective. I have the ability to grant food. Not only that, but I have the power to determine what kind of food she gets, how much she gets, when she gets it, and how long it is available to her. I have the power to punish. I have the power to reward. I even have the power to take her life from her if I see fit to do so.

And the things that I can do! How magical! I'm not talking about things like designing a nuclear reactor, flying into space, or even driving a car; those things she simply cannot even comprehend. I'm talking about things like picking up a stick and throwing it, or opening a door. Things that are so simple for me to perform that I can do them without thought, but to her, a creature who could not do those things no matter how hard she tried, things that must seem almost miraculous.

If I look at myself from her perspective and then consider her desire to constantly be near me, to gain my approval, and to show such enthusiastic joy just at being in my presence, I realize that this isn't how she treats another of her kind, this is how she treats her god!

Which begs a set of questions that I don't want to answer: Is that how I treat my God, the real, one true God? Is it my constant desire to be near Him? Am I constantly trying to gain His approval? And am I so ecstatically happy to be in His presence that unrestrained joy shoots from every fiber of my being?

Stupid dog. Who does she think she is? She has no business showing me my faults. And yet, against my will, my hand still winds up scribbling "Muffin Life Lesson #2" on the chalkboard: I should be showing my love to God the same way Muffin shows her love to me.

If you think about it, why would I *not* do that? Why would I even have to be told? Humiliating – again – to realize this from a dog, because I *wasn't* doing it and apparently *did* need to be told. But though I may not be the sharpest tack on the bulletin board, even I can understand something when it is shown to me in such simple, black & white terms.

I had learned a lot through all of this, and was confident that I could now pack up my books and leave this humbling classroom for the safety and confidence of my own life. But the school bell wasn't ringing yet. There was still another lesson yet to be taught. A review of sorts, on a subject that I understood quite well, but which had apparently gotten a little dusty in that unused corner of my mind where it sat year after year.

On January 1st, Muffin started dying.

We didn't know that at first. We had driven to Louisville that morning to take our daughter Lillian to the airport. The dogs were in the kitchen as they always were; they seemed fine when we left and fine when we returned, Muffin greeting us as she always did. But later that evening she threw up. A little while later she threw up again. If you have dogs, this is just one of those things that happens from time to time. It's no big deal.

And on Tuesday, when she didn't have her normal boundless energy, we knew she was a little under the weather, but dogs *do* get colds.

It wasn't until Wednesday that I started making eye contact with Catherine and knew that she was thinking the same unthinkable thing that I was: *it couldn't be. It just couldn't be.*

But by Thursday morning, it was obvious. She had no energy, wobbled badly when she walked, and would only take a few sips of water at a time, and then only when we all but forced her. She wouldn't eat anything; in fact, she actual *recoiled* when we put any sort of food in front of her.

I was absolutely beside myself. She was only 8 months old! How could she be dying? And from what? She was young and healthy and strong! She had her whole life ahead of her! And what were we supposed to do? Take her into the vet and have them tell us once again how sorry they were that they couldn't figure out what was wrong with our dog (though never too sorry to collect their fee)? Don't get me wrong, I'm not a cheapskate when it comes to those I love, but my trust in veterinarians had been raped so many times over the years that I had no confidence in them whatsoever.

There were a lot of prayers being said for that little dog in my house that week. There were a lot of prayers from many others who knew what was happening.

I felt so helpless and angry. I started to think about where I would get the wood to make another little coffin like the one I had made 6 months before, and it made me so upset just having that *thought* enter my mind that I couldn't stop the tears from running down my face.

And it was in that anger and helplessness that Muffin's 3rd lesson finally came home to me in vivid clarity: I am not a god.

If Muffin sees me as a god, then it's a paper god she worships. There is nothing behind the facade.

I have no power. Whatever "god-like" abilities I may have do not come from me, they go *through* me. I am nothing more than a simple steward. A middleman. Everything I have – all of my possessions, every person in my life, my very life itself –

are simply gifts that have been given to me, and sooner or later, I have to give all of them back.

I cannot give life. I cannot defeat death. Only God can do those things. He can do them with as little effort as it takes me to pick up a stick or open a door, but in doing them all I can do is stare in wonder. I know this, of course, but as I said, I think the concept had gotten a little dusty. I think I needed to be reminded.

By Friday morning, I knew Muffin would be dead in the next few days and I decided to take her to the local vet here in Liberty. I wasn't taking her with any expectation of her being helped – I didn't think they would be able to help her; I just couldn't bear the thought of letting her die without doing *something*.

The next few weeks were like being on a bad roller-coaster ride, where you desperately want to get off, but you can't because it just doesn't stop. It's hard to describe the state of constant emotional turmoil that existed in our household; the despair, the hope, the fear, the heartache. Three weeks, 2 veterinarians, shots, pills, blood tests, antibiotics – even IV's; we *fought* for this little dog. But doctors aren't gods either. Like the rest of us, they too are just stewards. No matter what our desire was, God's will had been set, and it would not be denied.

Muffin spent her last days at home with us, in a place that she knew with people that loved her. One of us was always with her, 24 hours a day, watching over her and letting her feel the warmth of our presence as the life continued to slip away from her little body.

She died on the 24th of January. Sarah's birthday.

It was almost as if Muffin was just trying to be there for Sarah, to hang in there long enough so that she could make it to her birthday, to sleep next to her one last time, and to wake up with her in the morning on that special day. Maybe that was her birthday gift to Sarah, and once she had accomplished that goal, she simply didn't have anything left to give. Her condition worsened so rapidly in those first few hours of the morning that we knew we couldn't let her go on any longer.

And through the tears that were flowing in our kitchen that morning as I watched my daughter finally lose all hope and accept what *must* be done, I learned the 4th and final lesson from this little dog; I do not *want* to be a god.

I do not want to have to make the decisions that He must make. I do not want to feel the pain that He must feel. Who lives and who dies, when to do nothing and when to intervene, who will be saved and who will be damned; just in the decision of having to put Muffin down – an act of *mercy* – I felt just a taste of what that power & responsibility must be like, and I hated it.

I know that the loss of a pet doesn't quite compare with the loss of a child, a parent, or a sibling, but it still hurts, and the questions are still the same. Like so many others have done before me, I couldn't help but ask, "*Why?*"

Why did this little dog have to die before her life really even got started? Why did my daughter have to lose this little creature that she had waited for so patiently and loved so much? What had this little dog ever done to anybody but love them? Muffin had no sin, no desire to hurt, no evil thoughts; Why hurt my daughter in this way, God? Why would You allow that to happen? How *could* You allow that to happen?

I puzzled over it a lot. In a world with so much bad, why did God let something that was *so good* – the love between a beautiful little girl and her beautiful little dog – come to an end after such a short period of time? It seemed so unfair, and certainly not something that a loving God would do.

After awhile, though, I started to think about it a little differently, because I know that God *is* a loving, merciful God, and a loving, merciful God would not go out of his way to hurt my daughter. So maybe it wasn't His intention to hurt her. Maybe the pairing of this little dog and my daughter had never been a gift for Sarah in the first place. Maybe it had been a gift for Muffin.

I certainly don't know, but I wonder if Muffin was simply doomed from the start; that her days were numbered from the very beginning. I wonder if the man at the shelter who had tried to talk us out of taking her home knew that she had a problem, or that she had the potential for a problem. I wonder if God, in His mercy, and knowing that this little creature did not have long for this earth, touched the heart of a little girl to pick Muffin out of all others, to take her home where she would be welcomed and loved, and to give this little dog the best possible life that she could live in the time that she had. Maybe God picked Sarah to be the steward of this dog because He knew that she would love her like no other could.

Would a loving God do that? A God who loves *all* of His creatures? Yes, I think He might. And if that was His intention, He was right to do so, because I know with all certainty that there are many dogs who live full, long lives that never get to experience the joy, happiness, and love that surrounded Muffin in her short months on this earth. She knew how to live, and she knew how to love. Boy, did she know how to love! I have to think that if all of the people in the world would treat each other with even *half* the love that that little dog showed, we would have no need for a Heaven, because we'd already be living there.

I remember sitting on our back steps with Catherine a few days after Muffin's initial treatment, a treatment whose results seemed to have been so successful that for a while we thought she was going to be okay. Muffin brought a stick up to my feet, wanting me to throw it. I didn't feel like playing fetch, so I didn't. I wish I had, because though I didn't know it at the time, I would never get another chance. How is it that I can know the lesson so well, yet still fail the test so miserably?

You have no idea how much I regret not throwing that stick.

24

Faithfulness

Marriages get rocked by a lot of issues; fights over money, resentments over "position" in the household, unhappiness over duties & responsibilities, and many, many more. Even though we often see these issues launching marriages into the downward spiral of divorce, in a strong union – one based on real love and Godly principles – they can usually be worked out to the satisfaction (or at least the acceptance) of both husband & wife. Most of them are nothing more than simple growing pains that should be expected to occur when two people are learning how to live as one; where they gradually put their selfish desires aside and start to live for the other, rather than for themselves.

Infidelity is another marriage killer, but it's a little different than some of its smaller, rambunctious cousins in that it is not a "growing pain" of two people learning to live as one, and it's certainly not "expected". It's a betrayal. A blunt rejection of commitment.

Catherine & I have very real expectations of each other in our marriage. We've worked through and learned from all of those "normal" issues that every married couple experience, and if anything, we've grown closer to each other because of them. We can tolerate a lot from each other; and we do (though I would wager her more than I). But faithfulness to each other is the one thing that we both hold the other to, that, unlike all the rest, *there can be no exception.*

I don't know what would actually happen should that ever occur; maybe we would stay together for the children, or try to "work things out", but I know that for each of us, even if we *wanted* to forgive the other and tried in our heart of hearts to do it, we would never be able to *forget*, and the bond of trust that would be broken from that one single act would alter things forever. In all likelihood, I don't think a recovery would even be a possibility for either of us.

But because we both clearly know that we have that expectation of each other, and that the consequences would be dire, life changing, and permanent, it's not something that we have had to face, nor is it something that I think we *will* have to face.

Do I know that for sure? Well, no. I mean, anything is possible. But just because something is *possible* doesn't mean that it has to be *probable*, and there are things that every married man & woman can do to minimize that probability to a point where it is so small it isn't even worth considering.

To me, one of the biggest contributors to having a healthy, faithful marriage is abstinence *before* marriage. That might seem weird, but if you think about it, it's not. Marriages always start with smiles, excitement, and good intentions. Isn't it odd then, that within the space of a few years, not only are the majority of those marriages dissolved, but the two people involved – who once vowed their eternal love for one another – now actually *despise* each other?

What happened? I'm sure part of it is that they didn't base their marriages on a Godly foundation, that they didn't have a clear set of priorities to guide them, and that they didn't have any realistic expectations of what they were going to be facing in the first few years together. (Before our pastor married Cat & I, he *required* us to attend a series of counseling sessions with him first. In those sessions he explained what our priorities needed to be in our marriage – God first, then each other, then our children – and he led us in very frank discussions on everything from our individual duties & responsibilities, disciplining our children, sex, money, etc.).

But all the counseling in the world isn't going to help if the two people shouldn't be getting married in the first place, and that's the danger of premarital sex; it can bring people together that would otherwise have *nothing* to do with each other, and when a marriage starts off on that foot, it is doomed from the beginning. I know this firsthand, because 20 years ago, in my first marriage, I lived it myself.

There are a few things that happen when a man & woman engage in premarital sex. The first thing is that sex becomes the center of the relationship, with everything before and after it just a prelude to the next sexual encounter. Rather than spending time getting to truly know about each other, finding out if their core values are similar, discovering what their dreams & aspirations are, and even just deciding whether or not they *like* each other, the relationship is built entirely on physical pleasure. Everything else is just noise around this limited and superficial core.

Secondly, because the focus of the relationship is on sex, the magnitude of things that they inevitably learn about each other that in any other circumstance would have them packing their bags, are downplayed and overridden by the threat of losing their source of instant gratification. They become blinded to what anyone else can clearly see.

Thirdly, when people engage in premarital sex, there is a very clear – but unspoken – message that is being relayed between both of them, whether they think they are saying it or not. Because if you have sex with someone without being married to them, you are saying quite clearly that sex outside of marriage is okay with you, that you condone it, and that there is no penalty involved. After all, if you don't care if they have sex with you without being married to you, why would you get all bent out of shape if they decide to do it with someone else that they aren't married to?

Lastly, and most importantly, it just cheapens the entire experience of intimacy, turning it from something special that should be cherished, into an action no more important or meaningful than changing the channels on the TV.

All of those things work together to lay a groundwork for disaster, and when marriages get off to a start like that, is it any wonder they collapse from infidelity, or anything else for that matter? The fires of passion *will* eventually die down, and if that's the primary core that the relationship is built on it will crumble as that happens, whereas a marriage based on true love, honor, and respect can still stand strong even if the fires should go out *completely*, since physical intimacy was only a component of the marriage – a single "window in the house" so to speak – not the entire basis of it.

What about infidelity in a marriage that starts out strong? Is there a sure-fire way to prevent that from happening, whether as a "one night stand" or a full blown affair? Let's face it, I really love hamburgers, but every day? Day after day? For the rest of my life? Would anyone be surprised that after so many years I might develop a craving for a chicken salad sandwich? I still really love hamburgers – that will never change – but, c'mon . . . that chicken salad is *right there*!

Obviously, maintaining a healthy physical relationship with your spouse is the best defense, and there are a lot of ways to make that happen, none of which I'll discuss here due to considerations of time and space. Let's just say that going up to your wife during halftime of the NFC Championship game and saying, *"Hey honey, we've got 10 minutes"* probably isn't the best way to go about it. I'll trust that you can find some better answers on your own.

But let's face it, a nice looking chicken salad sandwich has been known to shatter even relationships that are, in all respects, strong & healthy. Is there a way to keep that item off the menu entirely?

I don't have all the answers (many would argue that I have none), but I can share some things that have not only helped me keep my commitment to my wife, but have also kept me from thinking that there was any greener grass on the other side of the fence in the first place.

One of the things that I do to keep me on the straight and level is to not allow myself to ever take my wife for granted. Taking your spouse for granted is an easy trap to fall into when you see them every single day, but when you start taking them for granted, you also start to lose your sense of how valuable they are to you, and when that happens, "alternative options" that you would otherwise never consider suddenly have a little more appeal than they used to. Dangerous ground to walk on.

When I start to feel that way – and yes, that has happened – I take a few moments to think about my wife in a different way. How would I feel if she *wasn't* my wife? Would I still find her appealing? Would I want her *then*? I view a picture in my mind's eye of her walking along arm in arm with another man, smiling & giggling perhaps with this "other man who is not me", and

-SNAP!-

boy, oh boy, I can't begin to tell you how rapidly my mood changes! All of a sudden, I can remember quite clearly what she means to me and how lucky I am to have her, and just by getting that tiny glimpse of what my life would be like without her – and how I would feel should that happen – that whole "taking her for granted" business gets smashed up pretty good.

I also make sure that I don't forget what the consequences of my actions would be should I ever think it a good idea to stray from my wife. My life as I know it – and love it – would be gone. Catherine would not be here for me. Everything we've shared and spent our years together building would be cut into pieces. I would see my beautiful children only on weekends. And all of that would have been the work of my own hand! Is there anything so good that I would be willing to pay that price? Nothing I can think of.

Finally, I realize that no matter how much I love my wife, there are situations where, if I found myself, I might not be able to resist the lure of temptation. We are all human, and we are all sinners, and even the best of us can fall if the circumstances are right. A lot of "one night stands" fall into this category, where someone who honestly had no intention of being unfaithful made a "mistake".

I don't feel a lot of sympathy for these folks though. While it's true that those situations can occur, if you truly love someone, it is absolutely possible to prevent yourself from ever being led into them in the first place.

For instance, here's an imaginary, but not unrealistic scenario that might put me into that type of situation: My wife takes the kids and goes out of town for a few days to visit, and while home alone, I get a call from one of my single friends. *It's been a long time*, they say. *I never get to see you now that you're married. How 'bout we go out to a bar and have a few drinks for old time's sake?* So I agree. But my single buddy is single after all, and soon spots a nice looking lady that he'd like to get to know a little better. Trouble is, girls generally travel in pairs, so would I mind just sitting at the table talking to her friend to keep her occupied? Sure old pal, no big deal. But after talking for a while and having another drink or two, we suddenly notice my single buddy and his new found friend are gone, and I'm left sitting alone in this bar with a girl who seems to think I'm pretty interesting. At least that's what the alcohol is telling her, and who am I to disagree? Eventually she needs a ride home, so I offer. We get to her house and she invites me in for a cup of coffee. And suddenly I'm in one of "those situations". Nobody knows where I am, I'm feeling pretty manly since this girl finds me attractive, and the alcohol in my blood has made me forget everything that is truly important to me and is lying to me about all the rest: *Nobody would ever know!*

Could I walk out of that situation with my integrity and honor intact? Maybe a better question is this: *If I truly love my wife, would I ever allow myself to get into that type of situation in the first place?* I would suggest that by simply allowing things to get to that point, I have already been unfaithful, because I *did nothing* to stop the chain of events which led me there in the first place.

So rather than seeing that kind of situation develop and going along for the ride, whenever I can sense that something _might_ take me to a place I don't want to go, I stop it from happening before it can ever begin. Maybe in the above scenario it means that I say "No" to my single buddy's request to go out. Maybe it means I simply can't be friends with my single buddy at all anymore. That would be a sacrifice, yes, but love requires sacrifice (only fools think otherwise), and if you aren't willing to make sacrifices for the person who has made a commitment to spend their entire life with you – and to honor the commitment that *you* have made to *them* – should you even be married in the first place?

I don't know if all this helps. In hindsight, I think I probably took something very simple and made it a lot more difficult than it really is. All of the things I mentioned are good, I guess; getting married for the right reasons, not taking your spouse for granted, understanding the consequences of your actions, and making sacrifices when needed. But if you look through all the smoke & mirrors, it really boils down to one thing: Love.

My wife is not perfect, but she's perfect for me, and I don't ever want to lose her. And when you love someone with all of your heart, faithfulness isn't a burden you bear, it's a reward you receive.

Therefore shall a man leave his father and his mother, and shall cleave unto his wife: and they shall be one flesh.
Genesis 2:24

25

In Dependence

I had a disturbing experience the other day. Our little bottom-of-the-line printer that we use in our home office suddenly died. Since this piece of equipment is pretty important in the day to day running of our business, I headed out to Office Depot to pick up the latest & greatest bottom-of-the-line model.

At the checkout counter, the clerk rang up my total and I wrote him a check. He scanned it, pushed some buttons, and then said "Here's your receipt, and here's your check back, all voided out for you."

I looked at the check in my hand for a moment – the one I had just finished writing out – and asked, "You don't even send these in to the bank anymore?"

"Oh no," he replied, "The transactions are all done electronically now."

I rode home in the car very unsettled, asking myself the following questions: *If my bank account is going to be debited instantly even when I write a check, why am I purchasing checks and taking the time to fill them out and sign them in the first place? What's the difference between that and just using a debit card, other than the fact that I'm spending more money and time by going through the motions of using checks?*

That's what disturbed me, because there isn't one. Funny, my bank never bothered to clarify that particular point to me.

Catherine & I don't use debit cards for one simple reason: If someone were to steal my *credit* card information and then use that to make purchases, I can always dispute the charges and refuse to pay them. My money is still mine, and I'm in charge of it. But if someone were to steal my *debit* card information and then use *that* to make purchases, the money comes directly out of my own bank account. Sure, I can dispute the charges, but the money – *my* money – has already been spent. I would no longer be in a position to dispute whether or not I wanted to pay (I already *have* paid); I would instead be wholly at the mercy of the bank, completely subordinate to their decision of whether or not to restore my funds. .

I have never known banks to be very receptive to the idea of *giving* money to people.

The next day while watching TV, I saw a commercial showing a bunch of people in a store all smartly moving about as they made their purchases; a picture of streamlined efficiency, convenience, and happiness. And then someone came to the counter and wanted to pay with cash, and like throwing a wrench into rotating machinery, everything crashed to a halt. *Cash? You want to pay with cash?*

The commercial – for whatever credit or debit card it was promoting – was obviously trying to tout the convenience & ease of using it's product. But the underlying message it was telling anyone who saw it was very clear and very direct: *Cash is bad, plastic cards are good. If you use a card, things run smoothly, quickly, and everyone is happy. If you use cash, you just mess things up for everyone else. You are behind the times, archaic & un-cool, and your insistence on using money shows a complete lack of courtesy for others.*

Everything these days seems to be oriented towards "faster", "easier", and "automatic", and with regards to money, it seems as if the movement – if that is what it is – is pushing harder and harder to get everyone to buy into their methods. Visa is now promoting it's "smart card". Just wave it at the scanner as you go by; no need to waste all that time signing your name on a receipt. Everybody wants you to do your business online; pay your bills, do your banking, send in your tax return.

"*Save a stamp!*" they say. "*It's so much easier and convenient for you!*" Or even better, "*We'll pay your bills for you! Just sign up and all of that will be debited from your account each month automatically!"*

So much of our purchases are now done without the exchange of any actual cash, that using cash has actually become more of the exception than the norm. During the holidays I was in line at a K-Mart picking up a few gifts for the kids. A lady in line several places ahead of me made a large purchase and paid cash for it. It was amazing how everyone in line – including me – was just kind of staring at her as she peeled away twenty dollar bills from a wad of cash in her hand. And I know that all of us were thinking the same kinds of things: *"Boy, that's a lot of cash." "Why is she making such a large purchase with cash?" "Where did she get all that cash?"* It was so weird to witness! But the really crazy thing was that even though people after her made purchases that were far in excess of hers, *nobody batted an eye* when they used their credit cards!

Have we become so separated from reality that purchasing something outright instead of borrowing to pay later is now considered strange and abnormal? Doesn't that seem a little backwards?

We live in a world today where you could – quite easily – go through your entire existence and never actually see or touch any money at all. Ever. Every purchase you make *could* be made without any cash whatsoever, and more and more, paying without cash is becoming the *preferred* way.

Is there a day coming when that will be the *only* way? A day when not only will cash no longer be accepted, but will not even *exist*?

That is a day to fear.

I'm going to take you on a little trip here, and throw out a little factual information and quite a bit of speculation. It may seem a little paranoid, and I'll admit that it does to me as well. But whether or not you give any credence to the "whys" of what I'm going to explore, it doesn't change the outcome of the "whats".

Some of this will play into things that people have said for years regarding conspiracies, secret societies, and hidden agendas; I don't know what's true and what's not any more than the next guy, but I can observe *what* is happening even if there is no way to positively confirm *why*. So humor me a little; all I want to do is spark your own brain into doing some thinking of it's own; you're just as capable of that as I am. I would ask though, that as you're considering these things, please keep the following thought in mind: If you're crossing the street and you get hit by a car and die, would it really make any difference to you whether the driver of the car did it on purpose or if it was a complete accident?

The Federal Reserve

In 1913, the Federal Reserve Act was passed by congress and signed by President Woodrow Wilson, thereby transferring the power to control the creation & management of currency from the US government to a *private corporation* of bankers. The plan itself was originated by a group of 7 of the richest men in the world at that time. As of December 2006, the US national debt is over 8 *trillion* dollars. More than 40% of that is owed directly to the Federal Reserve. (Perhaps connected or perhaps not, 1913 was also the year that the 16th Amendment was passed by Congress, imposing a federal income tax on the wages of US citizens).

Think about that for a moment. The Federal Reserve is a private company – not a branch of the United States government – run by a small group of elite bankers. Can you even begin to imagine how much power this company has over the United States?

Start with the simple things, like inflation. Since we haven't been on the gold standard in decades, any money that is printed has nothing behind it; it is created out of thin air. Put more money into circulation to increase the supply, and the value of the US dollar drops, creating inflation. Take money out of circulation and the opposite happens. That's a lot of power for a small group of private citizens to have over everyone else. But that's only the tip of the iceberg.

If the US government needs more money than it takes in from taxes to pay for whatever social programs, defense spending, or pork projects it deems necessary, where is it going to get it? The Federal Reserve, of course.

So the US *borrows* money from the Fed which, of course, it now *owes* back to the Fed. As stated earlier, the US government now owes the Fed roughly $3,400,000,000,000 (plus or minus a few hundred billion, but what's that between friends?).

Forget for a moment that the government doesn't actually *do* anything to make money for itself and that that bill is in fact owed by the citizens of the United States; believe it or not, that's not what is really unsettling about it. The really disturbing part is this: If this group of bankers wanted something from our government, could our government say "No"? I mean, if the Fed holds the threat of not only calling in this current debt, but also to refuse to loan any more, could the government of the United States realistically stand it's ground and refuse them if they demanded something?

I'm not saying that the Fed *would* do something like that, but I feel it's important to understand in no uncertain terms that they absolutely *could* if they wanted to.

So *would* they ever use that leverage for a self-serving reason? To decide, I think you would have to question the motives of these Fed architects when they came up with the idea in the first place. *Why* did they want to create the Federal Reserve? I guess it's possible that they were simply a group of financial experts who realized that they had much more expertise in managing money than Congress did, and so, out of their concern for the continued well-being and prosperity of this great land, they offered their services to our country. But if that were really the case, why would such noble & patriotic men have allowed us to get into such tremendous debt? Is that how they handle their own personal finances? My guess would be "probably not".

So if they didn't create the Fed for benevolent reasons, is it possible that they did it for malevolent ones? And if this group of bankers controlling the money supply *did* want something, what could it possibly be? When you already have more money than you could ever use, what else is there?

"Give me control of a nation's money and I care not who makes the laws." - Mayer Amschel Bauer Rothschild

"Whoever controls the volume of money in any country is absolute master of all industry and commerce."
- President James A. Garfield

"I believe that banking institutions are more dangerous to our liberties than standing armies. If the American people ever allow private banks to control the issue of their currency, first by inflation, then by deflation, the banks and corporations that will grow up around [the banks] will deprive the people of all property until their children wake-up homeless on the continent their fathers conquered. The issuing power should be taken from the banks and restored to the people, to whom it properly belongs."
- Thomas Jefferson

This may be a stretch, but think for a minute about all the fictional "superhero" & James Bond villains from comics, cartoons, and movies. Think about all of the true life villains of history: Genghis Khan, Attila the Hun, Napoleon, Hitler, & Stalin. Think about the great empires that have risen and fallen throughout history. Whether real or imaginary, they all have a few very important things in common:
1) They wanted absolute power.
2) They tried to gain it and keep it by force.
3) They ultimately failed.

Absolute power. Totalitarian control. Some people just have a thirst for it, and history is littered with the corpses of

Pharaohs, Kings, Dictators, and Generals who have aspired to become gods among men. Is there any reason to think that that's not still true today?

"We will have a world government whether you like it or not. The only question is whether that government will be achieved by conquest or consent."
- Paul Warburg, chief architect of the Federal Reserve Act

So assuming that you wanted absolute power, how would you go about it if you already knew the dismal track record of those who came before you that had tried to get it and keep it by force? Maybe you don't try to get it by force. Maybe you take a different approach.

Instead of imposing your will over people, maybe you get them to subjugate themselves to you of their own free will. Maybe you put yourself into a quiet "behind the scenes" position where you have strong influence over governments and their policies, and then slowly & methodically lead everyone to where you want them to be. dependent on you and under your absolute control. And by the time any of them realize what has happened (if they even do), none of them will be in a position to do anything about it.

Crazy? Maybe. Maybe not. Nations and empires have a way of rising and falling, and history shows that time and again they have all followed the same general cycle:

1. People in bondage gain spiritual faith
2. Faith evolves into courage
3. Courage brings about liberty
4. Liberty results in abundance
5. Abundance progresses to selfishness
6. Selfishness turns to complacency
7. Complacency devolves into apathy
8. Apathy leads to dependence
9. Dependence brings the cycle full circle back to bondage

How dependent are we today? Most Americans do very little for themselves; for the most part, we work for other people, so that they can give us money, so that we can buy things from somebody else. If we were brutally honest, we would have to clarify even further to say that not only do we do very little for ourselves, but in fact we *couldn't* do very much even if we wanted to (which, of course, we don't).

We have become so dependent on the things that are done for us by something or someone else that the knowledge of how those things were done by our ancestors before us has been lost. We couldn't do them if we wanted to. We don't know how. The very technology that has made our lives so easy has also put shackles on what options we have left.

Grocery stores provide our food. Utility companies provide warmth and light for our homes. Machines wash our clothes, cut our grass, and transport us around. Ask yourself the following questions, and please use the term "survive" in it's most literal sense:

Could you survive today without electricity?
Could you survive today without the use of a bank?
Could you survive today if you had no car?
Could you survive today if you were not able to purchase things from stores?

These aren't questions we ever seriously ask ourselves, because these things are so much a part of our lives that our lives simply *wouldn't work* without them, at least, not the way we have become accustomed to living them. We've always had these things available to us so we take it for granted that they always will be. Sounds like a rather complacent attitude, doesn't it?

And if someone were to intrude into the entertaining convenience of our lives and start bringing up questions that were a little disturbing to think about, would we even bother to listen, or are we already gripped in the death throws of apathy?

National Identification Cards

On May 11, 2005, President Bush signed into law the creation of what is called "Real ID" to take effect in May of 2008. In the interests of protecting US citizens from the threat of terrorism and to aid in the control of illegal immigrants, all US citizens will be required to have a US identification card. The card will be tamper proof, will carry your vital information (age, sex, etc.), and will contain some method of positive identification (possibly a fingerprint). Without this ID card, you will not be able to travel on an airplane, open a bank account, or be the beneficiary of any government services (including social security). The Department of Homeland Security has the authority to add additional requirements.

"Those who would give up essential liberty to purchase a little temporary safety deserve neither liberty nor safety."
– Benjamin Franklin

This is just scary. Every American will be *required* to have this card, and if you don't have one you will technically not exist. It's truly an offer we can't refuse. How would we be able to live our lives as we have grown accustomed to if we cannot use a bank? In today's world – quite simply – we can't. The overwhelming majority of Americans today *cannot survive* without the use of a bank. It's not even a choice. I mean, what would we do? What *could* we do?

Absolutely nothing. To refuse one of these cards – even if that can be done without criminal repercussions – would be to permanently alter the convenient routine of our lives. We have been trained to avoid unpleasantness and inconvenience, and the vast majority of us have allowed ourselves to be put into a position where we simply will not be able to say "No".

But is that a bad thing? We already have other forms of ID; driver's licenses, social security numbers . . . so what if I have a card that positively identifies me as me? It proves that I'm an American, and keeps those pesky illegal aliens from taking a piece of my pie. Terrorists won't be able to run amuck and hurt me or my family. Identity theft will be almost impossible, which means my money will be safe. This doesn't sound like a bad thing at all. In fact, I want one!

. . . maybe you get them to subjugate themselves to you of their own free will . . .

The first problem with the National ID card is that you don't have a choice. Does that sound like an ideal of a free country? The second and much more important issue is what that card will inevitably evolve into.

Even if you have put yourself in a position where you *could* live without a bank and choose not to accept one of these cards, don't think you're out of the woods. What are you going to eat? If you raise animals for food, you'll have to have them – *every single one* – registered with ID cards to be in compliance with the National Animal Identification System (NAIS). Those tags cost money, and you can only get them from the United States government. No ID card, no government service, and without NAIS compliance, you're breaking the law by having unregistered animals that may be a threat to our nation's food supply.

Maybe you can hunt & fish for your food. Not without a hunting and fishing license you can't. To do so without a license is to break the law. Off to jail you go, troublemaker.

Maybe you can just forego meat altogether and *grow* your own food. That would probably work, as long as you don't get any genetically engineered seed in your garden. Those seeds are patented, and any plants that carry cells from a genetically engineered seed that are grown without a license are the property of the manufacturer, and you can be sued for patent infringement. And it makes no difference how those seeds got on your land or if you even knew about it.

Even if food isn't a problem, how would you cook it? How would you get paid? How are you going to pay for your mortgage? Your utilities? How will you get a driver's license? How will you do *anything*?

About the best that you could hope for is that you have some skill – either a service you perform or a product you make – that you could sell for cash. That assumes, of course, that no judicial action is taken against you and that it does not become illegal for people to do business with "non-card carrying citizens".

But even if you would be willing to put yourself into that position, what if it makes no difference? Because here's where everything swings back around full circle to what was so disturbing to me in the very beginning: What happens if there comes a day when cash is no longer accepted?

Ahhh! Checkmate.

Regardless of why all of this is happening, whether it is planned or just a random chain of events, there seems to be at least one logical termination point where all of this could be leading: a cashless society. A world where your ID card is everything.

Because it will be "you", it will be your ID card, your passport, your driver's license, your ATM card, your debit card . . . your *everything* card.Without it you will be nothing. That's a frightening place to be.

We live in a world today where we are constantly allowing our rights to be carelessly thrown away as if they are of no value. We continue to relinquish more and more of our freedoms & civil liberties to the government out of our own fear, complacency, and convenience – a government which may itself be governed by another – and in doing so we are unwittingly permitting it to change it's role from "servant" to "master".

But it doesn't have to be that way. None of this can happen without our consent; but by that I don't mean each of us individually, I mean all of us *collectively*. Not thousands, but millions – *tens of millions* – of people need to stand up and simply say "No".

Finding Liberty

" . . .But the proles [the masses]*, if only they could somehow become conscious of their own strength, would have no need to conspire . . . They need only to rise up and shake themselves like a horse shaking off flies . . . "* - Excerpt from *1984*, by George Orwell

If we do nothing, however, if we consent and allow ourselves to reach the point of becoming a cashless society - when every transaction for anything is merely an electronic shift of numbers - we will also take that final step into total and complete slavery.

Yes, *slavery*. Because just as these cards can be activated, they can also be *deactivated*, and when your very ability to survive depends entirely on the existence of that card, will it be possible for you to do *anything* against the will of those who control it knowing that they can, at their convenience, *turn you off*?

Think about that. Think *hard*.

When everything is virtual, nothing is real. In a cashless society, the emperor will truly have no clothes, yet we will have no choice but to extol the virtues of his garments, because to do otherwise would be to risk the disapproval of those who control the power of that card. They could ask us to do anything – *absolutely anything at all* – and we would have *no choice* but to comply.

"None are so hopelessly enslaved as those who falsely believe they are free." - Goethe

Absolute power is obtained when you have absolute dependence. And what better way to gain that than by having the ability to simply *turn someone off* if they don't do what you want them to do?

If this is all happening according to some plan, you really do have to admire the simplicity of it's design. In fact, one of its only few flaws is the actual card itself, since it still has the ability to be lost or stolen. But I would have to believe that that will only make the next logical step – that of having your ID microchip surgically implanted into your body – much easier for acceptance in the future. Don't laugh; this technology already exists today, and believe it or not, there are already people who are *volunteering* to have it done. Of their own free will.

I can almost see the credit card commercials of the future now . . . *Just wave your hand at the scanner as you go by; no need to waste all that time trying to get that card out of your pocket . . .*

And should *that* day come, how then will we interpret these words?:

And he causes all, the small and the great, and the rich and the poor, and the free men and the slaves, to be given a mark on their right hand, or on their forehead, and he provides that no one should be able to buy or to sell, except the one who has the mark, either the name of the beast or the number of his name.
- Revelation 13:16-17

I know that to some, I must sound like a paranoid nut, and in all honesty, I hope it turns out the be that way. I hope that the Fed is just a bank going about the business of making money. I hope that the people in our government – at all levels – aren't just a collection of pawns who have been bought & paid for by the highest bidder. I hope that common sense and basic human decency are not extinct. But hope, while a wonderful thing, is not much of a strategy.

Regardless of what validity my rambling speculations may or may not have, what I said about the creation of the Federal Reserve *is* true. The "Real ID" identification cards *were* signed into law, the cycle of rising & falling nations *has* been repeated over and over, and the NAIS *exists* right now.

Monsanto *has* been quietly suing independent farmers for several years for patent infringement with the courts ruling in Monsanto's favor, saying that it makes no difference *how* the seed got on the farmer's land – whether it got mixed in with other seed by accident, blew off of a passing truck, or even was cross pollinated by insects – the plants, *and all succeeding generations of plants*, belong to Monsanto. Most farmers settle out of court, with part of the settlement being that they are not allowed to discuss it.

Knowing that all of these things *are* real, does it make any difference whether the speculation as to *why* they are happening is right or wrong? I'll ask again: If you're crossing the street and you get hit by a car and die, would it really make any difference to you whether the driver of the car did it on purpose or if it was a complete accident?

Either way, you're still dead.

Since I wrote this, I've given a lot of thought as to what *my* motives were in doing so; I know *what* I wrote and I know that I felt compelled to write it, but *why* did I feel compelled? What am I trying to prove by painting such a gloomy picture? What gives me the right to speculate on the future?; I'm no prophet. And what "forward moving" purpose does it serve?

My first thought was, "Well, maybe we *should* be a little disturbed by all of these things so that we can start to *do* something about it." But while there may be some truth to that, the more I thought about it, the less important it really seemed. And too, do I really want to impress my views and fears on everyone else? I honestly have no desire for anyone to think I'm "important" or "wise", or "right".

So I kept thinking about it, and eventually, it dawned on me. This isn't about government, or conspiracies, or doom & gloom, or any of that nonsense. It's much, *much* simpler than that. This is about *faith*. More specifically, what we put our faith into. Because by putting ourselves in a position where we are dependent on banks, utilities, insurance companies, the government, corporations, and all the rest, we are in fact putting our faith *in them* to provide for us, and every time we move a little more of our faith into yet another man-made institution, we move ourselves a little further away from God.

Funny that we should do that, because all of those things

are "of man", and last I checked, mankind was a rather imperfect and unreliable creature. Is it any wonder then that things may go awry, whether on purpose or by accident? And should we be surprised to realize that if we had allowed God to drive that car that I've mentioned a couple of times, we would never have been hit in the first place?

In the end, there is nothing wrong with allowing ourselves to be in a state of dependence. The danger is when we put ourselves in dependence to anyone or anything other than God.

26

My Coat of Many Colours

Joseph got his from his father Jacob. Dolly Parton sang about the one her momma made for her. And I wear the one my son gave to me every day as I walk down the street.

Actually, it's black wool with leather sleeves and elastic trim around the wrists & waist, very much like the high school varsity jackets all the jocks used to wear. But that's just the blank canvas, and it makes the rainbow of colors stand out that much more. The front is adorned with campaign & memorial patches, and flags from countries where my son has made port calls stack one on top of the other in a line down each arm. On the back is a huge bald eagle overlaid on the vivid red, white, & blue of a American flag.

Technically, it's called a "cruise jacket", kind of a memento from a tour of duty at sea. I don't know what it cost my son Christopher to buy, but all money aside, I know the actual price was 13 months on an aircraft carrier driving across oceans, seas, and gulfs.

I normally don't look to seek attention, but I do get a lot of it when I wear this coat. People see it and become curious. They will stop and ask me what it is, where I got it, what it means. It's introduced me to a lot of folks that I probably never would have met or spoken with otherwise, and it gives me a chance to talk about my son. It's one of the ways that I can tell the world that I love him. That I'm proud of him. That I believe in him.

A few months ago, a couple of little old ladies saw me in my coat and stopped to ask me if I was in the military.

Finding Liberty

"No," I said, "my son is."

"Do you think he would mind if we prayed for him at our ladies group?" they asked.

Did I think he would mind?

"No, ladies," I said, "I don't think he would mind one bit. And I would be very grateful if you did."

I remember when I was a sailor, the first thing I wanted to do when I was off base was to shed my uniform. Not because I was ashamed of it, but because I wanted to blend in (as much as could be expected) with everyone else. People who live in cities with military bases often have a disdain for the servicemen who share those places. Many of them look down on the military, seeing them as a rowdy, troublemaking bunch that they would just as soon not have around.

I can understand that, especially in cities that have Naval Bases, where many sailors come home from months at sea with a penchant for excitement and a body whose alcohol tolerance is much less than they remembered. No big surprise that the battlecries would ring through the neighborhoods: *Turn off the lights! Stay off the streets! Lock up your daughters! A ship has come in!*

But for anyone presently in the service, just let me tell you this; do yourself a favor and get out of those cities every now and then. Go back to your homes in the Heartland, in New England, in the Southwest, in Big Sky country; wherever it is that you call home. Put your uniform back on and take a walk down the street, through the mall, or to church on Sunday morning.

Those stares you feel hold no malice. They are from people who rarely see the uniform that you have become so accustomed to, and who are saying to themselves *"That's one of them. That's one of those men who has made it possible for me to live my life any way that I want to."*

Those handshakes are from veterans who have done what you have done and are proud to see that young men still value our freedoms enough to serve as they once did. You have

175

absolutely no idea how many veterans are out there until you get out there yourself. You'll run into them in places you'd never imagine.

Don't worry about the rich folks in Palm Springs who are all bent out of shape because they think an American flag at one of their golf courses is an eyesore; that it's "too high". Those aren't the people you serve; they can *buy* their freedoms. You serve for the common man, the one who plows a field, drives a tractor trailer, or works a night shift on the assembly line.

Don't ever think that because many Americans are opposed to the war that you may be fighting, that they are also opposed to you. They are not. It is not you they oppose, but the ones who would callously treat your life as if it is nothing more than a pawn to be won or lost in a game. The farmers and the truckers and the line workers love you. They are proud of you. And they believe in you.

So when July 4th comes around this year, don't be afraid to leave the city for awhile and head out to one of those small towns nearby to join in the celebration that you help to make possible. If you have nowhere else to go, come on down to Liberty, KY. You'll be welcome here. And don't forget to bring your uniform, because we wear our colours proudly, and we fly our flags high.

27

Error Carried Forward

Twenty some-odd years ago, I found myself a fledgling 19 year old in the Navy Nuclear Power School in Orlando, FL, entrenched in a curriculum rich with theory, mathematics, physics, & chemistry, and noticeably absent of any electives such as "music appreciation" or "interpersonal relationships". It was a challenging place to be, and it didn't take long for me to lament that I hadn't paid at least a *little* attention in my high school algebra & geometry classes.

We were tested often in the various subjects, and the instructors had long since developed their own shorthand in which to provide written feedback to us students in a quick and efficient manner as they graded our exams. Along with the various marks and scribbles of red ink that would so often ruin our otherwise meticulously prepared answers would be acronyms ranging from "ATQ!" (answer the question!) to "CRI" (cranial-rectal inversion; a nice way of saying that our answer wasn't even close because our head was firmly planted somewhere that it shouldn't be).

The one acronym I became most familiar with was "ECF": error carried forward. In these situations, I had made a mistake at the beginning of a problem, usually something simple and stupid like "2 x 3 = 5".

The really gut wrenching thing about getting an ECF was that the rest of my calculations may have been performed in an absolutely flawless manner, yet because of that simple, fundamental error at the very beginning of the problem, all of those calculations – and the resulting ultimate answer – were completely & entirely incorrect. Yet in every single instance, I had worked the problems to completion, and to what I *thought* was a correct answer, all the while never even realizing that an error existed.

I imagine that centuries ago, when many things were still new and undiscovered, the process of scientific thought and invention was a fascinating thing. The minds of those who poked, prodded, tinkered, tested & observed had yet to be polluted by an excess of previous discovery and information; virgin minds were able to explore virgin territories simply for the sake of seeing *what would happen*, rather than expecting to witness a certain result.

Through this learning period of purely curious "cause & effect", many of the known laws of science were born, many of the theories of today were postulated, and many inventions that are now commonplace in our lives were made possible. Because of the work done by those who have gone before us, we do not have to do that work over again ourselves.

Such is the beauty of progressing technology; rather than cyclically relearning everything from scratch with the passing of every generation, each generation can instead build upon what has already been learned by the previous.

But progressing technology also has some very serious and inherent flaws built into it, and I sometimes wonder if we take them too lightly, if we even think about them at all. For instance, if the knowledge from yesterday – the knowledge that was passed on to us and that we are now building on for the generation of tomorrow – had a fundamental error in it of any kind, that error will be carried forward into every succeeding generation, and we may not even know it is there.

As the technology that is built upon that flaw progresses, we may even start to see signs that something is wrong (or at least, *not quite right*), but if we stubbornly refuse to even consider the possibility that the basis of our knowledge and technology could be in error, what limits to progress and delusions to truth would we self-impose on ourselves? Because there is evidence today that this has happened and is already clouding our perspective.

Sir Isaac Newton is one of the most respected and revered minds of the scientific community. Prior to his death in 1727, he pioneered many of the groundbreaking discoveries, theories, and laws that became – and still exist as – the basis of much of the scientific work being done today. He was a fascinating man with an incredible mind, and I make no claim to being even in the same ballpark as him when it comes to scientific thinking and reasoning.

But Newton did have one serious handicap; he lived 300 years ago. As such, all of his experiments, observations, and measurements were made using the tools of his day. Certainly no one would disagree that today we have instruments capable of detection and measurement down to a degree of accuracy that Newton couldn't even have imagined, and in fact, we have instruments and devices that are capable of detecting and measuring things that Newton, in the late 1600's, couldn't have even known *existed.*

It's interesting then that no one in the mainstream scientific community today will even consider the possibility that some of Newton's laws might be, if not completely wrong, then at least perhaps, *not quite right.* I say "interesting" because I certainly don't think it would be any fault of his – nor any shame – if he did get something wrong. It's amazing to me that his laws have held up as long as they have. But they are starting to show some cracks.

In the mid 70's, when computers had yet to start appearing on every desktop but had still become powerful enough to do some incredible things, a couple of scientists were doing computer modeling of galaxies.

What they found was that the galaxies, with the amount of matter that they contained by way of stars, planets, and debris, did not have enough gravity to hold together as they turned. In fact, the galaxies would completely fly apart in a single revolution.

They realized that in order for a galaxy to "hold together" as it spins under Newton's laws of gravity, there needed to be more matter to provide the extra gravity needed. The problem was that it wasn't just a little more matter that was required, it was a *lot* more; 60 to 70% more.

You might think that when confronted with an error in a proportion of that magnitude, they might have gone back to at least question the "laws" that their models were based on, but to do that would be to question Newton, and Newton is sacred in the scientific community. Instead, they protectively guarded Newton's laws and boldly exclaimed that there simply had to be more matter. 60 to 70% more. And even though they couldn't see it, it *had* to be there.

Their reasoning? Because Newton's laws *said* it had to be there.

As a result, they "invented" (their word, not mine) what is now referred to as "dark matter" to account for this majority of galactic matter that is unaccounted for, and they have been searching for it for over 30 years now. They have still not detected any of it.

To add to the mystery, it has also since been discovered that galaxies don't spin the way they should, and the Pioneer 10 & 11 spacecraft launched way back in the 70's are doing things that they are not supposed to do, and no one knows why.

So now we have 3 things (at least) which do not neatly fit into our known "laws" of gravity. Is it time to maybe start taking a closer look at these 300 year old laws, to see if maybe Newton might have missed something? We know his laws are pretty good; they have lasted 300 years after all, and have worked perfectly fine up to this point in helping us to accurately navigate space missions and predict many celestial events. But are they infallible, or is it even remotely possible that Newton didn't get something quite right?

Science is based on cause & effect. If something can't be observed, science would argue that it doesn't exist. But cause & effect can be a tricky business. Take rolling a bowling ball for instance. We can observe that if we push a bowling ball, it will roll in the direction we pushed it. If we can repeat that over and over, we can be pretty sure it will happen the same way every time, and we can write a law about it. However, while it can be observed that the ball does roll the same way every time, we can also observe that there are other effects as well. We can observe the sound that the ball makes as it rolls, the turbulence it causes as it pushes through the air, and the vibration it creates that can be felt through the floor. Those are all effects that we can readily observe with little or no extra equipment, except maybe a little smoke to mark the air turbulence.

If a scientist conducted this experiment 300 years ago, I'm sure he would have observed all of those effects – and possibly others as well – and considered them in any law he made. But would he have been able to observe the heat? Because in addition to the above, the friction between the ball and the floor is also creating heat as an effect, albeit in such a small amount as would be detectable only with an extremely sensitive measuring device.

What if the scientist didn't know about the tiny amount of heat that was being created, and what if he wrote his laws only on what he was able to observe? And what if that tiny omission of heat that he was unable to detect or account for in his laws didn't affect the usability of his laws or call any of them into question until many years in the future, when detection & measurement reached a point of such precision that the flaw in his observations finally started to become evident?

My point is, what if Newton had it *almost right*, but that there was something more, either something deeper and more encompassing or something he had no reason to suspect and no ability to detect, that created a tiny flaw in the laws he created, a flaw that would never be seen until centuries in the future. Would we think any less of Newton or his achievements if that were the case? I certainly wouldn't.

Please note that I'm not saying Newton was wrong about *anything*, but in all honesty, which is more probable: that we can't actually find 70% of the matter in our galaxies, or that laws made 300 years ago with the observations available at the time might be "not quite right"? Would it hurt to at least revisit those laws to see if they are correct and complete? Apparently, it would.

I'm using Newton as the example, but realize that this same type of situation can affect any of the known laws, theories, and facts of science, and in so doing, also permeate the technology & information that is built upon them.

Which leads into a few other problems with technology; namely the scientists themselves and the community they are a part of. For one, there is an arrogance among scientists that prevents them from even considering something that does not come from a "credible" source. Don't bother trying to bring something to their attention unless you have a degree from MIT and a dozen published papers in major scientific journals. Only scientists have the intelligence to think of or discover anything new. It's kind of a "catch-22" system; you don't have any credibility unless you are published, but you can't get published unless you have credibility.

Gone too are the days of free association, where it is acceptable to discover something by *accident*. Scientists no longer conduct experiments just to see "what will happen"; everything is pre-staged to either prove or disprove a specific theory, and the scientists themselves are so absorbed looking for the specific things that they *expect* to happen that they are undoubtedly missing – and understanding – what actually *does* happen, especially if it might embarrass the donor of their grant money.

Both of those things play into the system itself that the scientific community has turned into. It's a political system, it's played a certain way, and there are standards and rules that, if broken or questioned or deviated from, will cause you to be blackballed in a hail of ridicule. As just one example (of many available), in the mid-1800's, Dr. Ingaz Semmelwies came up with the preposterous notion that doctors should wash their hands before heading to the delivery room after they had been working in the morgue. The medical community of Vienna ran him out of town. He later died in an asylum.

For the modern day scientist, questioning the validity of Newton's laws of gravity would be one sure way to lose all of your hard-fought credibility. That's why over 30 years and millions upon millions of dollars later, we continue to search in vain for "dark matter". Nobody wants to lose their standing.

But if an error can be carried forward when it is made through innocent error or through arrogant vanity, "error" also has the potential to be consciously *chosen* so that it is carried forward *on purpose.*

You might ask, "Why would anyone ever consider doing something like that?" Well, you have to consider the *motives* of those who would be in a position to promote or repress new discoveries & inventions. And what is it that motivates most people to do *anything*?

Money & power.

Imagine if, more than a century ago, when electrical power generation was still in it's infancy and the infrastructure that now dominates how electricity is delivered to our homes had not even begun to be built, a wealthy entrepreneur looking to exploit this new technology was presented with two choices to invest in.

The first choice involved an elaborate system, in which electrical power would be generated in a central location and then distributed via a complex network to customers who would then pay for the electrical power they used. (Essentially what we have today).

The second (hypothetical) choice wasn't a system at all, but a self-contained machine which could be purchased by anyone, and was so cleverly constructed that it actually produced more power than it consumed, with the result being that each individual home & business could generate their *own* electricity for little or no operating expense.

As an investor, how would these options look to you? The "self-contained" machine could make you a lot of money; you would be able to reap profits from the sale of the machines themselves, from spare parts, and possibly even connection services. Not too bad, but after awhile, once the majority of homes & businesses have their own machine, sales & profits will start declining. And too, competitors will soon start to pop up everywhere, creating a price war.

Now compare that against the centralized system of electrical distribution. You spend more money upfront building the power stations and distribution system, but once you're up and running, your customers pay you not just one time, but *every month*, month after month, year after year. The money *never stops*, and in fact just continues to grow as more and more customers are added to your system. Your initial investment is paid off pretty quickly – you can still make money for all of those connection services too – and then you just sit back and watch your bank account continue to grow with little or no effort at all.

The infrastructure of your system is too elaborate and specific to invite much competition, and you control the price. If any of the little electricity addicts on your grid don't pay up on time, you just cut them off. You know they'll be back, because you're the only game in town, and the drug you have to sell is unbelievably addictive. They'll find the money. Junkies *always* find the money.

Now, I'm not saying that a perpetual motion generator ever existed, or that the above scenario took place, but assume for a moment that both did. If you were the investor in question and your goal was cashing in to the maximum extent possible, what choice would you have made? (If necessary, pretend for a moment that you have no Christian principles).

Exactly. Don't sell them the tree, just charge them for the fruit. In fact, the only threat that you could really face would be if people somehow found out that the perpetual motion generator existed, so you would probably go to great pains to make sure that never happened. You would probably go to *extreme* pains if necessary. In a world where people will kill each other for a hundred bucks, just try to imagine the measures that might be taken to protect a multi-*billion* dollar empire.

I sometimes wonder if there was a better option for creating usable energy than the monster we have created today, but that's not why I mention this little fictional scenario. The point is that, with regards to technology, the very real potential exists for technology to be built upon an option that is not necessarily the best one available; a *chosen* "error" that gets carried forward. And once that ball gets rolling, it's hard to stop.

It's that "hard to stop ball" that brings me to a final problem with technology, because while technology can be a very efficient process (since it builds upon previous accomplishment & discovery) and it can result in the creation of very complex things (since we are not "reinventing the wheel" every generation), it also *represses* new, independent, original thought. In other words, it gives us "tunnel vision".

Going back again to my days at Nuclear Power School, I vividly remember a salty old Master Chief coming in to talk to us on our first day in class. He started out his orientation session by telling us that a nuclear reactor, for all it's pomp & circumstance, was just a fancy way to boil water. I was floored. I couldn't believe it.

It boils water? That's it?

But he was absolutely right.

All of these nuclear reactors that exist around the world, with their massive structures, elaborate systems, strict security, and armies of engineers, do one thing and one thing only: they boil water. The water turns to steam, the steam turns a turbine, the turbine turns a generator, and the generator turns out electricity. Is that insane or what?

The funny thing though, is that after my initial amazement of making that discovery, I soon glossed right over it and never gave it another thought. Of course we use the heat it creates to boil water, what else would we use it for? And that's the problem with technological tunnel vision; no one is *asking* what else we could use it for because we're too locked in & focused on what we already know we *can* use it for.

Think about that for a minute. If there is one thing that we have a lot of, it's heat. We can get tons of it from the sun (and magnify it's intensity with magnifying glasses, Fresnel lenses & the like), and we can create it any number of ways, from burning natural resources to splitting atoms. In fact, it's *so* easy to generate heat that in most cases we create it by *accident* and then treat it as an annoying by-product that we purposely get rid of (such as with any internal combustion engine).

So here is an abundantly available resource, and yet, even after having it available to us for thousands of years, the only thing we've ever figured out to do with it is to boil water? It's fascinating that all of the other technology surrounding the "boiling water" seems to have advanced by leaps and bounds, from complex nuclear reactors on the front side to super efficient turbines on the other, and yet the "boiled water" aspect of it hasn't changed since Hero documented the first steam engine over 2,000 years ago.

Huh.

I wonder if there is anything else that you can do with heat besides boil water. I wonder if there is anything else you can do with sunlight other than power extremely expensive and horribly inefficient solar panels. I wonder if there is anything you can do with magnets other than incorporating them into existing electro-magnetic motors or the "Wooly-Willy" that I gave my son to play with. I wonder if, because we are so busy spending our time refining & improving the technology that previous generations have given us, we are completely missing a totally different way of doing things. A way that might be just within our grasp if only we'd take the time to look. A way that might be so *incredibly simple* that our complex technological advancements would look primitive by comparison. Imagine the "error carried forward" if *that* turned out to be the case.

But is this nothing more than naive, childish thinking? Scientists would tell me so. I don't know the rules. I don't understand the laws. I have no concept of the work that has already been done, or the experiments that have proven this, or the failures that have proven that, or the theories that specifically say so. I'm just being stupid.

You want to know stupid? Let me tell you about stupid: Right now it's about 20 degrees outside. I'm paying for gas to heat my home so that the inside temperature stays around 69 degrees. And then I'm paying *more* money to have a machine in this warm environment I've created that will keep my food frozen.

That's stupid. But that's just one of the places technology has brought me, and I promise you, I can rattle off at least a dozen more just as stupid right off the top of my head. If technology is supposed to make my life simpler, I'm confused as to how it's doing it, because the more technology I use, the more complicated my life gets. And all of that tells me one thing very clearly: I'm doing something wrong.

God does not make things difficult for us. He is not the author of confusion. I've mentioned before that I believe all great truths to be brutally simple and rooted in Godly principles. The Bible deals with very simple concepts: love, faith, selflessness, forgiveness. When it comes to the things that we must have in order to live our lives, why would we think that God would make them any more complicated?

The answers are all out there waiting for us to find. Answers to energy. Answers to health. Answers to ancient civilizations. Answers to how the universe works. Answers to *everything*. And I know – *I know* – that they will all be brutally simple.

In 1903, two brothers running a bicycle shop figured out how to do something that had stumped mankind for centuries. They did something that some scientists had already theoretically *proven* could *not* be done; they flew.

How many hundreds, if not thousands, of people had tried before them and failed? How many brilliant minds had tackled the problem and come up with nothing? How many convoluted contraptions had been created and scrapped? And why would these two average Joe's from North Carolina think that they had any shot at all of being successful when so many others before them had failed? They didn't know the rules. They didn't understand the laws. They had no concept of the work that had already been done, or the experiments that had proven this, or the failures that had proven that, or the theories that specifically said so. They were just being stupid.

But they were *successful*! How incredible is that? Two guys who fixed bicycles for a living changed the world because they figured out how to do something that the rest of the world *knew* was impossible.

And the key that made it all possible? Air flow over a wing. Brutally simple.

In fact, it's so brutally simple that in hindsight, it's difficult to believe that no one else figured it out sooner! But nobody did. Maybe everyone who had tried before just figured it *had* to be more complicated than that.

I know there are people who would say that this isn't true; that the Wright Brothers did use existing information, that they were *not* the ones who discovered the effects of air flow over a wing, and that non-powered flight (via gliders) had already been achieved. They were simply the first to figure out how to create *powered* flight that could be *controlled*.

That's all true, but don't cover the beautiful simplicity & irony of this event with mud. The fact is, it was *not* a brilliant scientist who figured out how to achieve controlled, powered flight; it was two dudes that owned a bicycle shop who understood a brutally simple concept and had just enough knowledge to be dangerous. Their thinking had not been clouded by *too much* information.

My theory, if I may be so bold as to make one, is that when we get too much information we become trained to see things *only in a certain way*, and in so doing, we can become blind to other things that are *right in front of us*.

As an example, take a look at the puzzle on the next page. In that paragraph, the titles of 30 books of the Bible are "hidden". The funny thing is, they aren't "hidden" at all; they're all right there in plain view.

"This is a most remarkable puzzle. It was found by a gentleman in an airplane seat pocket, on a flight from Los Angeles to Honolulu, keeping him occupied for hours. He enjoyed it so much, he passed it on to some friends. One friend from Illinois worked on this while fishing from his john boat. Another friend studied it while playing his banjo. Elaine Taylor, a columnist friend, was so intrigued by it she mentioned it in her weekly newspaper column. Another friend judges the job of solving this puzzle so involving, she brews a cup of tea to help her nerves. There will be some names that are really easy to spot. That's a fact. Some people, however, will soon find themselves in a jam, especially since the book names are not necessarily capitalized. Truthfully, from answers we get, we are forced to admit it usually takes a minister or a scholar to see some of them at the worst. Research has shown that something in our genes is responsible for the difficulty we have in seeing the books in this paragraph. During a recent fund raising event, which featured this puzzle, the Alpha Delta Phi lemonade booth set a new record. The local paper, The Chronicle, surveyed over 200 patrons who reported that this puzzle was one of the most difficult they had ever seen. As Daniel Humana humbly puts it, "The books are all right here in plain view hidden from sight." Those able to find all of them will hear great lamentations from those who have to be shown. One revelation that may help is that books like Timothy and Samuel may occur without their numbers. Also, keep in mind, that punctuation and spaces in the middle are normal. A chipper attitude will help you compete really well against those who claim to know the answers. Remember, there is no need for a mad exodus; there really are 30 books of the Bible lurking somewhere in this paragraph waiting to be found. God Bless."

Now, I like to think that I'm fairly intelligent (humor me a little here), and yet it took me over 2 hours to find all 30 names. *2 hours!*

C'mon! That paragraph isn't that long! I had my Bible open to the table of contents right next to me, and I knew there were some books like "Leviticus" and "Thessalonians" that simply couldn't be "hidden" in there at all. Yet it still took me 2 hours to find them. Why?

If my theory is correct, I had trouble finding them because I know how to read. In other words, my mind has been trained to view letters in a certain way, with each grouping of letters representing a specific thought that is distinct, complete, & separate from the other groups both before and after it. I've been trained so well that my mind simply can't see a "word" that starts in the middle of one grouping and then jumps a space to finish in the middle of the next group. Throw in some periods, commas, and capital letters, and it becomes even more difficult, because again, those things (in my trained mind) always separate a grouping of letters.

In case you're wondering, the very last book I found was "Ruth". A simple word, imbedded *exactly* as it's spelled entirely within the body of another word – no spaces or punctuation – and *I couldn't see it.* Yet, when I gave this puzzle to our youth group at church, every one of those kids found "Ruth" within a few minutes. So interesting. A bunch of kids who have only been reading for a couple years could easily find a word that I, someone who has been reading for *decades*, couldn't find until I had gone through the text carefully – literally letter by letter – *several times*!

If I were to compare myself, as a person who can read, with someone of the same average intelligence as me (be nice) who did *not* know how to read, I would probably think of myself as being "above" him, simply because he is illiterate. Since I know how to read, and have been doing it for years, I would know a lot more than he would about many things, and as such, I would probably have the ability to understand & explore ideas of a complexity far beyond what he would be able to comprehend. I might even consider him stupid. And yet, I have to believe that this same "illiterate" man would probably have found all 30 of those books *much* faster than I did, simply because he would be looking only for strings of letters that followed a specific pattern but had no other meaning to him whatsoever. Imagine that!

Is there any reason to think that the same sort of thing couldn't happen between a brilliant scientist and an average ordinary person if they were both to look at the same problem? There are a lot more of us average ordinary people around than there are brilliant scientists. Are all of us just leaving things to "the experts" to figure out simply because we don't want to look stupid? Is that really a good idea?

I'm going to allow myself to be stupid. I've got a jar of magnets downstairs that I'm going to play around with. I'm going to arrange them like this, and position them like that, just so I can see what will happen.

I know that scientists are going to laugh at me. They're going to tell me I'm wasting my time. They're going to tell me to leave the heavy lifting to them; to go sit back down on the couch and watch Jimmy Neutron before I hurt myself.

But I don't want to watch Jimmy Neutron, I want to *be* Jimmy Neutron. I want to *Think! Think! Think!* and see what I can come up with. And I'd love nothing more than to know that I'm only one of a million other kids (or kids at heart) around the world that have also chosen to be stupid. A million kids all starting from scratch with nothing more than their magnets, magnifying glasses, Fresnel lenses, telescopes, wires, glue, construction paper, Lego's, and just enough knowledge to be dangerous.

I know in my heart that 999,999 of us will accomplish nothing; that we'll only repeat the same mistakes that many before us have already made. Mistakes that we could have known would happen if only we had read our science books. But it's that one other kid that I'm thinking about; he's the one who interests me. He's the one who, perhaps quite by accident, will stumble across something brutally simple and figure out the answer to a question that has baffled mankind for centuries.

He's the one who's going to change the world.

28

The Shining

I've always liked a good name. Names for people, names for places, names for things; and as someone who loves to read (and tries to write), names for stories.

My favorite book title of all time is Ray Bradbury's "*Something Wicked This Way Comes*". I like it not because it refers to something evil, but because through a thoughtful arrangement of five normal words, the title, all by itself, invokes a very deep (though ominous) *feeling*.

Compare it as he wrote it to, say, "Here Comes Something Wicked", which sounds more like the name of "a delightfully witty" Broadway musical.

Snore.

If book titles were paintings, to me, that particular one of Bradbury's would be a Renoir.

Another of my favorite book names is "*This Far, No Further*". The book was forgettable, but even after ten years, its title still lives with me. It just feels *powerful*, like something God would say.

Back in the 80's, Stephen King wrote a book called "*The Shining*". Without regard to the subject matter of his novel, this is another title that I really like, simply because by taking an adjective and using it as if it were a noun instead, he created a whole different meaning. No longer are we using the word "shining" to describe something else, we're treating it as if the description itself is the actual thing in question. Something that is not static, but in *motion*. Something that simply "is", even if there is no good definition or rational explanation for it.

In the Bible, Joseph is a fascinating person. Genesis gives a lot of history and stories about Abraham, Isaac, and Jacob, but if you go through the post-flood history starting with Abraham, Joseph is the first one who actually starts doing things that really have an effect on a very large number of people. It's almost like God chose Abraham specifically because He needed him (as well as Isaac and Jacob) just so that He could finally get around to Joseph.

Joseph was different from his ancestors in a lot of ways, but the most interesting difference to me was that he seems to be the first person mentioned in the Bible that people could just *look* at and *know* he was a man of God.

Abraham, Isaac, and Jacob were righteous men also and were treated as such, but they were also *powerful* men, and it could be argued that some of the reverence they received from others could have been influenced by that.

Joseph, on the other hand, was a nobody, a slave. And yet, without hitting anyone over the head with a Bible or preaching the Gospels or shouting the name of Jesus Christ (and we know he *didn't* since none of those things would be around for quite some time) people simply *knew* he was with God.

In Genesis 39, both Potiphar (the captain of Pharoah's bodyguard) and the chief jailer (who oversaw Joseph when he was imprisoned) knew that Joseph was with God. So trusting were they of Joseph that they let him run the whole show. Potiphar made him overseer of his house and "*all that he owned he put in his charge.*" The jailer "*committed to Joseph's charge all the prisoners who were in the jail; so that whatever was done there, he was responsible for it.*"

This is pretty amazing if you think about. Both of these guys worked for Pharoah, one as the captain of his bodyguard, and the other as the overseer of the jail reserved for the king's prisoners.

From what I know about Pharoahs, they didn't have too much of a problem putting people to death if they felt like it (as the baker in Genesis 40 would attest to if he could). If either Potiphar or the jailer messed something up or displeased

Pharoah – and they were both close enough to Pharoah for that to be possible – they probably could have expected a rather blunt and unceremonious end to their lives, and yet they both put Joseph, a Hebrew slave, in charge.

What did they see in this guy? How could they be *so sure* of this man's integrity and godliness that they would (in all likelihood) put their own lives at risk by entrusting him with *everything*? We have the luxury of having the Bible to tell us that God was with Joseph, but how did *they* know?

I recently read a book called "*The Irresistible Revolution*", by Shane Claiborne. (I personally think it would be a good idea for this book to be mandatory reading for every Christian, but the vast majority would hate it, because the author does not even try to validate the comfortable routine that mainstream Christianity has become.) Shane lives his life in Philadelphia in what you might call an "inner city mission" located in a very bad part of town. It's a commune of sorts, though its focus is on Jesus Christ rather than "free love" & drugs.

One of the stories he told was about a trip to the grocery store he took with another member of their little mission. As they walked down the street they passed a disgustingly dirty woman in an alley, who, crutches and all, offered "her services". They declined, hurried to the store, and then hurried back home, giving the woman little more than a nod on the way back. When they got home, however, they found out that the bread they had bought was bad; they would have to go back to the store, and they didn't *want* to because they knew that they would have to walk past the woman again. (Is that the way God works in our lives or what? "*Sorry pal, you're not getting off that easy. Don't ignore Me. Go back and do My will.*" Just my thoughts anyway).

On the way back from the store the 2nd time, they finally stopped and started to talk to the woman, just to let her know that they cared about her. They invited her back to their house where she could warm up a little and have a snack. Back at the house, the woman started weeping and said, more of a statement than a question, "You're Christians, aren't you?"

The author was surprised that she had asked this because they had not said *anything* about Jesus or God or anything else, and their house didn't have any Christian paraphernalia (crucifixes, Bibles, plastic fish, etc.) laying around to tip her off.

She said, "I know you're Christians because you shine. I used to be a Christian. I used to shine like that, but the world is cold and dark, and it's beaten me down and taken my shine away."

Several months later, the author answered a knock at the door and found a woman he didn't recognize standing in front of him who obviously knew who *he* was. Before he could say anything she spoke first, "I know you don't recognize who I am. It's because I'm shining again."

In 40 years I have never impacted someone's life in that way. It must be an amazing feeling. They changed this woman's *life*! And they did it without hitting her over the head with a Bible or preaching the Gospels or shouting the name of Jesus Christ.

They talked to her.

They let her sit in their house and get warm.

They gave her a snack.

They *shined*.

I think that's the same kind of thing that Potiphar and the jailer saw in Joseph. I think he simply shined. Maybe not in a physical, "visible aura around the head" kind of way, but some kind of inherent *light* that came from within him that people could just *sense*. He might not have even realized he was doing it, but because he was in such a close relationship with God, I don't think he could have turned it off even if he had wanted to. It was just "there", and anyone who looked at him could see it.

When Catherine & I first got married, we attended a church in downtown Orlando for several years. The church building itself was made of stone, constructed sometime in the early 1900's, and it gave off a little of that "majesty" that older structures with stained glass windows can impart. You felt a little humbled in that building – like you were really, truly in God's house – and the pastor was just incredible to listen to.

The congregation, however – the *real* church – left a little something to be desired. Most of the congregation was made up of successful businessmen, doctors, and lawyers, and we never did feel a lot of warmth during our time there. In fact, I think that when our family showed up on Sunday mornings in our 10 year old Grand Marquis that looked like it was worth every nickel of the $1,500 that we'd paid for it, a collective sigh went through the more well-to-do crowd that drove up in their new BMW's, Mercedes', and Cadillacs (which was just about everybody else).

In the 5 or 6 years we went there, I can only remember 3 people who ever treated us like, well, *people*. One was a sweet older lady who worked at the church, another was the man who ran the Sunday Schools, and the other was a young lawyer about my age named Pete.

When I think back, I was always a little curious about Pete. At the time, I was just some schlep working for a company that made sewer equipment, but Pete, he was a *lawyer*. Like many other members of the church, he had money, he had a prestigious job, he was in a different class altogether. And yet, he would always say hello to me or even come up to me and start talking like we were best friends.

Sometimes, I used to even wonder if he was patronizing me; you know, like that one popular person at school who's nice to the geek because they feel sorry for them. But at the same time, I could tell – I could just *tell* – that that *wasn't* what he was doing at all.

The older lady and the Sunday School superintendent and Pete were all *for real*, they were simply *shining*. This "Jesus stuff" wasn't just words on a page to them; they believed it, they lived it, they walked it. I imagine that they would have been surprised that *I* was surprised, because to them, it had to seem like the most natural thing in the world. How could they *not* shine?

Three people out of a church of a couple hundred. I'm happy to say that the percentage is a little higher at the church I am a part of now, but it still makes me wonder; how come we all aren't shining? If we've really accepted Jesus Christ as our Saviour, if we've really made a true commitment to attempt to walk in His footsteps, and if we really believe that the light of Christ is in each and every one of us, how come we're not all shining? I realize that the world can be a cold, dark place, and we all go through trying times where it wouldn't be surprising that our shine might dim or flicker or even go out completely, but why are there so many Christians who don't shine *at all*? Ever?

Do they really *believe* all of the "Jesus stuff" that they profess, or are they just going through the motions of superficially "accepting" Christ as a logical business decision because they heard salvation was free anyway and Hell sounded kind of scary?

I know that we cannot "buy" our salvation; it is given to us as a gift. I know too that "our works" will not get us into Heaven. But I wonder sometimes if we don't preach those things a little too much, because knowing that I don't *have* to "do" anything as a Christian to get to Heaven (since my salvation is free) sure gives me a good excuse *not* to do *anything*. But while my works will not get me into Heaven, I have to believe that they might help *someone else* get there.

I wonder sometimes if we, as Christians, don't tend to focus on the parts of scripture that we like to hear, and ignore the parts that we don't. We do read the parts that we don't like, and we nod our heads and say things that we know God & everyone else will like to hear like "Yes, yes, oh absolutely, without a doubt!", but then we promptly forget what we read and go back to the parts that make us feel all warm and fuzzy, or the parts that we think justify our actions.

Funny that we should gloss over and downplay the role "our works" have in the big scheme of things, because Jesus sure does talk about them a lot. In fact, He spent a lot more time telling us what we *should be doing* than he did about *how we get into Heaven*, and though we seem to treat "our works" as optional, I can't find anywhere in the Bible where Jesus gave us a loophole.

Which comes back to the original question: Do we really believe this Jesus stuff? We say the words, we sing the songs, we speak with much reverence, but do we *really* believe it? Because if we do, how could we *not* do the things that Jesus has instructed us to do? If we have *truly* accepted Him as our Saviour instead of just making a superficial statement to cover our butt from the damnation of Hell, doing the things that Jesus told us to do wouldn't be annoying burdens that we were trying to avoid, they would be natural expressions of our love – of *His* love – that we *couldn't stop* doing even if we wanted to. We'd be *shining*. Whether we liked it or not.

Since I seem to have so much to say about this, you may be wondering if *I* shine. To be honest, I'm not really sure.

The movie *Schindler's List* was brought to my attention recently, and as it had been 10 years or so since I'd originally watched it, I decided to check it out from the library and watch it again. (If you haven't seen *Schindler's List*, please know that while it is an incredible film, it earns every single bit of its "R" rating; definitely *not* for the kiddies or faint of heart).

What impressed me about the film was that Oskar Schindler was not trying to be a hero. He was an opportunist, looking to exploit the war – and the Jews – for his own personal gain. His plan was to make as much money as fast as he could and then leave Krakow with his suitcases loaded with cash, and his plan worked to perfection. But he never left with the money.

Instead, something happened to this self-serving, gold-digging womanizer that made him do something that would make him one of the most unlikely of heroes. Over the years, something happened to him. Something happened *inside* of him. But it took time.

I do believe that some people are "born again" in an instant, that one day they are "who they are" and the next they are someone completely different, but I know too that there are other people who never experience that sudden "bolt of the

Holy Spirit" striking their souls in a sudden flash of righteousness. For some people, like Oskar Schindler, it takes time. I fall into this latter category.

I've always been a Christian, but I haven't always lived it, and because of that fact, I have to think that I haven't always really believed it. About 4 years ago, I really started to openly question what I was doing with my life and how I was living it. There was no specific day or time that I can put my finger on, just an approximate period when things started changing. I started changing. All of those things, those little clues, that I had been ignoring my whole life finally started getting some traction. I started to think about them; to think about what I valued, what I was doing, and how I was doing it. Even so, I still stubbornly refused to let go.

In late 2005, my career had reached newfound heights, with room yet to grow. No longer a schlep working for a sewer equipment manufacturer, I was now a sales manager at a global software company. I had a six-figure job, a title, status, respect; all of that good stuff. I drove to work in a red Corvette, crossed marble floors to a mahogany covered elevator that took me to a 4th floor office with a view of a manicured private golf course. I ate in some of the most expensive restaurants, attended conferences in luxury Las Vegas hotels, and vacationed with my family at our own cabin in the Georgia mountains.

And then one morning, quite unexpectedly, I blurted out something that I'll never forget, something that surprised me as much as it did my boss, because even after the words had left my mouth I still couldn't believe I had actually said them: *I don't think I want to do this anymore.*

And everything changed.

So here I am, a "struggling writer" (oh! I've always wanted to be a "struggling" something!) living in a little town in the middle of nowhere. No big job, no fat paycheck, no marble floors, no vacation cabin in the woods. I eat at McDonald's now, or maybe Shoney's or Cracker Barrel if I'm really upscaling it. I drive a 6 year old Ford Focus, if I drive at all.

In all fairness, I have to confess that I do still have the Corvette. It's currently sitting in a barn at my mom's house, an unwanted relic of a past life. Hey, what can I tell you? When you're running a little fishing empire the size that mine was, it takes awhile to cast down all of your nets. I had a lot of nets, and though the main warehouse has been cleaned out, there are still some back rooms (and a barn at my mom's) that I still need to purge.

I know some people here think I'm crazy for leaving "all of that" and coming here instead. I can see the look in their eyes, their longing to break free of the "shackles" of a small town, to experience the "excitement" and "opportunity" of a big city. I can tell that many of them think that they're missing something. They *are* missing something, but it's not what they think, and they probably wouldn't believe me if I told them.

I'm not crazy, I'm finally sane. I've never felt so free. I've never been so happy. I've changed a lot.

But do I *shine*? Well, I like to *think* that I do, but I'm not sure. Hopefully I have at least a little *glow* about me (or at least a persistent flicker) but even if I am shining, I also know that there's still plenty of room yet to jack up the wattage. As much as I like looking in the mirror at the man I have become today, I still yearn for the man who I will be tomorrow. God will take me there. I'm doing a better job of following now.

I think a lot of goofy thoughts sometimes. For instance, since I started bouncing ideas around in my head about this particular topic, a silly thought kept coming back into my mind, over and over. I kept thinking how cool it would be if we turned on the evening news at night and saw that all of the major networks were following a story that nobody could explain. A *new* story, something no one had ever seen before, something that had started fairly recently but was showing no signs of slowing down; in fact, seemed to be *growing* as more and more people were attracted to it like moths to a flame. A trend that had all of "the experts" baffled as they continued to witness hundreds of millions of Christians around the world all acting like the Christ they profess to believe in. A trend in which the sheer number of "insignificant" acts of Christian charity, love, and kindness going on in the world were causing supercomputers to melt down as they tried to keep track of them all. A trend in which all of the people involved somehow looked – as incredible as it may sound – almost as if there was a *light* coming off of them.

Instead of seeing all of those tired, old headlines on the TV screen like "The War in Iraq" or "Decision '08", each night the world was looking at a *new* headline regarding this worldwide phenomenon that, for lack of a better name, they simply referred to as "The Shining".

I don't know. Maybe I am crazy.

29

What He Won't Remember

We always felt fairly isolated in Orlando; homeschooling was frowned upon by almost everyone, churches were big & impersonal, and finding like-minded people who simply didn't care what the "Jones'" did were few and far between. Although it didn't really bother Catherine and I for ourselves that we seemed a little isolated, it *did* bother us for our children, because there were so few other kids around for them to play with.

I don't know where all the kids in the neighborhood went when they came home from school – to their TV's, computers, and video games, I guess – but they sure weren't outside. I'm not just exaggerating either; you *never* saw them.

One morning Catherine was talking to a neighbor across the street and our son David, who was about 6 years old then, came up and asked our neighbor if her boys could come out to play. She kind of hemmed & hawed and then said that *maybe* they could come out to play around 3 O'clock. Well, to David this was firm date set in stone, and as the hours clicked away our little boy got more and more excited. But Cat & I knew that this lady never let her kids play with anyone in the neighborhood, and even as David's excitement grew, we became more unsettled about what would actually happen.

3 O'clock finally rolled around, and David was ready to play. He was so excited! With something almost like dread, we took him outside where he ran to the end of the driveway and just stood there looking across the street – so excited and expectant – as he waited for a playmate who would never come. They weren't home. Of course they weren't home; she never

had any intention of letting her boys play with David. I had known that, and Catherine had known that, but David didn't.

I can still see him there; standing at first, then eventually sitting with his hands folded on his lap, so patient and happy, even as we tried to gently make excuses for why there would be no one for him to play with that day. *"Just a few more minutes Daddy"*, he would say, and then patiently continue to wait, eyes watching the empty house across the street.

My heart cried for my son that day. Why would you not want your kids to play with this beautiful little boy? He doesn't swear, he doesn't smart off, he doesn't bully; he's polite, he doesn't have a mean bone in his body, and he has an imagination that is pure and joyful. Isn't that the kind of boy you *want* your kids to play with? I don't care if you hurt *me*, but don't hurt my son. Not that way.

I mention that incident because shortly after moving to Liberty, David was invited to a birthday party. After living for years in a world almost sterile of friends for our kids, this was as much a joy for Cat & I as it was for David, and we wouldn't have missed it for the world.

When we arrived, the 8 or so boys already at the party were playing Whiffle-Ball in the backyard, and David was invited to join in. It came his time to bat, and after several swings he was able to hit the ball. I was so proud.

And then he just stood there. The other kids were screaming at him, *"Run! Run! Run!"*, and after a few confused moments and many pointing fingers he finally took off and made it to first base. I stood there watching and felt my heart crack a little.

The next batter came to the plate and hit the first pitch. And David, so excited to be included and playing a game with other kids, just stood there on first base, not knowing what to do. Again, the boys all began screaming, *"Run! Run! Run!"*, and my heart broke into pieces as I watched my beautiful little boy start running after the ball instead of towards 2nd base.

He didn't know how to play baseball. I had never taught him.

I stood there hurting and embarrassed for this little boy named after a noble king. I stood there helplessly, watching him flounder in bewildered confusion as he tried so hard to do *good*, while bearing the brunt of mockery and laughter and screaming, and not even understanding why.

If there could be this much pain involved just watching my son get *ridiculed* by others, how much more must there have been for God when He watched His get murdered?

To their credit, the other boys didn't give David too hard of a time, and once they learned that he had simply never played before, they did a pretty good job taking him under their wing and helping him out. In other words, doing what I should have already done long ago. And just where had I been all that time? What had I been doing?

Like so many of those around me in that past world, I had been doing all of those things which were important to *me*, but not to my son. David never cared whether or not his dad closed "that big deal", or that he was successful at "leveraging partnerships", or that his management skills resulted in "good synergy" within the workplace. Those aren't things that have any meaning to him whatsoever. They don't affect his life at all, and he won't remember me for them.

What he *will* remember me for is how well I've prepared him for this world that I brought him into. He'll remember me for what I teach him about life & love, anger & fear, and honor & integrity. He'll remember me for teaching him about losing with dignity & winning with grace, coping with rejection & acknowledging praise, doing what is right & leading by example, and standing your ground for what you believe in, even if others don't like it.

Regardless of how good or bad I may do those things, he'll at least remember that I *tried*, and if nothing else, he'll have a starting point from which he can then further develop his own ideas and values as he goes through his life. That's the only real legacy that I can give him.

To my shame, however, he'll never remember me for teaching him how to play baseball.

30

The Child Inside

I can still remember the day when I found out that my public education would continue through the 12th grade. I was in the 5th grade at the time, and while it may seem strange that I could advance that far in my education without ever realizing how long I would be continuing to go to school, the truth is that I had just never thought about it. School was simply something that I did, and though I was very conscious of all of those "adults" that I saw around me who "worked", it had just never occurred to me to think that one day, I too would stop going to school and join their ranks.

12th grade seemed so far off at the time! It was difficult – and a little scary – to even contemplate what being in the 12th grade would be like. High School kids seemed so . . . *big*. And they studied things like Algebra and Geometry, which by their very names were a little scary. To me, an awkward little 10 year old boy full of all the fears & anxieties of youth, High School kids seemed to be all grown up. They weren't kids anymore, they were, well, *adults*. And I wondered what that must feel like to be an adult.

A strange thing, though. No mystical transformation happened when I eventually reached High School. I was older than that 10 year old boy I had been, yes. My body had changed, yes. Certainly I knew more than I did then, had experienced more, and had become aware of many, many more things. But I didn't *feel* any different. I still had the same fear. I still had the same anxiety. I still felt that everyone else was more mature than me, that they knew more than I did; that somewhere, at some time, something had happened to *them* that, for whatever reason, hadn't happened to *me*. While everyone else seemed to have grown up, I was still the same child I had been years before, just repackaged in a different body.

High School is now just a distant memory; a tiny spark on a far away horizon. And yet I still wonder what it must feel like to be an adult. Because, although I kept waiting for it, that "mystical transformation" never did happen. That's not to say that I didn't *act* like an adult; I certainly did all of the "adult" things that everyone else was doing. I had jobs, bought cars, opened bank accounts, paid bills, mowed the grass, and voted. I married, divorced, and married again. I went to the hospital and watched as my children were born. I wore a tie to work, made business calls, hired some people and fired some others. But I always felt that somehow I was just going through the motions, *pretending* to be an adult amongst all of those who actually were.

I learned to live with the fact that, even though I *appeared* in all respects to be grown up, inside I was still the same little boy I had always been. My 20's passed into my 30's, and though I could then look back – with incredulity in some cases – at some of the things that I had done and accomplished, I still couldn't shake the fears and anxieties of that little boy. Regardless of whatever I had done before that might say otherwise, I still felt that nothing I had to offer would be good enough, and that there were some things that I simply couldn't do at all, even though in many cases, I had already proven that I could.

I wound up just faking my way through everything, always deferring to the knowledge and wisdom of those people who I believed actually *were* adults; people who were older, people who knew what they were doing, people who had more experience, people who – unlike me – *didn't* still have a child living inside of them, which was essentially everyone else.

One day in my late 30's, I was having a meeting with my sales team, just as I had done countless times before. But on this particular day, as I looked around at the faces of those people, answering their questions and giving direction for what we would be doing in the coming weeks, I was suddenly struck with a realization that I just couldn't believe.

They think I'm the one who knows what he's doing! They think I'm the mature one, the knowledgeable one, the one who is all grown up. They're deferring to me!

In that moment of insight, I could suddenly see the child that was hiding in all of them, that they too – *every single one of them* – were just like me! No "mystical transformation" had ever happened to any of them either; we were all playing the same game, living in a land of make-believe while hiding this child inside of us from the rest of the world. It was a shocking realization, but what was even more amazing to me was that, while I could plainly see the child in all of them, *they couldn't see it in me!*

I wanted to yell at them, *What are you looking at me for? I don't know what I'm doing! How could you possibly think that I'm an adult? I'm not! It never happened! I'm still the same kid I was in the 5th grade; I'm just faking it, I'm faking it all!*

As I look into the mirror today, I see that my hairline has receded a bit, and that the once bold shade of brown is now peppered with gray. My face has wrinkles that I realize are never going to go away, and my hands are no longer the hands of a young man. I'm getting old. And yet, that child is still there inside of me. The same one who once looked with awe at those kids in high school, the same one who felt the pain of being the last kid picked for the team, the same one who still thinks that what he has to offer couldn't possibly be good enough. A little boy whose yearning for affection and approval never went away. A little boy who still desperately *needs* to be *needed* so that his life will have purpose, and who *wants* to be *wanted* so that he may find some happiness there.

And you know what? I'm totally at peace with that.

31

The Greatest of These is Love

I'm no one in particular. Just a single man among billions of other people walking the face of the planet. There's nothing remarkable about me at all, nothing to set me apart from anyone else, and certainly nothing to make me think that I have any special power that would allow me to accomplish anything of a phenomenal nature. There are some very powerful people in the world who meet those criteria; I just don't happen to be one of them.

At least, that's what I have always thought. While I've touched on the topic of "power" several times in some of these stories, I haven't been too complimentary in my views about those who wield it, and I've always voiced those views from the perspective of someone who did not wield any power himself. However, I read a story that passed my way recently that shook up all of my preexisting assumptions about what power actually was, and more importantly, who has it. I'd like to share that story with you if I may – I don't know who the author is – and follow it with the thoughts it compelled me to think about, and the resulting conclusion that it led me to:

One day, when I was a freshman in high school, I saw a kid from my class walking home from school. His name was Kyle. It looked like he was carrying all of his books. I thought to myself, "Why would anyone bring home all of his books on a Friday? He must really be a nerd."

Finding Liberty

I had quite a weekend planned (parties and a football game with my friends the next day), so I shrugged my shoulders and went on. As I was walking, I saw a bunch of kids running toward him. They ran at him, knocking all of his books out of his arms and tripping him so that he landed in the dirt. His glasses went flying, and I saw them land in the grass about ten feet from where he landed. He looked up and I saw this terrible sadness in his eyes.

My heart went out to him. So I jogged over to him as he crawled around looking for his glasses and I saw a tear in his eye.

As I handed him his glasses, I said, "Those guys are jerks. They really should get lives."

He looked at me and said, "Hey, thanks!" There was a big smile on his face. It was one of those smiles that showed real gratitude.

I helped him pick up his books and asked him where he lived. As it turned out, he lived near me, so I asked him why I had never seen him before. He said he had gone to a private school before now. I would have never hung out with a private school kid before, but we talked all the way home, and I carried some of his books. He turned out to be a pretty cool kid.

I asked him if he wanted to play a little football with my friends. He said yes. We hung out all weekend and the more I got to know Kyle, the more I liked him, and my friends thought the same of him.

Monday morning came, and there was Kyle with the huge stack of books again. I stopped him and said, "Boy, you're gonna really build some serious muscles with this pile of books everyday!"

He just laughed and handed me half of the books.

Over the next four years, Kyle and I became best friends. When we were seniors we began to think about college. Kyle decided on Georgetown and I was going to Duke. I knew that we would always be friends, that the miles would never be a problem. He was going to be a doctor and I was going for business on a football scholarship.

Kyle was valedictorian of our class. I teased him all the time about being a nerd. He had to prepare a speech for graduation, and I was so glad it wasn't me having to get up there and speak.

Graduation day, I saw Kyle. He looked great. He was one of those guys that really found himself during high school. He'd filled out and actually looked good in glasses. He had more dates than I had and all the girls loved him. Boy, sometimes I was jealous!

I could see that he was nervous about his speech, so I smacked him on the back and said, "Hey, big guy, you'll be great!" He looked at me with one of those looks – the really grateful one – and smiled. "Thanks," he said.

When it came time for his speech, he cleared his throat and began. "Graduation is a time to thank those who helped you make it through those tough years. Your parents, your teachers, your siblings, maybe a coach . . . but mostly your friends. I am here to tell all of you that being a friend to someone is the best gift you can give them. I'm going to tell you a story . . . "

I just looked at my friend with disbelief as he told the story of the day we first met. He had planned to kill himself over the weekend. He talked of how he had cleaned out his locker so that his Mom wouldn't have to do it later, and was carrying all of his stuff home. He looked hard at me and gave me a little smile. "Thankfully, I was saved," he said. "My friend saved me from doing the unspeakable."

I heard a gasp go through the crowd as this handsome, popular boy told us all about his weakest moment. I saw his Mom and Dad looking at me and smiling that same grateful smile that Kyle had given years before, but not until that moment did I realize it's true depth.

* * *

Whenever I've thought of "powerful" people, my mind always conjured up images of presidents, world leaders, high-ranking military officers, business tycoons, and other "captains of industry".

All of those are indeed powerful people, no doubt. But as I began to think about those types of people in comparison to the boy in this story, some questions came to my mind about what *real* power truly is.

I would ask you, who is the more powerful person? The one who can accomplish something incredible because they have vast amounts of wealth, resources, people, and political influence at their disposal, or the one who can accomplish something incredible with almost nothing at all?

Who is really the more powerful person? The one who does something truly phenomenal because they have set that as a goal for themselves, focused all of their energies on it, and worked tirelessly to accomplish it, or the one who does something truly phenomenal with *so little effort* that they don't even realize what they did?

Our minds may think up many things when we think about what love is – it's warm and cozy, it makes us feel good, etc., – but I don't think we often consider love to be a *powerful* thing. But why not? 2000 years ago Jesus came to this earth and conquered it with love. 40 years ago Martin Luther King, Jr. conquered hundreds of years of bigotry & segregation with love. And not too long ago a 14 year old boy saved somebody's life with it. How many other times throughout history – and in our own lives – can we see the effects of what happened when the power of love was exercised? It's certainly very easy to remember the times when it was *not*.

Love *is* an instrument of power; *unbelievable* power. And the really crazy thing is that each and every one of us has that power inside of us! It's a gift from God. In His wisdom, He has granted each of us – *all of us* – the capacity to love.

It's interesting to me that those who have attained great power on this earth through other means rarely use the power of love. Maybe they don't feel that they need to use it. Or maybe because love is a power available to *everyone*, they would rather champion the other powers that they hold exclusive to themselves in an effort to divert the attention of "the unwashed masses." But even if they can succeed in distracting us away from the true power that all of us have at our disposal, there's nothing anyone can do to take that power away from us.

And unlike any other instrument of power – wealth, physical strength, military might, etc., – love has a unique characteristic that separates it from all others, and in my mind at least, reaffirms it's godly nature. Because the true beauty of love is that by it's very nature it simply *cannot* be used for evil intent.

Imagine that. An instrument of power whose use can *only* result in *good*. Knowing that everything on the earth that is "of man" can be used for either good or evil (and in some cases, evil only), that one characteristic of love proves to me beyond a shadow of a doubt that it is "of God". How perfect.

Another great thing about the power of love that I don't think we often realize is that we don't need anybody's permission to use it. We don't have to get "congressional approval" to love somebody. In fact, in John 13:34, Jesus not only *authorized* us to wield that power, He *commanded* us to. And who better to give us permission to use that power than the One who gave it to us in the first place?

"A new commandment I give to you, that you love one another, even as I have loved you, that you also love one another."
- John 13:34

Love each other. So simple. It makes you wonder what this world would be like if we actually did just that. Just do what Jesus told us to do.

All of us have personally seen & felt the effects of love when it was present, and all of us have personally seen & felt the effects of its absence. All of us have the *ability* to love, all of us have *permission* to love, and all of us have been *charged* to love. And I would guess that most of us – if not all – have also felt at least a *little* yearning to be thought of as a powerful person by our friends and neighbors.

So *knowing* we have that kind of power at our fingertips, and *knowing* what that power can do, and *knowing* that we have both authorization & direction to use it – to go *crazy* with it if we like – how come we don't?

Because we don't, do we?

We love ourselves, and maybe we love a select few who are close to us, and then we pretty much stop. Why do we do that? Are we afraid we're going to run out? That there's only so much love we have to share?

While that may be true of man-made instruments of power – money, bullets, people, & muscle – love is not man-made, it is "of God", and like God, it is eternal in nature. It always has been; it always will be. The well of love will *never* run dry. In fact, I suspect we would simply discover that love becomes even more profound the deeper into the well we dig.

I'm still nobody in particular, but after reading that story and then diving into the thoughts and questions that it made me explore, I realize now that I'm nobody in particular *with power*. We all are. We possess the greatest of all powers, the power of love. We *cannot* do wrong with it. We *cannot* run out of it. The only question that remains is, *will we use it?*

There may be only a select few in the world who have the ability to build a skyscraper, but each and every one of us has the ability to *change someone's life*. And I would ask you, which of those two would you consider the greater accomplishment?

<u>Statistics:</u>

* Suicide is the 11th leading cause of death in the United States (Homicide ranks 15th). Among young people ages 15 –24, suicide is the 3rd leading cause of death. (www.suicidology.org)
* Over 14 million Americans are alcoholics (www.gdcada.org)
* An estimated 3.5 million people in the U.S. are homeless in any given year (www.nationalhomeless.org)
* In 2001 the U.S. prison population exceeded 2 million for the first time. It continues to grow (www.ojp.usdoj.org)
* There are over 100 million orphans worldwide (www.zambian.com)
* Love never fails (<u>Holy Bible, 1 Corinthians 13:8</u>)

32

Dear John

Dear John,

I hope you are well. I don't know where you are at the moment, and I haven't had contact with you since we parted ways, but I still think of you often. You taught me a lot, and I know that that was a difficult thing to do seeing as how I already thought I knew everything I needed to know when you entered my life.

It's still amazing to me how much I learned from you – about being a team player, about being a leader, about being a mentor, about being a man; a massive amount of knowledge and insight gained in a very short period of time. We only worked together for 10 months after all.

I still remember – Oh! with vivid clarity I might add! – that first meltdown we had shortly after your arrival. How I had let my own selfishness turn me from someone who should have been your best ally & resource into your biggest and most pressing problem instead! I can still hear the fury in your voice as you spoke to me, and the glare you had in your eye that day is forever burned into my memory. I won't rehash the entire event here; I'm sure you remember it well, and anyway, I already wrote about it in a story I called "It's Nothing Personal". I was being a little clever with the title; "selflessness?" "It's Nothing Personal?" Get it? Maybe too clever.

What I *didn't* say in that article though, was how once that event was over, it was truly over. All you wanted was for me to resolve the problem, and once I finally did that, you let it go. You never held it over my head, never carried a grudge, never mentioned it again ever. I had "repented" of my ways, and the entire incident simply disappeared into the past, forgiven & forgotten. Life moved on.

I remember that time you took all of us out to lunch at a deli nearby. You & I were at the back of the line, letting the rest of the team go ahead. When it was my turn, I walked up to the counter, exchanged the usual pleasantries with the girl at the register, and placed my order. Nothing unusual about that. How many times had I done it before? This time, however, would prove to be different.

As soon as the girl walked away to prepare my order, you looked at me and said, "Why did you ask her that?"

"Why did I ask her what?" I replied, a little confused at the question.

"You asked her how she was doing. Why did you ask her that?"

Really confused at that point, I gave what I thought was a ridiculously obvious answer, the kind that's so obvious that you say it very slowly and phrase it in the form of a question. "Because I wanted to know how she was doing?"

And I'll never forget, you got right up in my face and said, "No you didn't. You had your eyes glued to the menu the whole time you were talking to her. You couldn't have cared less how she was doing."

I just kind of stood there, taken aback with the force and intensity of your words, and speechless as to what to say.

Then you backed away, shrugged your shoulders and said, "I was just curious why you would go to the trouble of asking someone a question when you don't care what the answer is."

And that was the end of it. Well, that was the end of it for *you*, but not for *me*. I couldn't forget about it, and wound up dwelling on it for weeks to come. Because you were right, I *didn't* care, I didn't care at all. To me, that girl was nothing more than an implement – a tool – that existed solely to get me something that I wanted, and once I had what I wanted, I had no further use for her.

Finding Liberty

I had treated her no better – and cared for her no more – than I did a computer terminal or an ATM machine. And what was worse, it wasn't an isolated event; that was how I was treating *everybody* that I came into contact with.

If they didn't work with me, if they weren't my friends or my family, they were *nothing* to me. Just necessary evils that I had to interact with on a daily basis to serve a specific purpose, and once that purpose was completed, I was done with them. It shamed me to realize that.

We live in such a big, busy world. There are so *many* people, it's easy to get lost in the mass of humanity, to feel as if, as individuals, we are nothing more than just another insignificant cog which wouldn't even be missed if it weren't there at all. And as if that wasn't enough to cope with already, here comes good ole' Blaine with his giant hammer of apathy to pound you just a little bit further down into the mire of nothingness.

I didn't like what I saw in myself, and though I'm not sure how or when I had become what I was, I knew I didn't want to remain that kind of person. So I decided to change. I started talking to people.

At the grocery store I began making it a point to look at the nametags of the people helping me. I would talk to them – calling them by their name – and try to engage them in a conversation, however short. I loved the way it felt when I walked away and they were still smiling.

Elevators are very interesting places to talk. Normally, you have all these people stuck together in this tiny little room, and nobody says a word. They look at their watches, their shoes, the floor numbers as they light up; everyone tries to look like they're *doing something* when in fact the *only* thing they're doing is pretending that the uncomfortable silence they are suffering through doesn't exist.

So I started talking to people in the elevator. It was a little scary at first (I felt like I was breaking some unwritten elevator protocol), but it got easier the more I did it. And I *liked* doing it, because every time it was like this unbearable tension would suddenly shatter. I discovered that people *wanted* someone to break that silence, it was just that nobody wanted to be the one to do it. The relief that swept over everyone was palpable. Even the people who weren't involved in the conversation seemed relieved; at least they now actually had something to do – listen – even if they didn't want to participate.

Nobody ever complained to me for talking. Nobody ever asked me to stop. So I kept doing it.

I started seeking out people I didn't know, introducing myself, and asking their names. What an amazing thing just to ask someone what their name is! So many of them look *shocked* that you would even want to know! And the *effect* it has on people when you ask, John. I know that *you know* what I'm talking about, but up until then I had never noticed it myself. They stand up a little straighter, they smile, their faces brighten – their whole *countenance* changes! – and then they say, "Well, I'm so & so."

Yes you are. I'm so glad to meet you.

One problem I ran into is that I was meeting so *many* people, I started forgetting some of their names. I used to avoid people when I couldn't remember their names, or just try to "cover" until I could ask someone else later who they were. I don't do that anymore. I just walk up to them and say something like "You know, I met you last week and I know you told me what your name was, but I can't for the life of me remember what it is."

And you know what they do almost every single time? They take the blame! Not only are they *not* offended, they act as though it's their fault! In most instances, they actually avert their eyes and say very apologetically, "Aww, that's okay."

And I have to tell them, "No, it's *not* okay. You are worth remembering. *I'm* the one with the problem, not you."

Such a magical thing. Just to ask someone their name. Just to let them know that you care enough about them to want to know who they are, even if there isn't a single reason in the world why.

Finding Liberty

You know, it's funny, but the people who know me here today wouldn't recognize me if they had met me a few years ago. Well, they'd recognize me, sure; I don't look much different. But aside from looks, I doubt they would believe they were dealing with the same person. They'd be right, too.

I'm not sure what people here *do* think about me; maybe they think I talk too much, or that I'm a little strange. It doesn't really matter to me though, as long as they don't ever think that I don't *care*. Because I don't ever want to make anyone feel like that again. I wonder, had you not drilled into me during lunch that day, would that still be true?

Oh, and do you remember that time when we were talking about that one employee on my team who had become my designated "problem child"? I was discussing all of the various problems and issues he was creating for me – what a laundry list *that* was – and how I was planning to address each one, when you suddenly interrupted and said, "Blaine, have you ever considered that maybe all of these issues are coming from the same place? Maybe the real problem is that this guy just isn't coachable."

Again, such a simple question, but such profound meaning! As I thought about it more and more, I realized that I was looking at all of the issues as separate problems, when in actuality, all of the "problems" were only *symptoms* of the *real* problem; sores that were all emanating from a single underlying disease and making their way to the surface.

No wonder I couldn't make any headway with this guy! All of my failures in working with him resulted from the fact that I was slapping band-aids on the *symptoms*, but because I wasn't addressing the actual problem, the *problem* never got resolved, and while it continued to fester away unnoticed, all of the symptoms would either return again in time, or, if I had put a *really good* band-aid on a particular symptom, they would simply surface in a different way.

What a valuable concept to understand; that what we see as problems may not be problems at all, but merely symptoms of an underlying disease. The only way we'll know the difference is if we take the time to probe down below the surface. I know, I know, it seems like such grade school stuff, such a simple concept to understand, yet nobody ever taught me that in grade school. I wish they had. I practice that concept all the time now, in every area of my life. I even try to probe into some of the problems our country faces and ask myself if it's really a problem, or just the symptom of a problem?

For instance, I question the legitimacy of the whole "illegal immigrant" problem that's splattered all over the news these days. *11 million illegal immigrants in the country and they continue to come across the border. How do we address this pressing problem?*

Is it really a problem, or is it a symptom of a problem?

I don't claim to know much about Hispanic culture, but I did learn a few things from working with many Latinos while in Florida. One is that they are a *hugely* family oriented culture (to a point that should shame most Americans). Another is that they are fiercely proud of their heritage and their countries. Americans often make the mistake of generically lumping all Latin Americans into one big pot, as if everything south of the U.S. were just one big country. But that's patently untrue. Puerto Ricans are Puerto Ricans, Cubans are Cubans, Mexicans are Mexicans, Argentines are Argentines, etc., and none of them likes to be mistaken for anything else. Are we any different in the U.S.?

So knowing that family is very important to Mexicans, and knowing that they love their country much as we do our own, isn't it at least a little odd that they would leave *both* behind to come into the U.S. illegally and live a life as a second class person? Why would they do that? Because this is the big payoff for that sacrifice: They get a chance to work at a job that most Americans don't want to do anyway for a wage that we would consider absolutely insulting.

So what's the real problem here? That Mexicans are invading our country with greedy selfish abandon, or that they come here because they can't scratch out a decent existence living in Mexico?

If the problem is the latter, building a billion dollar wall will only be a band-aid on the symptom, while the real problem will still exist. When the wall fails to resolve the problem (as it must since it only addresses a symptom), what then? Watchtowers, razorwire, & snipers?

If we're going to spend billions of dollars on the problem anyway, wouldn't it make more sense to spend it on the *actual problem*? Would it make more sense to use that money to help Mexico develop it's economy so that it can support it's own people so that they neither have the need nor the desire to cross the border? They're our next door neighbors; would we not do that for Canada if *they* needed assistance?

I don't know if I'm right about any of that, but I have to tell you, it bothers me that no one else seems to be asking a whole lot of questions about it. Nobody seems to be looking at anything deeper than what they can see on the surface.

I know I'm running off on a tangent again (I still do *that* a lot). The point is, I've learned to take a little more time when looking at problems rather than making knee-jerk reactions to any issue that comes my way. And I'm always amazed at how often I initially misdiagnose what the actual problem is when I have the patience to really think about it. I never would have started doing that if I hadn't met you.

Well, I'm getting wordy, and the postman will be at the end of the lane soon so I should probably wrap this up, but before I do, I did want to make sure that I took the time to say "thank you" for the influence you had on my life, because I don't think I ever said that to you when I had the chance. Maybe it's too late now, but maybe not. So here goes.

Thank you for showing me the destructive nature of my own selfishness. Thank you for pushing me to the extreme limits of my potential and not accepting anything less than my absolute best (I really hated you for doing that in the beginning, by the way).

Thank you for showing me – by your own example – that people are the only important things on this earth. Thank you for proving to me that while "realism" may be better than "pessimism", neither hold a candle to "optimism"; there is opportunity in any situation.

Thank you for showing me how to look beneath the symptoms to the underlying problem. Thank you for being a much needed mentor in my life and for never losing faith in me.

Thank you for being my friend.

As I think back, it seems like it was such a one sided relationship. I wonder, for all that I learned from you, did you ever learn anything from me? I was in such a reactive state during that time I was certainly not *trying* to teach you anything, but I sometimes wonder if I may have anyway, even if by accident.

I always worried about how much time you put into work, you know. I know that you were driven to help & inspire the people that worked for you – and that's not a bad thing; you had a positive effect on so many – but I worried your family was paying an unhealthy price for that to occur. You seemed so interested when I resigned; had so many questions about *why* I would walk away from my career and all the success I had achieved. You were intensely curious about where I was going, what I was planning to do, and more than anything, what my motives were for doing so.

Is it possible that with that one act – my resignation – I may have inadvertently placed a question into your mind that you then became obligated to explore for yourself? If so, I'd be curious as to what that question was, and where it led you.

I remember you telling us one Monday morning that you took your family to church the previous day, and that your youngest daughter, seeing a stained glass window depicting Jesus on the cross, pointed to it and asked out loud (much to your embarrassment), "Daddy, who's that man?".

I hope that you have not sacrificed your family for your career, regardless of how many other people you may have helped. I hope that your little girl now knows who "that man" is. And I hope that *you* know Him as well.

If I could go back in time and have the chance to pass just one thing on to you in exchange for all that you taught me, that would be it. To know Him. Jesus Christ. I wasn't strong enough to do it then, but I think I could do it now. I know I would at least have the guts to *try*, and to do my very best.

In the end, that's all you ever really wanted from me in the first place.

Best regards my friend. I hope you are well.

Blaine